James D. Atwater became a professional journalist at the age of sixteen while working one summer for the Westfield, Massachusetts, bureau of *The Springfield Union*. He graduated from Yale University and since 1950 has been a professional magazine writer and correspondent, having worked for *Time* magazine in that capacity, and also for the *Saturday Review* as a writer and a senior editor. During a three-year stint as a correspondent in London, he patrolled with the British Army's bomb-dismantling squad in Belfast. He returned to the United States and is currently writing for the "Nation" section of *Time*. He is the author of *Out from Under*, a history of Mexico, and has contributed articles to *Sports Illustrated* and *Esquire* magazines. A seasoned traveler, he has visited Poland, Israel, and all European countries. Mr. Atwater, an avid soccer fan, enjoys hiking and mountain climbing. He currently lives in Irvington, New York, with his wife, and he is the father of six children.

TIME BOMB

James D. Atwater

PENGUIN BOOKS

Penguin Books Ltd, Harmondsworth,
Middlesex, England
Penguin Books, 625 Madison Avenue,
New York, New York 10022, U.S.A.
Penguin Books Australia Ltd, Ringwood,
Victoria, Australia
Penguin Books Canada Limited, 2801 John Street,
Markham, Ontario, Canada L3R 1B4
Penguin Books (N.Z.) Ltd, 182–190 Wairau Road,
Auckland 10, New Zealand

First published in the United States of America by
The Viking Press 1977
Published in Penguin Books 1979

LIBRARY OF CONGRESS CATALOGING IN
PUBLICATION DATA
Atwater, James D.   1928–
    Time bomb.
    I. Title.
[PZ4.A8862Ti 1979]   [PS3551.T77] 813'.5'4   78-25593
ISBN 0 14 00.5023 X

Printed in the United States of America by
Offset Paperback Mfrs., Inc., Dallas, Pennsylvania
Set in VIP Baskerville

to my mother

TIME BOMB

Prologue ≈≈≈≈≈≈≈≈≈≈≈≈≈≈≈≈≈

THE SUBJECT, AS I remember, came up early that afternoon. Some friends and I were sitting around the bar in the Overseas Press Club in New York. We had all been American war correspondents at one time or another, and we were talking about the acts of courage we had witnessed during the past thirty years or so. A few recalled the June morning when the American infantry had run across the broad, sandy beaches of Normandy, heads bent forward, as though moving into a heavy rain. There was talk of Pork Chop Hill and Iwo Jima and guerrilla tactics in Vietnam. Then I brought him up. I said the bravest man I had ever seen had not been on a battlefield at all. He had done his work in the heart of London, and he looked like anything but a hero—a middle-aged man in a battered old trench coat, a gray figure who lived alone in a bed-sit in Fulham and waited for the telephone to ring.

Here is his story.

1

SQUINTING INTO THE gloom, he watched the lieutenant approach the box slowly.

"Careful, Roy," he said, flicking on the walkie-talkie clipped to the lapel of his coat.

There was a crackle of static, suddenly loud in the vast, empty space of Westminster Abbey, and then the reply: "Just ten more steps, sir."

Thomas turned to glance at the army technician who was squatting beside a large tape recorder on the stone floor. "You're getting all this properly?"

The sergeant nodded. "Both of you, sir," he whispered.

"Good," said Thomas. "I want every word on record."

Although it was August 24, there was still a damp chill in the Abbey, and Thomas shivered. He was a slight man with the long, thin face of an ascetic. Once, long ago, a woman had told him—was it in anger or admiration?—that he had the kind of face that belonged in the niche of a cathedral, and the thought, buried deep by the years, had stirred in his mind as he walked into the Abbey that afternoon. Now he looked at the retreating back of the lieutenant who was far into the shadows of Poets' Corner. We shall need lights, he noted to himself. Light shouldn't bother it, not unless they've become a devil of a lot more clever in the last six months.

Thomas lifted the microphone of the tape recorder and resumed his account of the lieutenant's slow walk up to the box. "Osgood is approaching the object . . . and now he is starting to lean over the box. . . ."

3

Again, a burst of static, and then the calm voice of the lieutenant: "I am now standing over the object. There are no visible wires. No visible fuse."

Although Osgood was only fifty yards away, Thomas raised his old binoculars to study every movement the lieutenant's hands made. This time he spoke into the walkie-talkie hanging near his shoulder. "Any marks on the box?"

"No, it appears to be just the same as the others, about two feet square, two feet high, fresh pine wood, nails neatly countersunk, as always."

"Any writing, Roy?"

"Bugger the Queen Mum."

"All right," said Thomas. "Back you come."

The lieutenant turned and headed back to Thomas. He was walking on tiptoe, bending forward as though he were leaving the bedroom of a sleeping child. He was wearing a bulky flak jacket, but it would do him little good if something went wrong. The sergeant who had been killed in Belfast had died with his guts in his mouth.

When Osgood was still ten feet away, Thomas could see the cold slick of sweat on his forehead. The two men stepped behind a pillar. They and the sergeant were alone in the Abbey. The police had chased out the last tourist five minutes after the bomb had been spotted. The only sound in the building was the faint whirr of the tape recorder as the sergeant rewound a spool. Thomas could hear the growl of a Number 29 bus as it lumbered around Parliament Square and picked up speed heading toward Victoria Station. That was fine. The police were following his advice: Keep the traffic flowing. Don't give the bastards the satisfaction of shutting down Parliament Square.

The captain from the Metropolitan Police had been a twit: "You'll guarantee that the bomb will not disrupt traffic or endanger pedestrians?" he had asked.

"Yes, damn it."

"No possible danger?"

"Not unless they've learned to put a bloody atomic bomb in a wooden box."

The captain produced a typed statement attached to his clipboard. "Then you won't object to signing this paper saying there *is* no danger."

Thomas had impatiently scrawled his signature on the sheet without reading it.

Now Thomas noticed Osgood listening to the sounds outside the Abbey. "Do you think our friend's standing guard?" he asked.

Osgood chuckled. "I expect he's delegated that responsibility," he said.

"Not a bad idea," said Thomas. "We ought to do that sometime." Thomas watched as the lieutenant lit a cigarette. There was no quiver to his hands. There never was in his case. Just the sweat on his forehead, and the dark stain of nicotine on his forefinger. A good man, Osgood. Thomas remembered waiting while the lieutenant had finished a cigarette standing in the iron-gray streets of Belfast. Then he had gone back into a Protestant pub where a bomb in a wooden box was waiting. He would let Osgood unwind a bit more.

As he waited, Thomas ticked off in his mind the number of bombs that had so far been planted in London and came to twelve. There was the one in Piccadilly Circus that hurt the boy, and the one in front of Selfridges that killed that woman—both going off while they were still working in Belfast. One in Victoria Station had been disarmed by Scotland Yard before it could explode. Three had damaged national monuments: Marble Arch, the statue of Queen Victoria in front of Buckingham Palace, and the main foyer of the National Gallery. Then there had been the disaster at the Fulham football grounds. Since returning from Belfast on July 15, Thomas and his men had disarmed four bombs before they could go off. The major himself defused the first, which had been left high in the Whispering Gallery of St. Paul's Cathedral. He had needed no walkie-talkie that day. The architectural genius of Sir Christopher Wren carried every word he uttered around the curved stone walls to the other members of the squad watching from the far side.

Now the twelfth bomb waited in Poets' Corner.

Thomas knew that some of the men on his squad liked to talk about their fear of the bombs. Osgood did not. He was quieter than most of the lieutenants Thomas had working for him, quieter and bigger, with huge gentle hands that carefully constructed delicate models of the bombs they had all defused so that they could practice their techniques. Watching the lieutenant finish his cigarette, Thomas realized he knew very little about him other than the fact that he had been raised in the country. Cornwall, was it? Devon?

"Right," said Osgood, stomping out his butt on the stone floor of the Abbey. "It's the same. At least it's the same from the outside."

In addition to the sticks of gelignite, the other boxes had contained a small battery, which was connected by wire to a cheap alarm clock. The minute hand was snapped off. The wiring was arranged so that the hour hand could be set to close an electrical circuit and fire a small detonator, which in turn would blow up the gelignite. The timer could be set to go off at any time during the twelve-hour cycle of the hour hand. So far, the terrorists had been setting the timer to go off within two hours after the device was planted. Thomas looked at his watch. It was 4:35. The bomb had been discovered at 4:10.

"No way we could sandbag it, I suppose?" Thomas asked.

"Not a chance. It's smack up against the wall. We could put sandbags around the three sides, but the wall would still be damaged. The scholars would have a fit. All that poetic tradition gone up in smoke."

Thomas looked at his watch again; he knew that Osgood was observing him.

"We'd best have at it then, sir," said Osgood. "Hadn't we?"

"Yes," said Thomas. "Yes, I'll go. It's my turn."

He had known he would say that from the first word that the bomb had been found in the Abbey—a frantic telephone call from a guard to his temporary office at Scotland

Yard. There was nothing else he could say. It *was* his turn. The words had come automatically, as though he were an actor on a stage. "I'll go." What was more, Thomas knew in advance just how Osgood would respond, how he would play the scene.

"I'd like to have a try at it, if it's all right with you—"

Thomas looked up at Osgood, trying to conceal his sense of shame and utter relief.

"Are you quite sure?"

Osgood was already moving toward his gear. The sound of his thick-soled army boots echoed in the Abbey. "A man has to keep in practice," he said.

Thomas strolled after him, and watched him strapping on his belt with the tools and the powerful set of wire cutters. "You know exactly what to do?"

"Of course. It's like the others. I'll pry off the top, the way we've done it before, and cut the bloody wire. Direct approach. Ten seconds' work should do it."

Ten seconds, thought Thomas. Maybe only seven or eight. No time at all, really, considering that the thing might be set to go off hours from now. The sooner done, the better. He was aware that he was trying to remove himself from the situation, to look down at the scene objectively, trying to find the right thing to do. Take the long view, take the broad view, do what's best for everyone concerned. You are too valuable to risk yourself every time. And, besides, you have done your share. You have been there.

To his surprise, Thomas found that he could look the lieutenant in the eye and sound completely sincere: "You're sure you wouldn't like me to go?"

"No, really. What is it the Americans say? 'It's a piece of cake'?"

Thomas nodded with what he knew to be grave approval, the leader taking quiet pride in the courage of his men. "Let the Americans come and eat it, then," he said.

Osgood stood up and adjusted his flak jacket. "What is that bit in *Hamlet* about if the job is to be done, do it quickly? Or was that *Macbeth*?"

"I wouldn't know," said Thomas. "But do it quickly anyway."

There was no shaking of hands. Thomas had decided against that a month before, when the bomb disposal squad was still in Belfast. Shaking hands solemnized things too much. This was the reason the men used among themselves. Thomas had a more personal reason for introducing the ban: He could not bring himself to be the last person to touch a man who might be dead in less than a minute.

"I'll buy you a pint when you get back," Thomas said.

"Right," said Osgood.

"Be careful."

"Right."

As the lieutenant began to go back to the box, Thomas raised his binoculars to his eyes. He could hear the tape recorder start to hum.

"He's going straight to the box," Thomas said. "Now he's squatting alongside. He's putting his left arm around it. He has his jimmy in his hand. I can see his hands. Now he's starting to pry the jimmy under the left-hand corner of the top—"

The flash came first. That was what Thomas would remember most sharply—the great flash of blue light. Then the sound, obliterating everything else, all other sensations, battering its way into his head. And then the force of the explosion blowing him back against the wall twenty feet away.

When he came to, the air was still filled with dust. Far away, he could hear a shout and turned his head to see the sergeant standing over him. The man's lips were moving. Thomas could hear nothing. The sergeant's lips were moving again. Thomas strained to understand. "Are—you—all—right—sir?"

Thomas nodded and struggled to his feet. There was a siren screaming somewhere. His mind was clearing rapidly, too rapidly. He could already feel the first waves of shame. He did not want to know, but he knew.

"Roy?" he asked the sergeant.

The man shook his head. "Dead, sir," he said.

Suddenly Thomas could feel something trickling down his face. He raised his hand quickly and his fingertips came away stained with blood. *Osgood's?* "Good Christ," he cried looking around. "Where is he?"

Thomas was staring wildly about when the sergeant grasped the cause of his fear. "No, no, sir," he said. "He's not over here. He's way over there." He pointed off to the right.

The sergeant began to talk soothingly. "No need to carry on, sir," he said. "You've got a bit of a cut over your eye. Must have been caused by the glasses being jammed in like by the explosion."

Thomas found the cut with his handkerchief. "Thank you."

"Would you like to go out to one of the ambulances, sir?" the sergeant asked. "Lie down for a bit?"

Thomas shook his head. "No," he said. "No, I want to be alone, if you don't mind. Keep them away from me for a moment, please."

Thomas walked away a few feet and slumped down with his back against a pillar. He could feel the dust in his nose and throat, and his ears were still ringing. He tried to concentrate on the physical sensation, but he could not. Osgood was dead. Osgood was dead because he had not the courage to walk to the bomb himself. Thomas knew that, and he suspected that Osgood had known it.

Thomas wished he could weep to ease the pain. He was alone with the knowledge that he was afraid. He was not a coward—but he was afraid. Terrified. And there would be other bombs.

Thomas would not think about it. "Right," he said to the sergeant, getting to his feet. "Let's have a look at Osgood."

2

THEY BURIED LIEUTENANT Roy Osgood in a tiny cemetery behind a Norman church in a village in northern Devon that huddled back from the cliffs overlooking the sea. During the service, the sheep in the adjacent field gathered behind the wooden stile that provided the only opening in the hedgerows that blocked off the pasture. The animals stared curiously through the mist at the little group around the open grave. Thomas watched them, while the Church of England vicar, an elderly figure with skin as white as his robes, talked about how the gallant men of the parish had been giving their lives for England for centuries. Thomas thought that Osgood would have remained unimpressed by that point, not being much for celebrating the valor of British arms, but he would have been amused and pleased by the audience of sheep in the field he had walked so often as a boy.

After the ceremony Thomas begged off going back with the family for tea. He knew he was being rude—he knew what was expected of him—but he could not bear to spend any more time with Osgood's resolutely composed parents, talking about the son that he had allowed to walk to his death in the gloom of the Abbey. There was business to be done, Thomas said, business that called him back to London. He shook the thick, rough hand of Osgood's father while saying good-by in the parking lot. Mr. Osgood, shorter than his dead son, was a dairy farmer. His black Sunday suit had become too small for him over the years. Mr. Osgood's open face registered disappointment, but he was too uncertain of himself to press Thomas to stay on. Mrs. Osgood simply bobbed, smiled, and held out her hand, and Thomas was free.

Driving down the narrow, twisting lanes to the station at Barnstaple, the thick hedgerows looming up on both sides,

Thomas shook his head in disgust. He had not even had the courage to break the news of the death of their son to the Osgoods. When a friend of the lieutenant's had volunteered to do the job, Thomas had hesitated—only long enough to indicate his realization that the job was really his to do—before saying yes. You're a man of immense courage, Major, Thomas said to himself. You let them volunteer to go and get killed, and then you let them volunteer to take the message to the parents. Pretty soon they can do the whole business, and you can sit back in your ruddy office drinking ruddy tea with the ruddy char.

At the Barnstaple station, Thomas quickly gave up his Godfrey Davis rented car and then walked along the platform beside the waiting train until he found a second-class compartment that was empty. Before long the train was wandering through the gentle countryside of Devon. The hills were bright green from the summer rains. Now and then in the distance, sometimes half-hidden in the gentle undulations of the landscape, Thomas could see the square towers of stone Norman churches like the one he had just fled. Bracing a pad of paper on his lap, he carefully began drawing the plans of the standard IRA bombs that he and his men had been successfully dismantling.

The drawings were meticulous, and Major David Thomas (Retired) was fond of pointing out that he was a meticulous man, knowing full well that over the years he had bored any number of chance acquaintances, not to mention his few good friends, by making the statement. But it was all too true. He *was* meticulous, and a good thing too, he would add, making sure that his listener got the point. If he were not, he would be dead. He did not mean to be priggish about the matter. It was fact, simply that.

Thomas was the man who had developed the techniques they had been using in the Abbey the day the bomb killed Osgood. In 1945 Thomas had been a twenty-two-year-old lieutenant in the Ordnance Corps who had been assigned, quite by chance, to the job of defusing German bombs left buried in the rubble while the war was being won. When one of his friends was killed working on the fuse of the same kind of bomb, Thomas had become incensed when he learned that no one knew why, that no one had thought to keep an exact record of what each man had done. Before the astounded gaze of a sergeant, Thomas had slammed into headquarters and chewed out his commanding colonel.

To his credit, the colonel had known when to smile, however thinly, and he had waited patiently until the slight young man before him had stopped sputtering with fury. Then he had asked what should be done. Thomas had told him. He said that they should record every move that the man at the bomb made so that the same mistake would not be committed twice. The suggestion had been quickly accepted, and made part of the standard operating procedures.

During those days the bomb-disposal squad developed the other basic techniques that were still being used—sending only one man forward at a time, planning every move in advance so that the disarmer need spend only seconds hovering over the bomb.

Thomas could remember clearly how much he had enjoyed the work. Actually enjoyed it. There had been no fear. It was long before the other thing began to bother him, the memory of what had happened to his father in the Welsh slate quarry. He had got the idea into his head that it simply was unlikely that he would be harmed by anything he did *after* the war was over.

In those days he had gone forward willingly, while the bobbies held back the passers-by, to climb through the shattered hulks of buildings in north London and descend into the holes that had been carefully dug around the bombs, leaving them exposed like oysters on the half-shell. Thomas would stretch out next to the bomb, sometimes having to toss his left arm over it to brace himself. Lying there, locked together with his adversary, he would begin to work on the fuse in the nose with his right hand. Once, as he labored with exquisite care, a fuse on a delayed-action bomb had begun to tick as quietly as a lady's watch. In the silence he could hear it quite clearly. Even then there had been no gush of fear. Only curiosity. Wondering what would happen next, he waited intently, conscientiously timing the interval on his watch, and described what was occurring over his walkie-talkie: "The sound is faint but very regular. I am proceeding as planned." Ten seconds later he had the fuse out in the palm of his right hand, which, he noted with pride, was not shaking. "I have it now," he announced. "It's quite all right." Back in the laboratory, they found that the timer had stopped with twenty-eight seconds to go.

For twenty years Thomas had stuck it out in the Ordnance Corps, a meticulous man, just as he maintained, but one who was also stubborn and blunt-spoken. Although he had become one of the most knowledgeable and respected experts on bombs and demolition in the British Army, he never was really a member of the officer corps. He was a loner, an individualist who gained his reputation with explosives not by ambition but by sheer skill, some kind of inborn talent that gave him the kind of feel for making and dismantling bombs that other men have for painting or music.

What Thomas did not have was a respect for fools, and since, in his opinion, he encountered many that outranked him during his years in the army, his career had been marked with bitter scenes and feuds. If he had not been so talented, if he had not been right so often, he would have been forced out of the service years before. But he had been indulged by a number of commanders until he finally refused to obey a colonel's orders to write a training manual in a prescribed way and had instead produced his own version.

That did it. The army forced him out at last. With no place else to go, with no wife or child to support, Thomas had returned to Wales and a job as a mining engineer in the quarry where, as a boy, he had first learned about the uses of dynamite from his father. There, he lived quietly and resumed his old hobby of collecting the tiny alpine flowers and plants that clung to crevices in the rocks on the heights of Snowdon and the Welsh mountains that look westward across the Irish Sea.

Thomas was as content, he had come to realize, as he was ever likely to be. But then the IRA began stepping up its bombing attacks in Northern Ireland in the spring. The phone call had reached him early one evening at home: Could he be in London in the morning on urgent business? No, the colonel was not authorized to say exactly what the business was.

Thomas knew what it must be, however, and he was human enough to gloat a bit while driving to London that night. Now they surely would have to make him a lieutenant colonel.

At eight-thirty on the morning of June 19 Thomas was ushered into the presence of an Ordnance Corps general in the military offices just off Whitehall. The two men had never met, but Major General Fitzhugh-Roberts—a bit more clever than the normal run, Thomas instantly decided—clearly knew all about his record. The general began straight off by saying that a lot of new and inexperienced men were getting in trouble in Belfast dealing with the trash that called itself the Irish Republican Army. The general pronounced the word "army" with disdain. Cowards who killed civilians, who never attacked head-on, who left bombs and dared you to take them apart. Well, the British Army, a *real* army, was taking them apart, but three men had been killed, and they needed someone with Thomas's experience to give them a hand, ease them over the rough spot in the road.

"We can sign you on as a civilian adviser, get you mess privileges, that sort of thing. You'd really be running the show, you know. A man with your knowledge and experience. Give it a try, would you?"

No promotion. Not even an offer to rejoin the army. For an instant, Thomas could feel the old rage boiling up in him. They could stuff their bloody bombs. He was on the point of rising from his chair and heading for the door when he realized that the general had said something else.

"Sir?" he asked.

The general leaned toward him. "I simply said what we both know—what you *must* know. You're the best man for the job, and the country needs you badly, very badly indeed."

The country needs you. It was a set speech every general could recite at will. How often had Thomas heard commanding officers use the same phrase to send men into danger? But the major, a man of no false modesty, could not ignore the point. He believed that he *was* the best man for the job, and it was plain that the country did need him.

"When would you like me to start, sir?" he asked.

The general hurried around the desk to shake Thomas's hand, as though afraid that he might change his mind. "Right away," he said. "Now."

That afternoon, Thomas landed in Belfast. He was assigned as a project officer to work with a handful of men, most of them about the age he had been when he was defusing blockbusters in the ruins of London. The men automatically addressed him with his old military rank of major, although he was one of the most unmilitary of men. Unlike many former officers, he did not betray his past by any hint of imperiousness in his manner or speech. His hair was long and he wore thick sideburns. He did not clasp his hands behind his back and sway from one foot to another while he talked, as though still addressing a parade ground full of troops.

Thomas's one visible link to his past was, characteristically, very unarmy, very much *not* the thing to do. He still wore his old officer's trench coat. Thomas was quite aware that the officers in Belfast thought he was sullying the uniform by wearing it as a civilian. He took malicious delight in the fact that he was offending them by an act of defiance, of breaking the code, because it was all the more appropriate. They had made it quite clear in the past that he was not one of them; why should he act as though he were?

To his surprise, Thomas had felt completely at home in the sooty streets of Belfast, with the pungent smell of smoke in the air, the blackened, tiny row houses crowding right up against the narrow sidewalks. The whole scene reminded him of the factory towns of Wales. The lowering gray skies, the constant drift of mist against his cheek, the feeling that rain was just about to fall—it all was very familiar.

Dealing with the bombs left in the middle of pubs or in the trunks of cars, Thomas had been able to rely on the simple technique of speed: go in fast, pry off the top, cut the wires. Very often, of course, the bomb exploded before they could get to it; but if they arrived in time they could handle it.

But this time Thomas was afraid right from the start. He did not know why it was so different from dismantling the bombs after the war. Was it more dangerous? Perhaps, but Thomas knew the problem went deeper than that. You're older now, you twit, he told himself. You're fifty-three. You're vulnerable, and you know it. Old people die, don't they? That's what old people do. No wife. No kids. You're marked.

Still, Thomas had forced himself to take his turns with the rest. None of his men were killed, although a few had died on other squads in the past, and the operation even became a bit of a lark for the young lieutenants. They were in more danger, they used to say, playing pick-up football on the field outside the barracks than they were taking apart the bits of garbage that the IRA was putting together. The men used to exchange IRA jokes, adapting familiar lines to IRA themes. Question: How does an IRA firing squad stand? Answer: In a circle.

3

FOR MONTHS THE English had been following the stories of the explosions and killings in Northern Ireland with growing disgust. The Irish—all they've ever been good for is blowing each other up. Never changed and never will. Then the IRA snipers began to pick off British soldiers on the streets of Belfast and the disgust hardened to hatred. The Irish. Always the bloody Irish. Pull out, is what we ought to do. Bring our lads home and let that lot kill each other off. The ruddy Paddies.

All the rage and frustration that had been building in the British erupted in an explosion of its own after the first bomb went off in London, killing two women and seriously injuring a small boy in the Piccadilly Circus Underground Station. The *Evening Standard* had managed to get to the surgeon who worked on the boy. Going home from work, crowded into the swaying cars of the Underground, Londoners read how the boy had still been alert when he had reached the hospital and had asked the surgeon, "You can still fix my arms all right, can't you, sir?" It was a scene made to order for the *Standard*, and the reporter had made the most of it. He told how the doctor had not been able to bring himself to answer the boy: "I stood there, holding his hand, until he went under the anesthesia. Then I took off both arms."

The story made the early-evening news shows on both the BBC and ITV, and a ripple of revulsion swept across not only London but the entire country. Ironically it was not the death of the two women that bothered people so much as it was the injury to the boy and the shattering of his child's confidence that the surgeon could make him right again. The bomb—the IRA—had destroyed innocence, a fact that made the outrage particularly unspeakable and unforgivable.

An hour after the television news programs, an Irish couple—he forty-five, she about thirty—had gotten lost while driving into London. The man made the mistake of asking for directions from a pair of boys on a street corner in east London. As it happened, the boys were "skinheads," young hoodlums who at one time had shaved their heads as a symbol of unity. The hair was long now, but the boys were still street fighters and they still wore the heavy boots known as "Dr. Martens" that they used as their main weapons in a brawl.

Before the Irishman had spoken five words to the boys, he was betrayed by his accent. Instantly a mob materialized. The skinheads pulled the couple from the car. The man went down under a swarm of fists and fell, unconscious, into the gutter. Then, with great precision and force, one of the boys kicked him in the stomach and genitals. The woman fainted as she watched and a member of the mob casually put his boot under her skirt and hiked it up over her broad hips as a gesture of contempt.

Later that evening a gang of young men in Liverpool invaded a pub in a working-class section that was patronized almost entirely by recently arrived Irish immigrants. Above the bar hung pictures of Pope John XXIII, President John F. Kennedy, and his brother Robert Kennedy. A half-dozen Irishmen were playing darts in the corner. One of them had just enough time to throw his mug of Guinness at the mob before he and his friends were overwhelmed.

The six were hauled outside, where a laundry tub full of warm, liquefied tar was waiting. When they saw the tar, the Irishmen struggled even harder, jamming their heels into the ground and shoving back. "Just like in the old country, isn't it?" said one of their captors. In succession, the men were flung flat in the middle of the cobblestone road and ladles of the steaming, black slime were poured over their heads and clothes, just as the Protestants and Catholics had been tarring each other for months in Belfast. The members of the mob had no feathers that evening, but they had a substitute: a pile of horse droppings that they rubbed into the hair of each of the six men with a long-handled laundry brush.

The Times and *The Guardian* were horrified by the two incidents. "The 'Irish sickness' is infecting England," warned the *Times*'s lead editorial the following morning. "Despite the provocation of the bomb that killed two persons and mutilated a small boy, we cannot wreak savage revenge upon the Irish in our midst and still ourselves a civilised people." Asked *The Guardian*: "Can it really be true that Englishmen were responsible for these acts of blind vengeance?"

But surveys by the popular press the next day revealed that a large number of Englishmen felt that the acts of violence, though perhaps a bit extreme, were entirely understandable. Indeed, the *Mirror* reported that the people in the East End, near the spot where the Irish couple was attacked, felt that the incident was completely justified. "Next time," said one shopkeeper, "maybe they'll think twice before they go about setting off their bombs and killing people and hurting children."

A week of anxious waiting, and then one afternoon a bomb exploded against the storefront of Selfridges on Oxford Street. Two women and three men were killed, and fifteen badly injured. Red gouts of blood smeared the sidewalk, and shoppers as far away as Marble Arch could hear the screams.

The force of the blast caught a middle-aged woman from Kew who had just left Marks & Spencer's and lifted her high into the air. Suspended like a puppet, she seemed to hang for an instant over the busiest thoroughfare in Britain before turning a lazy somersault and landing flat on her back on top of a passing truck.

An American tourist who had been buying some film in Selfridges ran out of the store and, hurrying past the dazed survivors, took a picture of the woman as she was being lifted down from the truck. The photograph was shown on television that night and appeared on front pages throughout the country the following morning. The woman was still clutching her shopping bag. A rivulet of blood was running down her arm and staining the upper part of the Marks & Spencer insignia.

The picture of the woman, who died on the way to the hospital, had a profound effect on the British. She had been killed with no warning while her mind was on the everyday business of getting on with the day's shopping. And because she had just left the best-known store in the Marks & Spencer chain, every adult and most children identified themselves with the woman—to their horror. The IRA had suddenly made violent death a stark possibility for everyone.

That was the point: the killings were completely at random. This was not a matter of hearing the wail of the air-raid warning and then going down into a shelter to wait for the Germans to end your life or let it go on. This was a matter of being taken completely by surprise, without a chance to say a prayer or reach for the hand of a friend. The maiming of the small boy showed how cruel the IRA bombs could be; the fate of the woman showed how capriciously they could kill. There was no place to hide.

No one panicked, of course. If for no other reason, the British would never have given the IRA the satisfaction of witnessing a public display of fear. The country soldiered on, but in different ways. The numbers of shoppers decreased markedly. Restaurants operated at half capacity. Tickets for hit shows in the theaters around Shaftesbury Avenue went begging. Even the crowds in the streets seemed to thin, and people walked more rapidly. Going down into the Underground was an ordeal. A stranger, looking at the anxious faces, would have guessed that the riders were listening for something.

An explosion in a Leeds pub killed five one evening. Three days later a Plymouth greengrocer was turned into rubble, the owner and his wife dead. Then a bomb detonated beneath the stands at the Fulham football grounds during an exhibition soccer game. Three skinheads were killed and five gravely injured. The ambulance crews found one Dr. Martens boot with a foot still in it. Climbing carefully through the wreckage, the police gently retrieved arms and legs that had been blown off by the explosion and put them into green plastic bags. There was speculation in the press that the attack was a reprisal for the earlier acts of violence against the Irish in Britain.

During this wave of attacks, which covered a period of twelve days, the bomb-disposal experts of Scotland Yard actually managed to get to four bombs—one in London—and disarm them before they could explode. Even so, the *Mirror* and then, more circumspectly, *The Times* urged the Government to bring back some of the army bomb-disposal units to cope with the attacks in Britain. OUR BOYS NEEDED AT HOME! proclaimed a *Mirror* headline. There was another reason to turn the job over to the army, at least in the major cities: so many suspicious-looking suitcases and boxes abandoned in public places were being reported by the public that the police had their hands full running down every request for help.

The order went out on July 14 to bring back Thomas and his men. There was no announcement and the request to the army headquarters south of Belfast was marked top secret, yet the word got out. The word was bound to get out: the offices were largely manned by civilians who went home every night to embattled neighborhoods. A Protestant could have spread the word out of worry that the experts were leaving, a Catholic out of glee.

It was midnight when Thomas's small caravan set out from their post in Belfast to drive to the airport. It was also raining, but that made no difference either. The young men were waiting for them on the street corner outside the gates. Thomas caught sight of them standing under the street lights, and at the same instant heard the two riflemen riding in the rear of the jeep cock their weapons. Up ahead there was a throaty growl of an engine as the Saracen armored car that was leading the way began to accelerate. A warning light on top of the vehicle began to revolve, and the beam of white, bright light reflected off the sullen faces of other men standing back in the shadows.

The jeers began as the jeep picked up speed. "Get the bloody hell out of Ireland!" someone yelled. A stone thudded against the hood. Thomas turned his head to see a tall young man raise two fingers to the departing British, but he paid him no special attention as the jeep shot away. At that point, there was no way for Thomas to know who the young man was.

Two days later Thomas and his men began disarming a series of bombs that the IRA had planted around London, leading up to the one that was left in Poets' Corner of Westminster Abbey.

4

THE MUD FROM Roy Osgood's grave was still on Thomas's boots when he walked through the front entrance of Westminster Abbey on August 28. He avoided stepping on the stone honoring Sir Winston Churchill and turned right to go over to the Poets' Corner. The damage was not as bad as he expected. The ancient stone pillars had withstood the shock without budging, although here and there a tablet commemorating a writer had been blown off the wall. Thomas noted that Ben Jonson's had shattered into three pieces. Looking at the blast marks, Thomas estimated that the bomb must have contained about ten pounds of gelignite. Easy enough for one man to handle. He could have dressed up as a workman and carried it right through the front entrance. God, the guards would have held the door open for him.

Thomas recognized the demolitions expert from Scotland Yard who had been assigned to work with him—Phillips, wasn't it? Yes, Phillips. Thomas walked over to the man, who was down on his knees, sifting through a pile of rubble. "Sergeant Phillips?"

Phillips scrambled to his feet, dusting off his hands on his coveralls. Thomas noted again with amusement the carefully trimmed mustache that gave Phillips an air of elegance. "Good morning, Major," Phillips said pleasantly. "I was just having a bit of a look around. Have been for a couple of days now." He nodded across Poets' Corner at three men who were also down on their knees. "We've been hard at it since eight this morning. Seems to be a good deal of pressure from up above that we turn up a clue or two on this one. Someone up there must be a lover of poetry, wouldn't you say, sir?"

Thomas liked Phillips. They were both professionals who wanted to get on with things without any superior fussing around them. What was more, they sensed their kinship immediately. There was working-class blood in each. The fact was implicit in their accents and the way they grasped their teacups, taking the whole bowl in the hand instead of holding just the handle. They had both gone to state schools and taken special courses at night to pick up their technical knowledge. Each knew—without asking—that the other bitterly resented the privileged who had gone to public school and on to Oxford or Cambridge.

Phillips was ten years younger than Thomas and hence had missed the war. Too bad, Thomas thought, as they stood talking in the Abbey. The war had helped the likes of them. Without it he too would have remained a sergeant. Still, Thomas realized that he expected to be called "Major" by Phillips. That was the system, and they both knew it.

"How big do you think it was, Sergeant?" Thomas asked.

"Close to ten pounds, I'd estimate. Could have been a bit more, of course."

"Yes," said Thomas, looking around, wondering what to say that would keep the conversation away from Osgood. "We were lucky that the blast wasn't confined more. It rather blew itself out, didn't it?"

"You might say, sir," said Phillips. There was the barest edge in his tone. "It rather blew out Osgood, I'm afraid."

Thomas flushed. Phillips had caught him talking like a fool. "Yes," he said. "Yes, it got Osgood, all right."

The point made, Phillips offered him a cigarette, which

Thomas politely refused. He had given them up long ago, partly to save money, but mostly to avoid becoming dependent upon something to steady his nerves. "Whatever you find will be helpful," Thomas said. "We need to know as much as we can."

Phillips nodded. "So far, we've found three bits of mechanism that look as though they came from the same kind of clock they've used in all of them—the one you can buy at Boots for about two quid."

"Anything else? Any special fuses, relays—anything like that?"

"No. A bit of wire or two. That's all. Nothing to speak of."

Thomas walked back and forth as he thought. Big Ben began to toll ten o'clock and all of the men automatically checked their watches. Deep within the Abbey someone started to practice a Bach fugue on the organ. He was having trouble with one run and kept repeating the notes over and over.

"So he was just unlucky," said Thomas.

"Sir?"

"Osgood. There was nothing new about the bomb. Nothing tricky. He just happened to be standing over the damn thing when it went off."

"Right," said Phillips. "The bomb is effective—there's no doubting that. It goes off. But it's not very sophisticated, is it? After all, we can disarm any bomb we can get our hands on. You've shown that."

As they talked the two men strolled through the Abbey and out to the main entrance, where they pushed through the swinging door and stood looking down Victoria Street. Behind them they could hear, faintly, the strains of Bach as life went on in the Abbey, just as it had down through the centuries, no matter what the state of the world.

Thomas could not argue with any of Phillips's points. If they could get to this type of bomb, they could handle it—barring a spot of bad luck, such as Osgood had run into. What was it that that sergeant used to say in Belfast? "You don't have to be lucky in this business to survive, but you can't be unlucky." There was a good deal of truth to that. Osgood had been unlucky. The bomb was standard enough: just a timer, a battery, and some gelignite. But just wait, Thomas thought. *Just wait.*

"It's almost too simple, isn't it," said Thomas. "The bomb is too bloody simple. That's what's frightening."

"Why?"

"Because I wonder, is this the very best they can do? And I have to say no, it can't be. They must have some clever chaps. God knows, they've got some brave ones."

Thomas felt better, having told Phillips that the unknown was frightening. He knew that the sergeant would interpret the remark to mean he was worried about what would happen to London, not to himself. Still, it was a confession of sorts, and Thomas always found it difficult to confess anything at all.

As two men talked, some boys from Westminster School came hurrying out of the ancient gate to the left, scarves flying behind them. They dashed to catch a bus, swinging expertly aboard just as the driver was pulling away from the curb.

The crackle of Phillips's walkie-talkie startled them both, and they missed the first few words. The sergeant asked for a repeat, and this time there was no mistaking the message: Army headquarters wanted Thomas.

Fifteen minutes later Thomas was learning about the new development in Belfast, and two hours later he was back in Northern Ireland under orders to find out what was happening. The major discovered that within the past few days the IRA had started using whole new families of bombs made out of unlikely materials and touched off by unlikely devices. Following standard procedures, some of the army experts who succeeded Thomas and his men had blown open the trunk of a car left in an off-limits zone and discovered, to their surprise, not the customary gelignite but two fifty-pound sacks of ammonium nitrate and two of sodium chlorate. Atop these sat a standard firing mechanism composed of a clock, a battery, and a detonator.

The device had been dismantled, and the whole contraption was waiting for Thomas in the squad room when he arrived. "They use this stuff on farms, don't they, sir?" asked one of the sergeants.

"They do indeed," said Thomas. "But if you put those chemicals together, and stick in a detonator, you'll get one hell of a bang, I promise you."

"Why use fertilizer instead of gelignite?"

"Easier to get, probably," said Thomas. "There must be tons of it scattered all over Ulster."

Not only had the IRA suddenly begun to make bombs out of commonplace materials but the devices were used with more cunning. Throughout the rural areas of Northern Ireland, one of the most common sights was a large metal urn of milk left by the roadside to be collected by truck. As an army patrol was passing such an urn one morning, there was a thunderous explosion. Two men were killed outright, and a third lost a leg. Searching the area afterward, the army found a thin wire that led back to a grove about fifty yards away, where the IRA men had waited until the soldiers were close to the urn before detonating it.

Whoever was designing the new bombs had an ingenious turn of mind, not to say a whimsical one. Army experts showed Thomas bombs that used a spring-operated clothespin as a timer. Electrical contacts were welded to the tips of each leg, and the clothespin was then tied open with a length of soft, malleable wire. The idea was that the strength of the spring would slowly stretch the wire until the tips of the legs eventually touched, the circuit was completed, and the charge went off.

But the device that amused even Thomas was a fire bomb that appeared the day after his return to Belfast. A cardboard cigarette package was tucked into the pocket of a man's suit in one of the city's largest stores. From the top of the box dangled a condom filled with acid. In the bottom was a mixture of potassium chlorate and sugar. When the acid ate through the rubber, it would drip down into the chemicals and start a fire.

"Bloody sacrilegious," said a sergeant.

"What?" asked Thomas.

"Using a Durex. What would the Pope say?"

Later that night, as he tried to fit all the new events into a pattern, Thomas realized what a serious turn the fierce, small war with the IRA had taken. The rebels had suddenly acquired an explosives' expert of their own. He had to assume that; too much had happened too quickly for any other explanation.

Thomas was concerned about handling the new bombs; but that was not his deepest worry as he lay on his cot in the darkness, waiting for the field telephone to ring with news of another incident. What bothered Thomas was that this new man—whoever he was—had an imagination. He not only was a chemist of sorts but he was clever. And that meant he could do more—much more, indeed. He could design a bomb more deadly than any he had put on the streets of Belfast so far.

That was the prospect that kept Thomas awake. When the new bomb was designed, the major knew that he would be the one who would have to take it apart.

Thomas wrote up a lengthy report on the new bombs, noting that they might well have all been devised by the same man, since they had appeared in such a short period of time and had been far more imaginative, technically, than anything employed by the IRA to date. The major returned to London on August 31 to discover that a cigarette-box incendiary had just been found tucked down into the cushion of a sofa at Harrods. While showing the piece of furniture to a customer, a clerk discovered the box and casually opened it then and there, burning his fingers with acid. Thomas had expected as much. The contagion spreads, he thought, and waited for the next surprise.

When it came, it was from quite another quarter: a phone call summoning him on the morning of September 9 to the office of Major General Fitzhugh-Roberts. The time he had persuaded Thomas to go to Belfast to take over the bomb-defusing operation, the general had been almost deferential. Thomas had then been a civilian he badly needed. But the major sensed the change in mood the moment he walked through the high doorway and began to cross a Persian rug that was the size of a parade ground. The general was in command now, and he was angry. After all his years in the army, Thomas could tell that by the way the man was tapping a forefinger against a document he was holding. Also, he was standing. Generals don't stand for burned-out majors unless something is on their minds.

"I've started reading this report of yours," the general said. "This business about all the new bombs the IRA is using."

"Yes, sir."

"Do you mean to tell me that they are making bombs out of fertilizer and using condoms in incendiaries?"

"Yes, sir."

"That strikes me as being rather bizarre. Are you quite sure?"

"Quite sure." The edge in the general's voice was beginning to stir old resentments in Thomas. "If you follow on, sir," he said, "you'll also see that they use clothespins."

"Clothespins?"

As Thomas explained how the IRA used a spring-operated clothespin as a timing device, the general walked around the desk and stood in front of the major. Instinctively Thomas stood erect and pulled in his chin. His heels came together and his toes turned out at the proper angle. He was braced at attention.

"You're not putting me on, are you?" The general's voice had the flick of a whip in every syllable.

"No, sir."

"What puzzles me—and I will wait for your explanation—is how anyone reduced to using condoms and clothespins can make bloody fools out of you and the British Army."

Too late, Thomas saw the trap he had built for himself. "I don't follow, sir," he said.

"They've got you on the run—is that simple enough?" said the general. "They've turned London upside-down. Do you understand that?"

Thomas did not know what to say. For an instant he thought of quitting on the spot, but that was impossible. They might even be expecting him to do that, and he would not give them that particular pleasure. But there was another reason that kept him there: the wrath of the British Army was concentrated in the general's glare. Uneasily, Thomas realized that he was being intimidated.

After a moment the general snorted and moved off to stare out of the window at the traffic dodging down Whitehall. The instant the words were out of Thomas's mouth, he wished he could have retrieved them. "Some of their bombs do explode, you know."

The general whirled and came back. He looked curiously at Thomas. For ten, twenty, thirty seconds, the general let the silence stretch taut. Then he said, very softly, "Is this business getting to you, Major?"

"No, sir."

"You're sure you are still up to the job?"

"Yes, sir."

"They tell me that you're the best we have. I said that to you once myself. I hope to God I was right."

Thomas was still standing at attention. He knew his face betrayed no emotion, but he also knew that the general had seen through him. " 'Some of their bombs do explode, you know.' " He had blurted out a comment that the general had instantly recognized for what it was: a confession. He was afraid. Of course the fucking bombs explode.

"This job of yours," said the general, "it's a question of leadership. You have to give your men the confidence to do the job. You have to show them it can be done. Yourself. By what you do."

"Yes, sir."

"That man Oswald—should he have been handling that job in the Abbey?"

" 'Oswald?' "

"Wasn't it really your responsibility to handle that one yourself, given the circumstances?"

Thomas understood the thinly veiled accusation: he was a coward. But he seized upon something else. Oswald. My Christ, he doesn't even know Osgood's name. They never do. They never really bother about the men who die. Thomas's anger drove all the other thoughts and emotions out of his mind. He was back on familiar ground now. The major turned his head and looked at the general. "His name was Osgood," he said.

"Oswald, Osgood—what difference does it make?"

"Rather a lot to Osgood, I should think. He's the one who's dead." Thomas glanced around. "Look, do you mind if I sit down? I'm damned tired." Without waiting for a reply, he sank into a chair in front of the general's desk.

The general hesitated for a moment, and then walked around behind his desk and sat down himself. The two men stared at each other appraisingly across the brightly polished walnut surface. "You've gone through a rather sticky period, I'm afraid," said the general after a while.

"You might say," answered Thomas.

"I'm sorry about getting Osgood's name wrong."

"But you still think that I'm afraid of the job."

"I didn't say that."

"What *did* you say?"

"I only meant what you already know very well—that a job like this requires personal leadership."

"And I haven't been giving it enough."

The general carefully removed a thread from the sleeve of his coat. "Perhaps not."

Thomas no longer felt ashamed or defiant. He was just tired. "Maybe you should get someone else."

The general shrugged. "They say you're the best there is," he said.

"Well, maybe they're wrong."

"Maybe they are, but one has to proceed on the faith that the experts know what they're talking about."

"I'm supposed to be an expert, and I don't have the slightest idea of what I'm talking about."

The general smiled and leaned forward. "As long as we're talking like this," he said, "let me put you in the picture. There's enormous pressure from the Home Office to get this thing stopped. Enormous, I don't mind telling you. They don't care how, they just want the bombing over and done with. You can guess who's been getting most of the pressure on this, and now I'm going to put it on you."

"I already have that impression," said Thomas. "Quite clearly, as a matter of fact. And how do you suggest I stop it?"

The general stood up. The session was over. "That's your job, isn't it?" he said briskly. He rapped the table with the knuckles of his right hand. "But you'll have to get into it more yourself. Up to your ears."

Thomas was trying to think of something to say that would get him out of the room as painlessly as possible when the signal unit on his belt began to buzz. His office used the device to notify him to ring up immediately.

"May I use your phone?" Thomas asked.

The general nodded.

The major dialed, identified himself, and then listened for a moment. His dark-brown eyes were focused on a print of a battle scene across the room. He said, "I'll be right there."

The general was waiting. "Well?" he said.

"It's on Tower Bridge. In the boot of a car."

"How do you know?"

"Someone claiming he was the IRA phoned in a warning," said Thomas. "He said it would go off at eleven-thirty." The major checked his watch. "We've got fifty minutes. Plenty of time."

Then the idea flashed into Thomas's head. He knew that he should consider it, but he was afraid he might hesitate if he did. His instinct told him to ask the question: "You wouldn't like to come along, would you, sir?"

The general hesitated.

"I think you'd find it interesting," Thomas went on. "We used to handle these things in Belfast. They're rather tricky." Thomas was up and walking toward the door. He paused and looked back. "Can you get away, sir?" he asked politely.

"I can think of nothing I would like better," said the general. "We can use my car."

They did not try to make small talk during the twenty-minute drive to the bridge. Thomas pretty much knew what was awaiting them. A car bomb was not all that complicated, really. One problem was getting to the thing, since the trunk of the car was usually locked. Then there was the psychological problem. In addition to the fact that you could not tell exactly when it might explode—you could never be sure of that, as Osgood had discovered—there was the knowledge that you were working on a bomb that might contain not ten but two hundred pounds of explosives. That was the beauty of using the car: they could pile the stuff in like firewood. Thomas knew all too well that he could be killed just as dead by one stick of gelignite as a hundred. But a hundred would splatter him, flak jacket or no flak jacket. That was the difference. There would be very little left to pick up. Thomas minded that very much.

The car was parked in the middle of the bridge between the two great towers—Victorian marvels of decoration and engineering—that lifted the central span so that ships could pass up and down the Thames. Thomas remembered a postcard of the bridge sent him by an aunt off on holiday. He had pinned the card to a beam in his bedroom, where it hung for so long that the yellowing of the photograph had finally blotted out the famed towers, as though some marvelous, strange fog had crept up the river from Greenwich and turned the scene into a painting by Turner.

"Pretty, isn't it," said Thomas.

"What?"

"The bridge. It's pretty."

The general glanced up at the towers. "I dare say," he said. He was holding tightly to the strap on his side of the rear seat. Their car stopped and Thomas led the way up to a policeman, who stiffened with surprise when he saw the general. There was a barricade blocking off traffic and pedestrians about fifty yards from the entrance to the bridge. Thomas could hear a faint cry of sirens and then, like an answering echo on the opposite bank, another wail. The ambulances and the fire brigade were on their way. That was cold comfort. Whatever happened, he would have no need for them.

As Thomas had expected, the car was a black Ford Cortina. "They like Cortinas for some reason," he said. "One of the Paddies must have something against Ford." His concentration was wandering. His mind did not want to grapple with what he had to do in the next half-hour.

A police car braked to a halt, and Phillips got out on the run. Thomas felt better immediately. Phillips looked at the general with surprise, and Thomas quickly introduced the two men. There was a perfunctory handshake. The general was looking over Phillips's head at the car.

A crowd was beginning to form behind the barrier. The first arrivals stared curiously at Thomas, Phillips, and the general. Thomas saw a woman nudge a friend. Then they both looked at him and nodded. Yes, thought Thomas, I'm the one what does it. How could they tell that? A black angel over my head? Thomas frowned. He was doing very badly.

Automatically, he turned to Phillips. "How does it look to you?"

Phillips moved a step closer. They were shutting out the general, the stranger. "It's like the others you've had, isn't it? The ones in Belfast, I mean. Car parked by itself in a place like that." Phillips nodded at the bridge. "You handled those easily enough."

"Yes." Thomas had disarmed two of the three himself. The job could be done; it was important to remember that.

"Shall we get on with it?" he asked the general, who had strolled a few yards away.

"By all means," said the general. There was an elaborate casualness in his tone. He knows I'm going to try to stick it to him, thought Thomas. He knows, and now he's ready.

Thomas led the general and Phillips over to his unit's Land-Rover, where his three men popped to attention. The stomp of their boots on the cobblestones seemed out of place, the sound of authority in a setting where men made small talk as a ritual to build up their confidence.

Thomas explained to the general how the team worked, how every move of the men who went forward was described and recorded on tape by others watching through binoculars. He handed the general a flak jacket and pulled one on himself. Then, as lightly as he could, Thomas said, "We start out by simply walking past to see what we can see. Care to come along, General?"

There was no hesitation: "Delighted."

"Good."

There was a faint mist moving up the Thames. Thomas could feel the cool wetness on his cheek. He noticed that the tide was out, exposing glistening brown flats of muck along either bank. The artists and photographers must always work at high tide, he thought. Two seagulls soared above the far tower. There was no other movement. The bare bridge with its abandoned car looked like a stark stage setting, something for a play by Beckett or Ionesco.

Thomas started to walk toward the car. The general was at his shoulder; the prerogatives of rank had been left back at the Land-Rover. The two men did not talk. Still, because they were so alone—isolated by the silence and emptiness of the bridge—they looked like old companions. Watching, Phillips was struck by the effect. You'd think they were friends, he said to himself, old friends out for a stroll.

5

THOMAS HEADED STRAIGHT for the trunk of the car. When he was about eight feet away, he veered to the right, walked the length of the vehicle, and then circled back toward the Land-Rover, lengthening his stride as he went.

The general took three quick steps to catch up. "Is that all?" he asked.

"It was enough," said Thomas. "The lid of the boot is latched—maybe locked. There was nothing else in the car."

"When do we get down to it?"

Thomas turned his head and saw that his companion was frowning. " 'We,' " the general had said. Good, thought Thomas. I've got him now. He's committed himself.

"First we figure out how we're going to do it," said Thomas, leading the way over to Phillips and the other men by the Land-Rover. Phillips was holding the binoculars. "Well?" he asked.

"It's latched," said Thomas. "We'll have to blow it." He turned to the general: "It's very simple, really. One man carries up the explosive charge attached to a wire, and the other goes along with some tape to fasten the packet to the boot. We slap it on and get away fast. Should only take four or five seconds. Not much risk—from what the Paddies said, it shouldn't detonate for another thirty minutes or so."

"I'll go," said Phillips. He started to hand the binoculars to a sergeant.

"No," said the general. "No, I'll go. I insist."

Thomas had expected some gritty show of nerve, but the general had composed himself completely. He was rocking back and forth from the balls of his feet to his heels, legs spread apart, hands on his hips, as though he were watching a unit of his men go through a particularly engrossing maneuver. His face was bright with interest. "Which do I carry—the explosive or the tape?" he asked.

"The tape," said Thomas. He reached into the Land-Rover and pulled out a wide roll of the stuff, which had a special surface that would stick to almost anything. Swiftly Thomas ripped off three pieces that were about a foot long. He reached over and fastened one end of each piece to the general's flak jacket. Then, very slowly and in great detail, Thomas explained just how they would go about blowing open the lid of the trunk. The general, who was several inches taller than the major, was leaning forward to catch every word. All of the aloofness and condescension in his manner had vanished. Thomas did not allow himself the luxury of gloating about the change. He understood. He knew what happened to men who suddenly felt the full impact of the fact that they were about to put their hands on a bomb.

When they were ready, Thomas turned to Phillips. "Here we go then," he said with a nod, and set out at a brisk walk. The general was right beside him. Thomas was holding the charge in both hands as though he were carrying a cake. The explosive contained a detonator that was attached to a wire, which in turn led back to a reel held by one of the sergeants. As Thomas strode forward, the reel turned quietly and the wire lengthened.

Thirty yards from the car, Thomas nodded and both men began to run. Thomas reached the trunk first. He knelt on the pavement and pressed the charge against the crack at the bottom of the door. The general was panting and his knees cracked as he joined Thomas. With one deft motion, he pulled a length of tape from his jacket and pressed it down over the explosive. Then, in quick succession, he added the other two pieces of tape in a crisscross pattern.

Thomas took away his hands and the charge stayed in place. "Right," he said, and began to turn. As he rose from his crouch like a sprinter, the fear seized him. He started to run, as planned, but he could not stop when he got out of range of the bomb. His arms were flailing awkwardly and there was a hot pain deep in his chest. Suddenly Thomas was conscious that his men back at the Land-Rover were standing absolutely still and staring at him. *Oh my Jesus*, thought Thomas. The humiliation halted him within three strides.

Even before he turned to look, Thomas knew what he would see, and he was right. The general was strolling away from the car with long, casual strides, as though he were off to get some lemonade at one of the Queen's garden parties. Thomas braced himself for a barely lifted eyebrow, but what he got was far more caustic. The general's lean and tanned face with its thin line of a mustache was perfectly deadpan. His face, the set of his body, his whole being professed a total lack of surprise that Thomas had cut and run.

The general nodded as he approached. "Shall we get on with the rest of it, then?" he asked genially.

Thomas said nothing.

When they got back to the Land-Rover, the lieutenant and the two sergeants were busying themselves with their equipment. They did not look up. Phillips waited until the general's back was turned. Then he winked at Thomas and lifted two fingers to the general. Immediately Thomas felt a surge of gratitude for Phillips. He nodded his appreciation. But he was still not under control. He rubbed his hands together to try to stop the trembling.

"And now?" asked the general.

"Now we explode the charge and see what happens," said Thomas. He turned toward one of the sergeants who was avoiding his eyes. "Would you please touch her off?" he said.

There was nothing to it. The little knot of men stood staring into the gathering fog that was beginning to obscure the black car and watched. The sergeant pressed a button, the explosion was sharp and short, as though an antitank gun had been fired just down the way and, obediently, the trunk lid swung up and open. "A nice bit of work, sir," said Phillips to Thomas.

"Yes," said the general, who was studying the car through the binoculars. "First-class, I must say."

Thomas could feel his confidence slowly coming back—why, he did not know. Why should he be feeling better when he knew what lay ahead? Thomas had always been baffled by his emotions. He knew that he did not control them; it was the other way around. They had a life of their own and, whimsically, they could make him do incredibly brave or cowardly things. He wondered which it would be this time.

"Now we take another walk," he said to the general, and started again for the car. As they approached, Thomas could see that the trunk was completely open; at least they would have no trouble getting at the stuff. And there it was, in plain view, just as he had been fearing, six large sacks made of thick, corrugated paper, all neatly piled in the trunk, and tied to the lot was the small wooden box that they would have to deal with. Six bags at fifty pounds each—three hundred pounds in all. No wonder the car was sagging on its back springs.

They were past and circling back, this time at a controlled walk, when the general sniffed and asked: "Fertilizer?"

"Exactly," said Thomas.

"What's in the box?" asked the general as they approached the Land-Rover.

"I hope just a Boots alarm clock wired to a set of batteries, and the detonator. Maybe something else. I hope to God not. The other is plenty enough." Thomas glanced at his watch and did a quick calculation. "We've got about twenty-five minutes to disarm the thing—if our lads managed to set the clock correctly and if they can tell time."

"Time enough, I should say."

"Time enough, if we get on with it. That's what you wanted, I take it."

"Of course." The general smiled again at Thomas, who turned away.

The bland condescension suddenly aroused the old combativeness in Thomas, and he remembered why he had lured the general out there: to scare the shit out of him. All right, he thought, all right. After that last scene, what did he have to lose? He would raise the ante and see what happened.

"Move this whole unit back about fifty yards and get some cover," he ordered the lieutenant. "If those bags go off, there will be pieces of Ford coming through here like shrapnel. That car will disappear."

The general was watching the two seagulls as they glided overhead. "Shall we get on with it?" he asked. "What do we do?"

Thomas smiled at the general. "It's very simple," he said. "We take it apart. We take the top off the box and cut the wire."

"Is that all there is to it?"

"That's all—*if* there are no surprises inside the box. If there is a surprise, we'll find out soon enough."

Thomas sensed that he was becoming melodramatic and paused. Not only did he hate theatrics but he knew that melodrama would not work on the general. It would not intimidate him, and if the mission was successful it would only make Thomas look silly. Still, the situation had to be discussed: "If there's something new inside the box, we'll cope with it as best we can right there, or we'll come back here to think it out. There's not much we can do about the second problem. If our friends have been careless when they put the bomb together, anything can happen when we try to open it. Wires can move around, timers can go bonkers— that sort of thing. We just have to hope they took some pains with their connections. Any questions?"

The general shook his head.

"Right," said Thomas. "Now, I propose that you grab hold of the box and hold it firmly on top of the fertilizer. I'll pry open the lid, reach in with a pair of clippers, and cut the wire. Very simple, as I say. Is that all right with you?"

"Certainly," said the general. He was looking at the car that was now all but hidden by the fog. "Anything you suggest, Major," he said, turning back to the others with a smile. "You're our expert."

Thomas tried to shake that condescending confidence.

"Sooner or later, someone has to go to the bomb," he said. "This time, I'm afraid the 'someone' is us."

"Precisely," said the general.

"Shall we go?" asked Thomas, and set out for the car. With a quick step the general joined him.

Peering through the binoculars, Phillips kept track of the two men as they gradually faded from sight into the thickening fog. The car was nowhere in sight. "Bloody useless," said Phillips. He put down the binoculars and, holding a walkie-talkie close to his ear, paced back and forth beside the Land-Rover, listening intently to Thomas's running commentary.

Sooner than Thomas expected, the car loomed out of the mist. He walked straight to the trunk and took out his jimmy. His fear had disappeared. All he felt was an overwhelming desire to shatter the composure of the general. "Well?" asked Thomas.

The general did not move. Thomas looked up at him. The man was staring at the small wooden box on top of the sacks of fertilizer. He was absolutely motionless. There was no expression on his face.

"Shall we get on with it?" asked Thomas, and turned toward the trunk. Suddenly the general moved. He took a quick step forward and clamped his hands on both sides of the box.

"Easy," said Thomas. "Easy."

He began to work his jimmy under the right-hand corner of the lid. The box moved slightly.

"Damn it, hold it steady!" Thomas ordered. "Press down!"

The general was taking long, deep breaths, as though he had just surfaced after an underwater swim.

"Steady," said Thomas. "Push down harder."

Thomas began to open the lid. As he felt it coming loose, he automatically closed his eyes and turned his face away.

Nothing happened. The only sound was the clink of a nail falling on the macadam. Thomas looked into the box. It was just what he expected. There was the Boots alarm clock wired to a battery with wires leading to a detonator. The hour hand of the clock was at seven, about an eighth of an inch away from the terminal wire welded to the face. They had about ten minutes to spare. He felt in the pocket of his overcoat for his clippers, reached into the box and cut the wire.

"There," he said.

For a moment, he did not understand what was happening. There was a scuffling sound beside him and then the heavy pounding of feet on the roadway. Not until Thomas turned his head did he see that the general was running. He barely caught sight of him disappearing into the fog.

"My Jesus," he murmured, and then realized that his walkie-talkie was transmitting everything back to Phillips and the others.

Later that night Thomas would remember how close he had come to ruining the whole thing—to making some comment over the radio that would have explicitly described what the general had done. Something that would have shown them, when they played the recording later, that Thomas did not know how to play the game. That he had deliberately tried to humiliate the general. But some instinct that Thomas did not know he possessed saved him, not an instinct to be generous, he was to decide later on, but quite the opposite—an instinct for the jugular. An instinct to win the contest of nerve and breeding.

At the moment, Thomas felt only the enormous sense of relief he always experienced when a disarming job was completed. He was walking toward the Land-Rover when he nearly bumped into him. The general was standing in the middle of the bridge with his arms folded across his chest. Thomas looked up ahead; the Land-Rover and his men were completely hidden in the fog. Thomas felt a wave of sympathy for the other man. He switched off the walkie-talkie. "Shall we go back?" he asked.

The general did not answer for a moment. He had his back turned to Thomas. "I'm sorry," he said. "I don't know what happened."

"That's all right," Thomas said. "Believe me, it's all right. It happens to all of us."

The general considered the point. "That's good of you to say," he finally replied. He looked beyond Thomas into the mist. "I would hope we could keep this quiet," he said. "You didn't—" He gestured at Thomas's walkie-talkie.

"No, no. There's nothing on the tape about what happened."

"Good. I'm very grateful to you. You've behaved admirably, I must say."

"Thank you, sir. But don't be too hard on yourself, really."

"I'll try."

The two men began walking together toward the Land-Rover. They were met halfway by Phillips and the rest. "Congratulations, sir," said Phillips, sticking out his hand. The general kept on walking. In a moment, they could hear his car pull away. The other men clustered around Thomas. "Well done, sir," said one of the sergeants.

Thomas felt some of the adulation he used to receive from the crowds awaiting him after a mission in north London just after the war. The affection warmed him like a blanket, but there was something else in the mood of the group, a sense of loyalty and pride that Thomas had not detected before.

The major did not understand. He looked questioningly at Phillips.

"The radio, sir," said the Scotland Yard man. "We heard everything."

"I didn't say anything," said Thomas quickly.

"You didn't need to," said Phillips. "That's a very sensitive little set."

"What?"

"The running," said Phillips. "We could hear him running. We heard him clear out."

"Really?"

Phillips smiled. "You won," he said.

Thomas still did not understand. "What do you mean, 'won'?" he asked.

"We knew," said Phillips. "We knew what was happening out there."

"But I ran, too," said Thomas.

"Yes, but not at the end—not when there was nothing to run from."

Now all of his men were smiling at him. "What a balls-up," Thomas said at last. "It's all right to run, so long as you're not the last one to do it. Is that right?"

"Precisely," said Phillips.

"Jesus," said Thomas. He wanted to say something to increase or prolong the rare feeling of camaraderie he had with his men, the sense of intimate isolation that was helped by the fog that cut them off from public view. But nothing occurred to him that seemed appropriate.

"You're all mad," he said. He handed his wire cutters to a sergeant. "Let's go and find a pint. Maybe it will sober us all up."

6

"DON'T BE DAFT," Thomas said into the phone. "The Home Secretary?"

"Honestly, Major." He could detect the concern in the voice of the young girl in the office "They just rang up. The Home Secretary's office, they said. They want you there at eleven-fifteen."

"Who does?"

"The Home Secretary himself. Really. That's what his secretary said. She told me to be sure you were there on time."

No one had ever played a practical joke on Thomas. For a few seconds he asked himself who might be putting him on now. It was September 14. Just five days had passed since the incident on Tower Bridge. Would the general play a trick on him? Hardly. Phillips? No, never. One of his old friends from the army? No one knew he was in town. Perhaps someone in the Ordnance Corps who was jealous of his assignment? Possibly, but he could not go on that assumption. "His secretary, she didn't let on what this was all about?" he asked the girl.

"She wasn't exactly in a chatty mood. She rang off on me. Very prim, she was."

Thomas glanced at his watch. "Right," he said. "It's half-past ten. I'll be there on time. I'm taking the tube." Then he hung up and ran.

The train was just pulling into Westminster Station when the thought occurred to him. Immediately he tried to dismiss the idea, but it would not go away: the Home Secretary had called him in to say that his name would be on the next Queen's Honors' List. Skeptically, Thomas examined the proposition and had to admit, even to his cynical self, that it was a possibility. Defusing all those bombs for England. The irony of the situation appealed to Thomas—they were going to give an award for bravery to a man who was scared to death. Thomas actually broke into a smile, startling the woman taking tickets at the head of the stairs, as another thought crossed his mind: the reaction the news would cause in various officers' messes of the Ordnance Corps. "Thomas?" "On the honors' list?" A stunned silence, and then someone finally saying, "Well, he had really put on a proper show, taking those bombs apart." Then a respectful pause broken by someone asking with a snort: "Do you suppose he will wear that coat to Buckingham Palace?"

At precisely eleven-fifteen Thomas pushed open the heavy oak door of the Home Secretary's office and a secretary immediately rose. Without acknowledging his presence, she walked noiselessly across the carpeted floor, opened a far door, peeked in discreetly, and then beckoned to Thomas. "Won't you please come in, Major," she said. As he walked by, she deftly took his coat, which was folded over one arm.

Thomas tried to judge the man who was waiting for him

with a genial smile. The Secretary was still a powerful man, thick shoulders stretching the blue worsted of his suit as he extended his right hand. If he was so strong, why was his handshake so weak? Soldiers shook hands as though they meant it; you could feel a man's character in the bone and muscle. But these civilians all shook hands like women. You could not tell what was there—*who* was there. Thomas looked again at the man's shoulders. Rugby, he recalled. Rugby for Oxford, and then a stretch with the Harlequins, bashing heads at Twickenham in the big stadium that was like a jolly private club—everyone in the stands knowing someone on the field. Oh so proper. But, give him credit, the man had also played six times for England. That was something. Thomas vaguely remembered a gray news photo of the Secretary coming off the field twenty years before after a victory over the French, the clever froggies, with the blood streaming down his cheek and his right eye completely closed. But he had been bellowing in triumph. Head back and howling like a Hun. Now a dead-fish hand-shake and a nervous silence while the preliminary rituals were performed.

Tea? Yes, very nice, yes of course. Tobacco? No, sir, no thank you. There was a pause while the Minister's secretary delicately poured. Milk? Yes, please. No sugar, thank you. A mention of the weather, a mention of the batting prob-lems that affected the Marylebone Cricket Club. Bugger the cricket, thought Thomas, bugger the games. Let's get on with it. Thomas allowed his mind to play with the idea of the Honors' List. On the appointed day, you crossed the crackling gravel courtyard of Buckingham Palace into the inner square that no one ever sees from the outside. You went up the broad, dark staircase just to the left inside the big glass doors, past all the portraits of royalty, past the Guardsmen standing as rigid as statues on the landings, dress red tunics, polished silver helmets with feathery plumes. Marvelous. Bloody marvelous. The Queen would be waiting with a smile to shake his hand and speak of her gratitude for what he had done for England.

The Secretary turned sideways to stare out of the tall window, the small, old, elegant panes polished as brightly as diamonds. Thomas noticed that the man was whistling under his breath.

Suddenly the Secretary began talking in mid-sentence: ". . . absolutely incredible nerve to do things like that. When you consider the risk. When you consider what is at stake. What *could* happen." The Secretary turned toward Thomas, his round jowled face blank with amazement. Then he chuckled abruptly. "But you realize the cheek of it better than anyone else, of course."

Thomas stared at the Secretary. The "cheek of it"? Defusing a bomb was "cheeky"? He said, "I'm afraid that I don't follow you, sir."

"The bombers," the Secretary replied impatiently. "The bombers, whoever they are. They could go to jail for the rest of their lives if we catch them. Damage all over the place. Civilians killed. One fine young officer killed, a man I assume you knew." Thomas inclined his head slightly without changing his expression. "Damage in the hundreds of thousands of pounds. Our national treasures all threatened." He gestured in the direction of Parliament and Westminster Abbey. "That business on Tower Bridge the other day. They want to stop life in this city. They *can* stop life in this city. If we don't give up in Ireland, they will try to blow us to pieces. That takes nerve, remarkable nerve, Major. These are daring men, Major. I think we must acknowledge that."

Thomas continued to stare at the Secretary. So that was what was behind the limp handshake—a bloody fool. As he listened, his hopes had turned to astonishment and then to rage. He recognized the familiar danger signals. He was on the edge of telling the Secretary what he thought of him.

"A cheeky lot, sir," said Thomas, and quietly sipped his tea.

The Secretary nodded. "Very cheeky indeed. I must admit that the Irish are gutsy. Always tough in the scrum. I recall one time at Twickenham—" his voice trailed off. "I don't suppose you ever played rugby in school, Major?"

"No, sir. Football was more our game, you might say."

"Good game, football, in its way. I suppose it can be rough enough."

"So they tell me, sir."

"Yes, well—the point is that we are faced with some very brave men, some very determined men, and the problem is that the way things are going now we cannot stop them."

Thomas shifted in his chair. Why not, he thought. Why not lay it out? "I think the 'them' is a 'him,' sir," he said. "Or at least it's one man we have to worry about."

The Secretary turned to peer at him. "Do you really? One man doing all this? Planting all these bombs?"

"No," said Thomas. "Probably several men are actually doing that. That's the easy part."

"What do you mean?"

"Someone they've got to design the bombs. Someone they've got rather recently."

"Fascinating." The Secretary scribbled a note on a pad, then looked up perplexed. "But that bomb in the Abbey, it was perfectly standard, wasn't it? Just like all the others?"

"True."

"Then I don't see how you know there's one man—"

Thomas saw the problem and felt free to interrupt: "You haven't had a chance to see my report yet?" he asked.

The Secretary shook his head and gestured at a pile of papers on the side of his desk.

"Well," said Thomas, "put very briefly, the IRA has started to use all kinds of new bombs and techniques in Belfast. The change came very quickly, about three weeks ago. I think one man's behind it—the thinking, the imagination—everything's different."

"But not here as yet?"

"Sir?"

"I mean, the bombs they're using here are still normal."

"They used fertilizer on the bridge, and there was that

fire bomb in Harrods," said Thomas, "but basically the devices are the same. In particular, the time bombs are pretty standard."

"Do you think they'll change—that they'll improve?"

Thomas nodded emphatically. "I'm sure they will."

"How?"

"I wish I knew," said Thomas. He was rather warming to the Secretary. He liked the way the man cut through to the basics. "But I tell you one thing. I'll know it when I see it."

"So things could get worse for us—the bombs, I mean. They could get more complicated."

"Oh yes."

"And you think one man may be behind whatever happens—that he's already at work."

"I think so, yes," said Thomas.

The Secretary was leaning forward on his elbows, staring intently at Thomas. "Fascinating," he repeated after a moment. He began cracking the knuckles of his left hand, one after the other. "Absolutely fascinating. One man. Let me think about that."

The Secretary turned his back on Thomas and stared at the walnut paneling of the nearby wall. With time to think, Thomas guessed that the Secretary had not yet learned what had really happened on Tower Bridge. Perhaps he never would. The general surely wouldn't tell him. Good enough, thought Thomas. Let that sleeping dog lie.

Thomas took the opportunity to look over the objects on the Secretary's desk. There was a miniature set of rugby goal posts with an engraved inscription on the base that he could not make out. And there was a smiling picture of the Queen. It was carefully turned toward the front of the desk so that a visitor, sitting in Thomas's chair, could see that it was signed "Elizabeth R."

The Secretary began talking before he had completely turned away from the wall: "One man, you say. If you're right that could change everything. We have a man-to-man contest."

"Sir?"

"They have their man—and we have you. Man-to-man. You against him."

Thomas did not know where the conversation was heading, but all of his instincts, so well developed over twenty years in the army, told him that something was wrong, very wrong indeed. A man with power had become enamored with one of his own ideas, dazzled by his own brilliance. That was always dangerous. Thomas did not like the Secretary's triumphant smile.

"There are a lot of men helping me, sir," Thomas said. "I'm really not alone, you know."

The Secretary waved an impatient hand in the air. "Yes, yes, of course, I know that," he said. "But essentially you are alone. Or at least we can make it seem that you work alone."

"Why in the name of God should we do that?" Thomas asked loudly—too loudly.

But the Secretary seemed to take no offense. "To lure him in, to take his mind off his proper business, to end this whole ghastly affair—to catch the bastard when he makes his mistake."

Thomas stirred uneasily. Suddenly he was acutely conscious of being utterly alone with the Secretary, isolated in the large, somber office, cut off from the world outside and the distant rumble of traffic. With one finger, Thomas slowly traced the grain in the arm of his chair. He could hear the quiet tick of the glass-encased antique clock on the shelf behind the Secretary. What was this pompous ass up to?

"I'm afraid I don't follow, sir," said Thomas.

The Secretary could not hide the trace of condescension in his voice. "Perhaps I went too fast," he said. "Let me explain. I take your point that we are dealing here with one man, or at least one designer. You had better be right, of course, because the whole scheme is built on that theory. In any event, we assume we're dealing with one man—a brave and clever man, I think we would both agree.

"As things stand now, he has us. He can set his bombs all over London. Occasionally we could get to one before it went off and disarm it, but then he could always choose to have them explode within minutes after the time he left. He can disrupt London. He can control London by fear. People afraid to ride the tubes and buses, shop in Oxford Street, pop into a pub for a pint, take a train to Victoria Station, afraid to do anything at all. What is more, the bomber could strip this country of its heritage. He has already shown himself clever enough to get through the security at St. Paul's. True, we got that device before it exploded—"

Thomas broke in: " 'We,' sir?" he asked.

The Secretary nodded. "Yes, yes," he said. "More accurately, *you* got that one. But what if he plants five or ten more in the Tower or the Abbey? What then? And he will plant them. He will find a way to get through a security net—he can wait for months for his chance. And there are plenty of other targets. What about Piccadilly Circus? Are we to stop and search everyone going to Piccadilly Circus?"

Thomas waited.

"So," the Secretary said, "what it all boils down to, doesn't it, is that the bomber has us if we allow him to play his game. We must make him play *our* game."

"And how do we do that, sir?"

"By making him try to kill you."

By making him try to kill me. Thomas repeated the thought to himself, then considered it abstractly, conscious that the Secretary was studying his face for a reaction. But Thomas had no trouble disappointing him. His face stayed perfectly blank. He had known something like this was coming. Something like this always did happen when the man in charge talked to you alone—alone and so fervently, so full of himself. "You're the only man to do the job," the colonel used to say, before sending him in to defuse the great blockbusters. And he had gone without a protest to lie in the rubble beside a ton of TNT and feel with his fingertips for the fuse.

"Marvelous," Thomas said. "And how do we get our clever chappie to try to kill me?"

"Just because he *is* clever," said the Secretary, getting up from his desk and beginning to pace the office with great rolling strides. "Just that. We challenge him. You go on the telly and say that you've figured out how to disarm his bombs—that you can always keep one step ahead of him, that you can take apart any bomb he can make if he will give you time to get your hands on it."

"Bloody marvelous."

"Then he begins to design and plant his bombs not to force us out of Ireland but to get you."

Despite his resolve, Thomas could feel the resentment and bitterness rising again. Goddamn them. Goddamn them for thinking like that, pouring out a cup of tea and then asking you to risk your life. The sheer arrogance of the casual approach. Old school tie. Never a flicker of emotion. Play the game. The Germans are over there. Do be a good fellow and pop over and bring back one or two.

Thomas was aware that the Secretary had stopped pacing and was waiting for him to say something.

Finally the Secretary spoke: "Don't be concerned," he said. "There's no need to worry. The bomber will rise to the fly. Say what you will about the Irish, but they will always respond to a sporting challenge. I remember the time we were playing Ireland in Dublin, terrible fog, terrible conditions, blood all over the wet grass, very slippery and this little man of theirs, Murphy, I think, told me . . ."

Thomas began to talk very quietly. "Go*damn* your bloody nerve!" Thomas was conscious that the Secretary was standing still. "Good Christ, no wonder the Irish hate us so, dealing with fools like you. 'Go and have a nice little romp with that clever Irish chap who makes those nasty bombs. And don't worry. He'll play the game.' We're all Gilbert and Sullivan characters to you, aren't we? Funny little plots and funny little people. And not to worry. Nothing to worry about. Just that he might be clever enough to blow my guts out—that's what happened to Osgood, you know, the one who was killed. You thought I might have known him? I was there when he died."

Now Thomas was on his feet. His rages in the army had

always been explosions of temper, but this time, to his surprise, he was staying perfectly cool. He said, "Go and play a fucking game of rugby with one of your clever chappie's bombs."

The Secretary examined a fingernail, glanced at his watch, and then said, "Are you quite through?" Thomas nodded. "Good," the Secretary said. "You realize, of course, that your little outburst . . ." He paused for a second as though trying to find the kindest phrase ". . . was insubordinate, to say the least."

Thomas shrugged.

"But we'll let it pass."

"Why?"

"Because we need you. You're the only one who is capable of taking on our bomber friend man-to-man."

Thomas waited.

"Ah, yes."

"What is more," said the Secretary, "you know that you will do it. You have to. There's no other way."

Thomas had been waiting for that. Now there was nothing to do but get on with it. Honors' List, hell. You'd be lucky, boyo, if they hang your medal on the bloody tombstone.

Of course he'd do it. Even as he began to walk to the door, Thomas realized why there was no other way for him. Part was patriotism, a sense of duty, a sense of loyalty to country. But more than that, deep underneath, Thomas knew he would do it because *they* had asked him. The Secretary, the general, and all that lot, the ones he had been raging against all his life, the ones who not only controlled the country but who *assumed* they had the right to control the country. They thought he might bolt and run. Thomas knew that. Could he stay the course, that chap Thomas? Bloody right he could.

The two men paused at the door. "Do you think it will work?" the Secretary asked.

"Perhaps. It's worth a try."

The Secretary stuck out his hand. Thomas shook it and

was startled to feel a warm, firm grip. "You can do it all right," said the Secretary. "Good luck."

The door closed and Thomas found himself standing in the cavernous hallway outside the office. He hesitated there for a moment. Passing secretaries glanced at him curiously, and one finally asked politely if he was lost. He said no and began walking toward the great ornate entrance at the bottom of the marble staircase.

Did the Secretary really care what happened to him after all? Had he misread the man all along? Made a fool of himself again? Walking slowly down the curving staircase, Thomas decided that it made no difference. The Secretary wouldn't be with him the next time he put his hand on a bomb.

As he thought about it, Thomas could feel the fear again. It was not just the thought of the bombs that would be waiting for him. The Secretary's plan was going to make him a celebrity, the man to save Olde England. That was what he was afraid of—the adulation that would make him do anything. Long ago he had loved the cheers of the Londoners after he had dismantled a bomb, and he remembered the sensation all too well. The Secretary could not possibly have concocted a more ironic scheme. He would hear the applause and go to the bomb with a smile.

It would be quite a show for "The News at Ten." Thomas began to think of what he could say on television that would make the bomber want to give up destroying London and try to kill him.

7

THE ARMORED CAR was marooned in the circle of traffic twisted tight around Trafalgar Square. Opening the door, Thomas stood erect and swore. All he could see were taxicabs and double-decker buses, red islands in the sea of black. The driver of a nearby cab stared curiously at

Thomas and then at the armored car and its camouflage of browns and grays and greens. "Wha'cha, mate," he said amiably. "There's a war on, is there?"

Thomas ducked back inside and slammed the heavy door. "Piccadilly is bloody useless," he told the driver. "Go down the Mall." Then he grabbed the radio microphone to speak to the lieutenant who had already gone on ahead to the Albert Hall. "Brewster," he said. "Can you see it?"

Brewster's voice was soft and calm through the static. "I have the glasses on it, sir," he said. "It looks exactly the same as all the others."

"Where is the damn thing?"

"Bang in the middle of the auditorium. About fifty feet from the podium. It's in full view. The guards must have been sleeping when he hauled it in."

Thomas thumped the metal dashboard with his left hand. Next time they'll put one in the Queen's lap at teatime. "Leave it alone, Brewster," he said. "I'm coming as fast as I can."

"Leaving it alone might not be advisable, sir."

"Why not?"

"There's no telling how long it has been here. We may be running out of time."

With a spurt, the armored car jerked free of the traffic, swung in front of a battered Morris Minor and sped under Admiralty Arch. As the heavy car picked up speed going down the Mall, siren wailing, Thomas shouted into his microphone: "No holes in the top? Nothing showing?"

"Nothing at all, sir. I've been past twice. Just a little message for us: 'Bugger the Queen Mum.'"

The car swerved as the driver swung left around the Victoria Memorial and then curved around in front of Buckingham Palace. The date was September 21—a week after his talk with the Home Secretary. Thomas caught a glimpse of the guardsmen walking their post. Nannies pushing black prams with glistening wheels were turning to stare as the armored car passed Green Park. The vehicle began bulling its way through the traffic around Hyde Park Corner. Thomas decided it made sense to let Brewster do the job. He had tried to get there. His conscience was clear. A delay was too dangerous.

"Brewster," he said, "I guess you'll have to take it on."

"Yes, sir." Thomas could detect the pitch of excitement in Brewster's voice.

"From what you say, it sounds like all the others. Go in fast, pry the top off, and cut the wire."

"Right. Phillips is here to watch and make the recording."

"You'll be fine. Just hurry."

"Right. I'm off."

As the car sped along beside Hyde Park, Thomas leaned down close to the radio receiver, but he could pick up no sounds. He could imagine Phillips crouched in the back of the hall watching Brewster walking quickly toward the box.

Seconds later Thomas could see the memorial of Victorian gingerbread that the bereaved Queen had erected in honor of her departed Albert. Then, to the left, the rounded front of the Albert Hall, a great hatbox that someone had set down opposite Kensington Gardens. To one side, he could see the BBC mobile broadcasting station and the waiting crew.

A policeman waved them through the barricade set up across the road. Thomas's watch read 4:23. He was out of the door and running before the car stopped. He burst up the side steps used by concertgoers, then turned right and dashed past a pair of startled policemen and into the great, wooden auditorium itself. He very nearly bumped into Phillips. Strolling toward them, grinning with delight, was Brewster. He was holding aloft a section of wire.

The tension drained from Thomas in an instant. It had all worked out. He had let no one down. No one was to blame for anything.

Brewster was holding out the wire. "The show must go on, isn't that what they say, Major?" he asked.

"What?"

"The concert tonight. The Berlin Philharmonic, I believe. Now it can go on."

Thomas considered taking the young man down a peg, then remembered how elated he had felt years before after disarming a bomb in north London. It was like being drunk on two quick pints. He stuck out his hand. "Good work," he said. "Very good work."

"Too bad in a way it didn't explode," said Brewster. "I mean, with the acoustics in this place, think how it would have sounded."

That was too much. "Next time, perhaps," said Thomas. "Maybe our friend will oblige with something special. Just for you."

Brewster caught the tone and stopped grinning. He handed Thomas the wire. "Anyway," Brewster said, "this one was standard enough. Just like all the others."

Thomas inspected the wire. It was common stuff—no clue there. "Let's take another look," he said, and walked down the aisle to the box that lay on its side. The splintered top was off to the left. Thomas righted the box. It was standard, all right. There was the clock, the wires, and the stick of gelignite. Twenty pounds at most.

"Not very complicated, is it, sir," Brewster said, peering over his shoulder. "I don't suppose they're capable of doing much better."

Thomas picked up the bomb and put it under one arm. "I wouldn't count on that," he said. He started up the aisle toward the entrance where he knew the BBC crew would be waiting.

"I wouldn't go out that way," Brewster said. "The press is out there, sir."

"I know," said Thomas, and pushed open the door.

Standing directly in front of him was a BBC interviewer whose face he recognized instantly.

"Right this way, Major," said the well-known voice, and Thomas obediently followed the man to an area protected from the street where the cameras were already set up. He was conscious that Brewster had stopped deadstill and was watching them leave.

"We're going on live with this," said the interviewer.

"We'll do it just the way we discussed when we talked this morning. I'll just ask you some questions and you just say the natural thing that comes into your head. No need to be nervous."

Thomas nodded. He was not nervous. He was numb. He could not really grasp the point that he was about to talk to this familiar stranger about taking bombs apart with the hope that in the audience of hundreds of thousands— millions?—the right man would be watching. When the Secretary's aide set up the arrangement with the BBC that morning, Thomas had assumed that at least a few days would pass before another bomb turned up. It was all happening too fast.

There was a camera pointing at him with a red light flashing on and off. Thomas heard the resonant voice of the announcer lauding him theatrically as a man of unparalleled courage, the fearless explosives expert who was doing so much to save British lives and the British heritage.

"Major Thomas," asked the commentator, "was there anything special about this bomb?"

He started answering too rapidly: "No, nothing special at all, really. Perfectly standard, I would say."

"Would you describe the bomb for us, Major—that is, if you wouldn't be giving away any classified information?"

Thomas saw the camera move downward to focus on the box he was holding in his hands. "I don't suppose we can tell the enemy anything he doesn't know already," Thomas said. His voice sounded very odd, as though it were coming from a third person somewhere far away. "The bomb is really very simple, almost primitive, you might say. The electric circuitry is connected to the hour hand of this alarm clock, and when the hand hits this little electrical point that has been welded on the face of the clock, the circuit is completed, the electricity coming from these small batteries here ignites the detonator here, and that ignites the gelignite. Nothing to it, really."

As he talked, Thomas tilted the box to give the camera a

good view. "What we do," he said, "is take the top off the box and cut this wire."

"No danger in taking the top off, is there?"

"No, none so far."

"Then why was Lieutenant Osgood killed?"

Thomas hesitated a second. He had not realized that the interview would veer this way. "We believe he was simply unlucky—that the bomb just happened to explode while he was standing over it."

"The hour hand reached the contact point while he was working on the box?"

"I'm afraid so, yes."

"A delay of a few more seconds and he would be alive today?"

Thomas cleared his throat. This was the cue that he had hoped the reporter would give him. He started to reply, then paused. Brewster had suddenly appeared behind the camera crew. He was standing there with his arms folded across his chest. There was no expression on his face as he watched Thomas. Phillips was standing beside Brewster.

"Yes," said Thomas. "If Osgood had had a few more seconds to work with, he'd still be alive. That's just the point, you see. If we can get our hands on these bombs, we can disarm them. There's no trick to that. Every one we've reached before the time it was set to go off we've handled with no difficulty."

"But what if the IRA were to design some new kind of bomb?" asked the interviewer. "Would you still be so confident?"

"Oh, yes." Thomas heard himself say. "From what they've shown us so far—their level of technical competency—I know I'm safe in saying we can take care of anything they can put together, if they just let us get to it."

"You could disarm them yourself, Major?"

There was no stopping now. "Yes of course I can deal with them myself. No problem whatsoever. And I have other men working with me who can do the same." Brewster did not move a muscle.

The interviewer was finishing up rapidly and switching back to BBC headquarters. "Good job," he said to Thomas. "You were smack on."

Thomas shrugged and walked over to Brewster. "I can't explain now," he said. "Sometime soon, I hope, but not now."

"Really?" said Brewster. He still had his arms folded.

"Yes, really," said Thomas. He hesitated. "I didn't really say I disarmed that bomb today, you know."

"That was rather the impression I got."

"I promise—I'll be able to explain someday."

Brewster was already walking away.

Thomas was left with Phillips. "You know how these things are," he said to the Scotland Yard man. "I just can't talk about the bloody thing now."

"I dare say, sir," said Phillips. "I'm sure it's something we would understand."

"You don't believe me, do you?"

"I'm trying to, sir."

Bloody hell. The whole thing was impossible. He had thumbed his nose at the IRA, made himself out to be a bloody hero, made himself a bloody celebrity, all because of the half-ass scheme the Home Secretary had thought up. Now he was humiliated in front of his men.

"Stickier than I thought it would be," Thomas told Phillips.

"It often is, Major," said Phillips.

There was a pause while the two men stood there on the sidewalk trying to think of something to say. The crowd had begun to disperse. Thomas glanced around helplessly. He could see two kites rising high above Kensington Gardens, and he studied them for a moment.

"Why don't you give it to me, sir?" Phillips said.

"What?"

"The bomb. Why don't you let me take it down to the laboratory to see what they can pick up. Maybe there's a fingerprint or two."

Gratefully, Thomas put the box in Phillips's hands.

"That's very good of you, Sergeant," he said.

Phillips turned to go. "It will all work out, I'm sure of it," he said.

"Yes," said Thomas. "Maybe so. It's nice to think so, anyway, isn't it?"

There was nothing to do but take a staff car back to his bed-sit in Fulham. He was very tired. He knew IRA could do better than put together a bomb with a bloody alarm clock. He was not dealing with fools.

On October 4, thirteen days later, a tall young man appeared at the main entrance of the Tate Gallery. Under his left arm were squeezed a small easel and a folded canvas stool, and in his right hand he carried a large box liberally daubed with paint. His red hair was all but covered by a large Scots beret, and he was wearing dark glasses.

"All right, are you lad?" asked a policeman at the door with a smile.

The visitor grinned and glanced down at his loaded arms. "Should have been a photographer," he said.

A second policeman looked up with interest. "American?" he asked.

"I thought my accent was perfect."

"You might say it was—for New York."

"I'll have to practice," the young man acknowledged. He stood in the foyer and looked around. "Where are your Turners, gentlemen?" he asked. "I've come to copy a Turner."

"Wait a bit," said the second policeman. "Let's have a look in the box."

The visitor put down his box and flipped up the lid. The interior was a jumble of paints and brushes and rags.

"You'll be lucky, you find anything in there," said the policeman.

"You should see it when it's messy," said the student. "May I go in now?"

With genial nods, the two policemen waved the young

man toward the gallery. Finding his spot, he set up his easel and stool, leaving the box with the lid open and wandered off for tea. When he got back, the guards were passing through the gallery warning that they would be closing in twenty minutes.

The young man slowly packed up and then, after everyone had left, sneaked into a nearby men's room and hid in one of the stalls. At 11:30 p.m., when the gallery was completely quiet, he removed the top tray of his paintbox. Then he reached down and carefully lifted out a small, heavy wooden box. The initials "IRA" were scrawled on the cover.

For a moment, he listened at the door of the men's room. There was not a sound. Carrying the box in both hands, he walked quickly into an adjoining hall filled with Turner's huge, shimmering canvases. He set the box down against a wall. Then he leaned over and slowly removed a metal rod that was protruding from a hole in the top.

Two minutes later, loaded down with all of his equipment, he thrust a shoulder against an emergency exit. It held, and he swore silently to himself. He lunged again. With a clatter, the door swung open. Instantly, an alarm sounded and a red light flashed on in the guards' office. Harry Johnson, one of the night-duty men, snapped alert just as the young man was disappearing into the night.

Johnson was sixty-two years old, squat and heavyset, but he managed to trot the sixty yards to the door that the signal board showed had been opened. Finding it closed, he began to search the area. A minute later he turned the corner into the hall and saw the wooden box.

Johnson knew the procedure he was supposed to follow when he found a strange object. He had been drilled by his superiors about the need to leave everything alone and to call Major Thomas's office. Johnson knew all that, and he promptly forgot it the moment he saw the box in his gallery. He had been with the Tate for forty-two years. For longer than he could remember he had patrolled that particular hall, watching over the Turners and their predecessors. He had come to think, not unnaturally, that the gallery was more his than the curator's.

Quickly Johnson decided what must be done. He did not even wait for the other guards, who were then converging on the spot from throughout the Tate. He would pick up the bloody thing and carry it outside. Then it could damn well go off, for all he cared.

Grunting, mindful of his bad back, Johnson knelt in front of the box. He began to work his hands under the bottom. He was concerned about hurting a small cut on his right thumb.

Then Johnson saw the blue flash. The noise of the explosion was overwhelming, but he did not hear it. His eardrums were shattered in a fraction of a second, and he already was unconscious when the enormous energy of the twenty pounds of igniting gelignite lifted him into the air and hurled him against the far wall. He slid to the floor and lay motionless, obscured by a sudden storm of dust and powdered stone. Three of the Turners fell from the wall, but none was damaged seriously. Johnson had absorbed the full force of the explosion. He was dead when the ambulance got him to Westminster Hospital.

8

HIS NAME WAS Patrick Reilly. It was at once his curse and his pride. Growing up in Belfast, he had only to say it, or write it on a piece of paper, to damn himself in the eyes of every Protestant he met. There was no escaping the legacy of hate that was his heritage. The Protestants were the enemy. England was the enemy. They were one and the same. It was what a Catholic boy in Belfast grew up knowing, grew up *feeling*, it was so much a part of him. England had given the Protestants control of Northern Ireland, given the Protestants control over true Irishmen in what was rightfully their own country. You grew up waiting, hoping, for someone to beat England in something. It did not much matter what—football, the Olympics, World War II.

He was raised in a Catholic ghetto known as "the Bone" because the short, curved streets in the neighborhood rather resembled a set of marrowbones. His family lived in a two-story row house so blackened with soot that not even the eternal, soft rains of Belfast could wash the stains away. You could stand on the sidewalk, put your elbow on the window sill, and stare right into what passed for the living room—worn, brown linoleum on the floor, a crucifix on the wall over a weary sofa. In the rear was an outhouse, and down the street was Oldpark Road, the great divide, for on the other side was where the Protestants lived.

From the beginning of his life, so far back that he could not remember when it started, except that it had surely begun before he could speak, he had hated the bloody Prods. One of his first memories was of his father sitting at the kitchen table, a mug of tea cradled in his huge hands, slowly and quietly cursing the personnel manager at Harland & Wolff's shipbuilding yard who had just denied him a job. Wolff's was a Protestant bastion in Belfast, a link to the home country across the Irish Sea.

He never saw Protestant children his own age unless he was fighting them. They went to separate schools. At the end of the day, they went home on opposite sides of the street, hurling rocks at each other all the way.

He had been twelve the day they got him. It was the eve of July 12, 1963. For hours the Belfast lodges of Orangemen had been marching to celebrate the day that the Protestants, under William of Orange, beat the Catholics in the Battle of the Boyne in 1690 and kept Northern Ireland safe from the Pope. The vindictive scream of the fifes had filled his head all day, and he was edgy when they found him. He ran, which was just what they wanted. There were six of them, all his age or older, and they caught him easily. He waited to be beaten, but no one hit him. Instead, they took an orange sash and tied his hands behind his back. Then they turned him loose. Years later, he could still hear their laughter and feel the flush of humiliation—a Catholic boy running home through the streets of Belfast with his hands tied by a strip of flaming orange.

Pat Reilly grew up knowing that as soon as he was able he would leave Belfast. Two older sisters had disappeared into England, and a brother had gone off to Canada; he sent back postcards for his mother's birthday that always read the same: "Getting along fine and hoping this finds you well. Weather cold here." Pat Reilly might have stayed in Belfast just to be near his mother, but as he grew older he could not bear to watch her turning gray and shapeless with the futility of her life. His father kept urging him to go when the time came. "You're the clever one. Make something of yourself. Don't end up like me, slaving down on the docks, me with a bad back, trying to keep up with lads half my age."

School was an ordeal: hour after hour of droning lessons in dusty classrooms, while nuns, pinched with age, boxed his ears and called him "bone-lazy." They nearly killed his only passion—a love of chemistry and physics. In particular, Reilly was fascinated by explosives. His avocation had nothing to do with the IRA—he was by no means planning ahead. When Reilly and his friends were in school, they paid little heed to the IRA, which at the time was quiescent. Reilly simply wanted to know how and why certain chemicals exploded. He used to make gunpowder of a sort by using whatever ingredients were at hand—saltpeter, sulfur, lamp black, and sawdust. Reilly knew that it would never do to set off an explosion in Catholic Belfast, no matter how inactive the IRA had become, so he used to bicycle out into the countryside and send empty beer cans soaring into the gray sky. Dabbling with electricity, Reilly built his own wireless, repaired friends' sets for free, and designed and installed an electric-eye system that sounded a chime when anyone walked in the front door, much to the delight of the neighbors' children.

At the age of sixteen, he easily passed his Ordinary Level

Examinations in physics, chemistry, and mathematics, but let the others slide, barely bothering to answer half the questions. There was no sense staying on in school, trying to get more "O's." He would never be going to college—that hope was an absurdity—so he apprenticed himself to a Catholic electrician. For the next two years he repaired lamps and soldered wiring in houses, tasks he could perform in his sleep. Relief came suddenly and unexpectedly. A cousin in Boston wrote a letter: Would Pat like to come live with her for a while? Help around the house in exchange for room and board?

When he arrived in Boston Pat Reilly had just turned eighteen. He got a job as a laborer with a construction company and soon maneuvered himself into the demolitions unit, clearing out obstacles and blasting foundations for housing developments around Boston.

By the time he was twenty, Reilly already was so expert with dynamite that he was allowed to plan the razing of an ancient and towering factory chimney in Lynn. Instead of just knocking it down all at once, Reilly designed and set the explosives so that the top fifth went first, curving gracefully down into an empty parking lot. Section by section, the rest of the chimney followed, so that the structure seemed to be diving into the ground. WBZ-TV covered the event, and Reilly—his busy red hair sticking out from under his white hardhat—pleasantly and expertly explained what he had done.

To make some extra money, Reilly worked three nights a week as a salesman in a store selling cut-rate carpets. He had charm and a glib tongue and an accent, gentle and lilting, that fascinated the wives of the factory workers from Somerville who came hunting for bargains.

But he also had a mimic's ear and in time he picked up the local accent well enough to pass for a Boston-born Irishman. He was quick to adapt his talent to help his work as a salesman. "Where do you think I was brought up?" he'd ask his customers, when he could see them losing interest in his wares. Everett? they would guess. Malden? Medford? A boy like you, looks and sounds like you, must be from around here somewhere. Am I right? Brockton, maybe?

Then Pat Reilly would laugh and begin to speak in his Belfast accent, letting the words gush out in a stream, the way the people spoke back home in the Bone, so that the women would stare blankly at him for a minute, and then begin to laugh themselves, pleased that they had been fooled so completely. But they still could not guess—they had never heard the like—and he would have to tell them he was from Belfast.

Belfast? Some of the Italians and the Poles were not sure just where that was, but the Irish women all knew. They knew, all right. Most of them had never met anyone from Belfast, and the torrent of words and strange accent fooled them, too. Their people, all from the Republic of Ireland, all from the south, had spoken much more slowly and distinctly. The Irishwomen would look at Pat Reilly with great interest, then ask him casually, "Catholic, are you?"

Yes, he would say with a grin, and they would smile back, allies against the British and the Prods, three thousand miles away across the sea. Usually the new bond was enough to induce the women to take one more look at the shag rug they had been considering.

This link with the American Irish made Pat Reilly feel very much at home in Boston. He used to love to cruise the city in the old Pontiac sedan he was buying on time, ending up in a bar in Irish south Boston where, after a lonely beer or two, he would reveal his origins and become an instant celebrity.

When he was twenty-one, he gave up the attic bedroom he had been occupying in the house of his cousin —although she had been more than friendly to him, wanted him to stay on, in fact—and moved into a large, second-story apartment in south Boston along with two other salesmen from the store and a young painting contractor. By then he was six feet two inches, a height accentuated by his leanness. He was known by his roommates as "the operator," not so much because of the deals he always had working—knowing, for instance, where to get a pair of flashy new shoes at half-price—but for his style. He was very slick, very poised. For a young man on the make, he managed the neat trick of ingratiating himself with people without fawning on them. His lack of education was no obstacle. Above all, he was shrewd. He retained the knack, learned on the streets of Belfast, of sensing who had power and who did not, who could benefit him and who could not, who could be exploited and who could not.

Not until he was twenty-five did Reilly feel any compulsion to go back to Belfast. A series of brief, worried letters from his parents had begun to nag at him. Mother and father wrote separately; each worried about the other's health, and each suggesting that the decent thing to do was to come home, at least for a little while. To his suprise Reilly also felt himself being pulled back to Belfast by ties he did not know existed. He was curious to see what had happened since he left, curious to see the effect of the IRA bombings that he'd been reading about. On June 11, Reilly quit his job and that evening caught a plane for Shannon. He arrived home carrying his savings: a certified check for $7500.

Pat Reilly was stunned by what he found in Belfast. The impact struck him moments after landing and walking into the airport building with its forlorn and ironic exhibitions of a few machine tools in the lobby ("Northern Ireland Proudly Builds for the Future") and a coffee shop that immediately showed how firmly the past still had a grip on the six provinces. There, waiting for a slattern of a girl to pour out some tea, stood a British paratrooper in full combat gear: green-and-brown camouflaged fatigues; high, heavy boots, and a proud red beret that negated the stealth of the uniform, a beret that raised two fingers to the hidden gunmen.

The paratrooper must have just come off patrol; his lean, hollow-cheeked face, slightly pimpled around the mouth, still bore the traces of black greasepaint, another attempt at concealment mocked by his red beret. The para reached

for a cardboard cup of tea, then turned and handed
a second to Reilly. "Wha'cha, mate," he said pleasantly.
"Take milk, do you?" Reilly usually did lace his tea heavily
with milk, but he instinctively shook his head at the man
and turned to go without a word. Then Reilly saw the
others: three paras chatting up some girls at a corner table,
while all around them people sipped tea and talked and
stared out of the window at the drizzle, just as though four
men in combat gear were not in their midst, just as though
the soldiers had not carefully stacked their automatic rifles
under the table (out of the way, but not too far out of the
way), just as though the coffee shop at the Belfast Airport,
for all its customary bustle, was not on the edge of hysteria.

My Christ, thought Reilly, staring around him, they've occupied us. The bastards have occupied us again. Just like
always. British uniforms in Belfast to help the bloody Prods.

He swigged down his tea and headed for the bus that was
going into town. The countryside was still as peaceful as he
remembered it—herds of cows, long since inured to the
Irish rains, calmly chewing their cuds in fields of green. But
then, in the middle of nowhere, the bus clanked to a stop.
Looking up ahead, Reilly saw a short queue of vehicles and,
beyond, two gray armored cars, squat and ugly. Standing in
the road were four British soldiers. They had rifles over
their arms.

Suddenly the woman across from Reilly cackled with
laughter. Reilly saw that she was rather shabbily dressed
and guessed that she was riding back into town from her
job at the airport. She was sitting erect in her seat and staring at the soldiers. "A roadblock," she called out gaily to her
fellow passengers. "Hide your bombs, lads!"

A nut, thought Reilly, a Catholic nut, but a nut. He did
not like scenes. There was a mutter of disapproval from the
front of the bus, and two men turned, eyes narrowing, to
see who had made the remark. At that point Reilly felt a tug
of empathy for the grinning woman sitting opposite him
and tipped her a quick wink. She winked back and Reilly
braced himself for her to make some announcement about

him ("Here's one of our brave lads now!"), but she contented herself with a second wink and then, as polite as you please, held open her canvas bag for the soldier who was working his way down the aisle.

"Identification?" the soldier said to Reilly, who held up his passport. Bored, the other glanced at Reilly's face, compared it to the picture, and handed the document back. Reilly found that his hand was trembling slightly, but the soldier had not noticed or did not care.

Minutes later the bus swung into the gray maze of Belfast, but there was no delighted instant of recognition for Reilly, no feeling that he was home. Nothing was familiar. No, that was not quite it. Reilly struggled to make the connection, then made the leap back into his memory: Belfast looked like the pictures of the war the nuns used to pass around, telling how the bombers had come over on four nights between April 8 and 15 in 1941, leaving the harbor area in flames and then, as carelessly as throwing handfuls of confetti, had scattered fire bombs across the rest of the city. Over nine hundred persons were killed, and the damage amounted to more than £20 million.

The destruction was not nearly as bad, of course, but the mood of the city struck Reilly as being much the same as the one conveyed by those fading newspaper clippings that he remembered being so carefully preserved in a green scrapbook kept in a special place of honor on the headmaster's desk. There were few people on the streets, for one thing, and they appeared strangely isolated and furtive, like the stunned figures in the old pictures. There were blackened ruins in every block where bombs had exploded and started fires. Storefront windows were crisscrossed with heavy tape, just as they used to be. Many shops and houses were abandoned, their windows and doorways sealed off against the outside world by concrete blocks cemented into place.

It's a ghost town, said Reilly to himself. They've made it a ghost town. While riding through the barricaded and besieged streets of Belfast, Reilly felt the resentment beginning to build. Not against the bombers, not against the

IRA. They were not the ones who were destroying the city, not really. Reilly knew how things had always been. It was the British who were to blame, forcing the Catholics to take such drastic action. The Catholics had the right to do something to get free of the bloody Prods.

Suddenly the bus lurched. Reilly stared around him and again caught the eye of the old woman across the aisle. Bright as a sparrow, she grinned and said, "Slows you down so you can't throw a bomb at Her Majesty's bloody forces."

Looking behind them, Reilly saw that the bus had just crossed a rounded concrete hump in the road that would have torn out the guts of any vehicle that did not creep over it at dead slow. "Over there," said the woman.

At first Reilly saw only an elementary school, bleak and gray as a penitentiary. Then he half-rose from his seat in astonishment. There, by the front entrance, was a fort. There was no mistaking it. A fort had materialized in the center of Belfast as though the dingy street was a jungle trail and the Japanese patrols were only half a mile away. The sandbags rose to a height of about five and a half feet. A galvanized-iron roof slanting upward from the front protected the redoubt from grenades or mortar fire. A coil of barbed wire blocked off the immediate area, and the whole structure was covered by camouflage netting. Two narrow slits faced the street. As the bus paused to haul itself over a second hump just down the way, Reilly saw the glint of a gun barrel as an unseen marksman kept them in his sights. Welcome home, Patrick, he said to himself. Home sweet home, and God bless our glorious Queen.

Walking to his old home from the bus depot down behind the railroad station, Reilly kept coming across surrealistic incongruities, as though the whole city of Belfast had gone daft. He took a detour to see what was happening around City Hall, a Victorian pile that dominates the city like a very wealthy and very sour dowager, and discovered that he could not get anywhere near the place. A block away, a soldier waved him on; the entire area was cordoned off. Reilly could barely glimpse one of his favorite sights in the city of his birth—the monument on the grounds of the City Hall that was erected to memorialize the fact that the *Titanic* had been built in Belfast. The tablet had always made Reilly smirk. What fuck-ups the Protestants really were. What a loser of a city, to commemorate its failures.

Reilly turned away and was soon in a Catholic neighborhood. There was a soldier—a sentry—standing on a street corner, and as Reilly approached the man was surrounded by a group of children three or four years old. One grabbed the sling of the soldier's rifle and tugged on it, and then, as if on cue, they began to sing:

> If you hate the British Army, clap your hands.
> If you hate the British Army, clap your hands.
> If you hate the British Army,
> Hate the British Army,
> Hate the British Army, clap your hands.

The children stared solemnly up at the soldier and began to clap. The man caught Reilly's eye as he approached and shrugged his shoulders. There was not much difference in their ages, and for an instant Reilly could not help sympathizing with the other. Still, he hurried on past without a word.

9

PAT REILLY WAS nearing his old neighborhood when he noticed a patrol of British soldiers creeping down the city street. Seconds later a teen-age boy came around a corner, gliding at a half-trot and controlling a battered soccer ball with his instep. He dodged an old man, who turned, muttering, to stare at him, and caught up with the patrol. "English bastards," the boy said, not raising his voice, nor showing any temper, but not easing the sting with a smile or a wink.

Reilly watched as the boy dribbled the ball straight at the

last soldier in the patrol. The man uneasily shifted his rifle, walking backward all the while. His job was to guard the rear of the patrol from a sniper, and his eyes never stopped roving the roofs of the tenements while the boy approached at half speed.

Teasing the ball along, feinting with his shoulders, the boy slowly moved close to the soldier, and then began to describe aloud the scene and action, adopting the English accent of a BBC sports announcer heavily laden with working-class undertones not altogether scrubbed out by some red brick university. "Shea coming straight on at Ingleby of England, daring him to take the ball, teasing him, teasing him"—voice suddenly rising—"and oh, what a cheeky move!"

At that instant, the boy darted so close to the soldier that his elbow hit the butt of the rifle. The boy faked to the left, then spun sharply to the right, the ball magically appearing on the other side of his man, the dribbler in full flight now, yelping with delight, swinging around the soldier, leaping over the boot finally thrust out to trip him, and shouting back, "Bloody English bastard!"

The other British soldiers glanced around, eyes widening slightly, ready to dive for cover. Reilly had read that there usually was no warning—the sight, the glimpse, more likely, of a hand holding a revolver appearing from around a wall, and then the sharp crack-crack-crack of the shots, fired quickly and without aim. Most often, not even that much warning: just the report of a sniper's rifle from a rooftop blocks away.

The boy was still controlling the ball, still broadcasting his account of the scene. "Shea has the whole English defense hypnotized," he cried, dodging around one soldier, dragging the ball along like bait in front of a fish. "And now Shea, the dauntless Irishman from Belfast, is sticking the buggering ball up the arse of England!"

The soldiers stopped in their tracks. They watched the buildings around them, guns up high and ready. There was no chance of trying to kick the ball away, although one or two were tempted—Reilly could see them bending their knees slightly, ready to have a go. The boy kicked the ball up into the air, bounced it off one knee, then the other, doing his tricks as he moved through the squad, flicking the ball back and forth from his knees and then high into the air to be caught on his forehead and bounced once, twice, three times. And as he moved, he kept repeating a chant set to a staccato rhythm that every soldier knew because it was the basis for dozens of incantations—mostly obscene—shouted out every Saturday afternoon at soccer games all over Britain. Dum dum-de-dum dum dum-de-dum *dum-dum*. "You're going to get your bloody heads blown off!" chanted the boy, smiling, innocent as you please.

He was repeating the chant, heading the ball in time to the rhythm, when the lieutenant took out his pistol. As the ball reached the top of its arc, about eighteen inches over the boy's head, the lieutenant fired. The sound of the shot crashed off the stone fronts of the houses that crowded the sidewalks. The boy had been looking upward at the ball when it disintegrated right before his eyes. He dropped to one knee and turned to stare at the officer. He moved his lips but no sound came. He tried again. "You dumb fuck, Mister," he said.

The lieutenant bowed slightly. "England one, IRA nil," he said.

Reilly could hear the laughter of the soldiers as the terrified boy started to run. Hatred of the British surged over Reilly as though the lieutenant had slapped him in the face. For a moment Reilly very nearly intervened to curse the officer, a man no older than himself, but he caught himself in time. That would have been disastrous, questioning right there on the street, followed by an interrogation at the army headquarters and maybe internment without charge—just because he was suspicious, belligerent—at the camp he had read about called Long Kesh. So Reilly looked the other way and kept to his side of the street and ignored the hoot of laughter as a corporal repeated: "England one, IRA nil."

When he finally reached home, Reilly was so shaken with

rage that he botched his reunion with his mother, who thought that he was somehow angry with her and burst into tears. By the time Reilly had that sorted out, and got her peacefully settled with a cup of tea in her hand, his father was standing in the small doorway. My God, Reilly thought, he's shrunk. He's an old man.

"It's fine to see you, son," said his father right off. "But I'm sorry to see you."

Reilly understood. "That bad, is it?" he asked.

"That bad," said his father.

It was indeed. That night Reilly was snapped awake by the roar of a helicopter swooping low over the neighborhood. The flash of its searchlight swept through his window, blinding him as he sat bolt upright. He realized that the pilot must have been hunting for snipers prowling the rooftops. As he lay in bed, listening to the roar of the engine growing fainter, Reilly heard a dull explosion far off in the distance and then, a minute later, the faint but insistent moan of a siren on the other side of town.

The next week, making courtesy calls around the neighborhood, looking up his old buddies, Reilly learned how the war with the British was hurting the Irish Catholics he had known all his life. Six houses in the area had been entered in the middle of the night, the only warning a heavy pounding on the front door.

In each case, so Reilly was told, the soldiers acted like brigands, ripping things apart, even prying up floor boards. They were looking for arms. "Guns, Pat," the neighbors would say, giving him a nudge. "Can you imagine—looking for guns in our house? They never found any—not to say," with another nudge, "that they didn't come close. The bastards."

There was a unit of the IRA operating in the neighborhood—holing up by day, dodging the searchlights of the helicopters by night, waiting, waiting for the instant when the cross hairs of their telescopic sights rested on a soldier at the outpost just down the road and the shot would ring out and bring instant silence to the street. Even the dogs would stop barking. When the British patrols came to investigate the next morning, the housewives would grab the lids off their garbage pails. Beating on the metal with sticks, they would march alongside the soldiers, raising a din of warning that could have been heard in Dublin.

Two of the boys that Reilly had gone to school with had been seized and thrown into Long Kesh. One friend had died in a brief but bitter skirmish with British troops. And another, he learned, had been obliterated one night when a bomb that he was assembling exploded in his cellar.

When he had been growing up in Belfast, Reilly had never been attracted by the IRA—the legend of the solitary gunman challenging the entire British Army. The whole thing was too romantic. It didn't make sense, and Reilly had always been sensible—shrewd, really—since he was a boy. Get ahead, was the thing. Look out for Number One.

To his surprise, considering all that, Reilly found that he was being drawn more inexorably to the IRA the longer he stayed in Belfast. He certainly had not become a romantic. Bugger that, he told his mates over mugs of Guinness. What began to win Reilly over was far simpler and much stronger: it was loyalty to his people, loyalty to his class, loyalty, even, to his religion, although he had stopped going to Mass in the States and only went in Belfast to please his mother. People he knew were suffering at the hands of the British. His father now worked for a trucking firm owned by a Catholic, praise be, but lived in fear that he would be laid off and have to go, literally cap in hand, to apply for a job with one of the Protestant firms that controlled the commercial life of Belfast.

Reilly worked as an electrician—he had easily gotten a job with his old boss, who was delighted to see him—and at night he sat in a neighborhood pub and talked with some of his mates, damning the English and their soldiers who surrounded the old neighborhood as though it were under attack. The pub itself was prepared for war. Oil drums filled with concrete lined the curb in front to prevent any raiding Protestant from parking a car with a bomb in the trunk by the door. Concrete humps to slow traffic crossed the road on either side of the pub, as though some great mole had tunneled beneath the pavement.

Late one night, just before the bartender rang the warning bell for those who wanted one more round before closing, Reilly noticed that a small, elderly man almost hidden in a nearby booth was listening intently to his group's conversation. Half gone with ale, Reilly rose to challenge the eavesdropper, only to be pulled back down on his stool by one of his friends. "Not to worry, mate," the friend said. "That's Cassidy."

"Cassidy?"

"The same." Then a pause while the friend waited for a reaction. Reilly shrugged. "Jesus," cried the man, "you have been away, haven't you? Bloody Boston is on the bloody moon, isn't it?"

His friends told Reilly about Cassidy, the man who financed half the IRA operations in Belfast, the man who had the British on the run. "Owns an electrical-supply store that's a perfect front. Fit you out with anything, he can, and buy it legal too. Proper businessman with a branch office in London, and smart, smart, you wouldn't believe. That's who Cassidy is. He wants to listen, you raise your voice, boyo. One of us, he is."

All Reilly could see was the glint of thick spectacles back in the gloom of the booth as he walked out, but he nodded, briefly, and the spectacles bobbed up and down and then the voice, astonishingly deep and resonant and tinged with amusement: "Good evening, my lad."

That was all until two days later. Then an envelope thrust under the door when Reilly came home from work. "Mr. Cassidy takes pleasure in inviting Mr. Reilly for tea." Jesus, he's a bloody toff, thought Reilly. But he changed his shirt and went, curious to see what manner of man was backing the fight against the British.

He knocked hesitantly on the heavy oak door of the basement apartment. A squeak and then the sallow face of a woman at the crack. "Yes?"

"Reilly's the name. I've been invited for tea."

The woman looked at him closely. "You might as well come in," she said.

The blinds in the flat were drawn. A teakettle was whistling, and he heard the rattle of china as the woman moved about in the tiny kitchen to the left. Then the swivel chair in front of the big desk turned slowly. Reilly looked closer, but he could not tell who was sitting there.

"Mr. Cassidy?" he asked.

There was a quick movement and the desk light flicked on, casting pale yellow light on a jumble of papers and books and revealing, faintly, the outline of a man all but hidden in the chair. Will you look at the size of him, Reilly said to himself. Jesus, he must be all head.

Again, the voice was astonishing—an actor's voice, something from the telly, and again the edge of amusement, as though the huge voice realized the joke it was playing on its tiny master: "So you've come. Good. Very good indeed. Please take a seat and forgive me for not rising. I seem to be welded into this blessed chair."

Reilly found a seat and stared at the man before him whose feet barely touched the floor. A pair of thick-lensed spectacles dangled on his chest from a lanyard that went around his neck. The face was as round and free of wrinkles as a baby's. An ancient Kewpie doll.

"I'm pleased to meet you, sir," said Reilly.

The woman interrupted to serve them tea, slopping some into Reilly's saucer without apologizing. Cassidy's wife? That didn't seem right. He could not connect the sullen woman with the man examining him from the depths of the chair by the desk. He's like a fox holed up in that thing, thought Reilly. All you see is the gleam of his eyes.

"Housekeeper," said Cassidy, matter-of-factly. "Comes in eight to five. Her conversation is as elegant as her tea." He made no effort to lower his booming voice. The woman must have heard.

My Christ, thought Reilly, who is this charmer?

"I'll come straight to the point," said Cassidy. "That's the way they do it in the States, I'm told. I'm right—you have been in the States?"

Reilly nodded.

"Larger than Ireland, I understand, but not nearly as green. Correct?" He leaned forward slightly, but Reilly, puzzled, did not answer. "Correct. Now, the business at hand. I have heard you and your mates speak slightingly of England, our mother across the Irish Sea. I share your opinion, I assure you. I have asked around about you. You have a good reputation, you'll be pleased to know. Reliable, they say. Bright, they say. Talented, even. And hates the bloody British. Am I right?"

Waiting, fascinated by the drum roll of the little man's voice, wondering what was going to happen, Reilly sat absolutely still.

"I am right, I believe," said Cassidy. "Let me plunge in, forthwith. You could help us, I am sure of that. *Would* you help? Can I persuade you to help?"

"Help what?"

Cassidy delicately sipped his tea. "Oh, come. No fencing, please. Surely you know the answer to that. To drive the fucking British out of Ireland."

The effect of that great, round, mellifluous voice uttering the obscenity startled Reilly. He did not know what to think. He did not know how to cope with the strange man eyeing him from the depths of his chair. He struggled to find something to say, and found himself saying more than he wanted. "How could I help?"

Cassidy reached behind him for a small plastic container, and then sprinkled something into his hand. "Do you know what this is?" he asked, holding out his palm.

Reilly leaned closer. Cassidy seemed to be holding some thick grains of brown sugar. He looked up at Cassidy questioningly.

"Smell," said Cassidy, "the smell's the thing."

Reilly rose, took a step or two and sniffed carefully at Cassidy's tiny hand. He detected the scent of almonds immediately. "Jesus, " he said, "it's gelignite."

"Right you are," said Cassidy. "You may have heard that we make bombs out of it."

Bombs. Reilly felt his stomach convulse. He had not known what to expect, but he had not expected this. He was not ready for this, not at all. He liked the idea of doing something to get the British out of Ireland. He had come to Cassidy expecting to be asked to do something. But not bombs.

"You could help us," said Cassidy.

"How?"

"By designing bombs. A lad like you, with your background in explosives. Oh, yes, I've heard how good you are. You could be invaluable to us."

Cassidy was speaking very slowly and casually now. The woman turned on a faucet in the kitchen. The sound of a television program came through the wall behind his head. The BBC News. The Prime Minister had been badgered at question time about the North Sea oil. And in front of Reilly the little man waited with the grains of gelignite in his hand. The whole thing was unreal.

"You're daft," Reilly said.

Cassidy was unruffled. "Hardly that. Many things, but hardly that."

"I'm not your man," said Reilly. "I'm just not." He had a vision of a newspaper photo of a young woman after the explosion at a restaurant. She had lost a leg. A policeman was cradling her as though she were a child. "I couldn't build a bomb."

"You're not interested in beating the British?" There was a glint of sarcasm in the beautiful voice.

Reilly flared. "Jesus Christ!" he said, hearing his voice rise and not caring if he lost his temper. "You've got some bloody nerve—deciding what everyone else should do. Who the hell are you to say? I'll help, but not with bombs. Not me. They mess up too many people."

Cassidy delicately brushed a finger over the grains of gel-ignite on his palm. "You sound like the Home Secretary himself," he said.

"Oh, shit," said Reilly. He turned to go.

"Wait," said Cassidy. "Now just wait a minute. I'm afraid you feel superior to us—about the bombing, I mean."

"Maybe."

"Well, I advise you to guard against that. Wait until you've been with us a bit longer before you decide on the morality of bombs."

Reilly turned at the door. Cassidy was struggling help-lessly to get up. He can't even get out of his chair, thought Reilly. He's going to get the British out of Ireland? Bloody ludicrous. The whole thing was bloody ludicrous.

"I'll see you around—like they say in the States," said Reilly, and left.

Reilly found himself going over the scene with Cassidy time and again, wondering if he had been really honest, wondering if perhaps the reason that he had refused to get involved with bombs ("They mess up too many people") was not basically a lie. Perhaps he was just too afraid to do any-thing. What if Cassidy had asked him to become a sniper? Would he have done that? Reilly found he could not an-swer.

He had never been accused—even indirectly as Cassidy had done—of being a coward. He had never analyzed his own character. Nor, for that matter, had he ever thought very much about what he believed in. Values? Get your finger out, mate, and get on with it.

Later, when what happened next was long enough past so that he could consider it calmly, Reilly was to decide that his expedition may have been partially a show of bravado to convince himself—to show Cassidy—that he was not a cow-ard. That and a desire to prove to himself that the Prods had not intimidated him for life on that night, so many years before, when they had sent him home, weeping, with his hands tied together behind his back by a sash of orange.

In any event, for whatever muddled reason, Reilly got cleaned up after work on the evening of July 11 and headed for the Protestant section around Sandy Row. It was the biggest night of the year for "the Billies," the eve of "the twelfth," the anniversary of the Battle of the Boyne.

Five blocks away, Reilly could already hear the Protestant bagpipers playing "The Sash My Father Wore," and he could see the glare in the sky from the arcades of lights stretching across the streets and the bonfires. The flame and smoke were what he remembered from his childhood. The first smell of burning wood brought it all back. Reilly ran a nervous hand through his red hair and pressed on.

He turned a corner and there was the first fire—a great victory beacon ignited in the heart of Belfast to the glory of a king who had been dead for over two hundred and fifty years. The fire was burning in the middle of a street inter-section, the flames shooting up higher than the roofs of the two-story brick row houses—very much like his own, Reilly realized—that lined the narrow street. A group of children cavorted around the blaze, daring each other to get closer. Their parents stood back, watching and smiling and oc-casionally shuffling their feet or even strutting for a few yards to the wild music of a bagpipe coming from a nearby pub.

Reilly could feel the blasting heat of the fire on his cheeks as he struggled through the friendly crowd that filled the street. He was jostled, pounded on the back, and offered a drink at every corner by people treating him like one of their own. Any other night of the year, he—as a stranger—would have immediately been asked, "Are you a Paddy or a Prod? Are you a Mickey or a Billy?" But on the night of the great Protestant celebration, with the flames dancing higher and higher, it never occurred to anyone that a Catholic would walk down Sandy Row.

Everywhere Reilly turned he was confronted by the Union Jack. The flag hung from buildings, decorated light poles, waved from the windows of upstairs bedrooms. Old ladies caught up and spun around by the throng waved little Union Jacks in Reilly's face. A crippled boy in a wheelchair had a Union Jack wrapped across his legs, like a blanket, and held another aloft in his hand while his mother pushed him down the middle of the road.

Reilly had never seen such emotion before, a blend of patriotism and religion, and a kind of savage exultation that had its ugly side. "Up the bloody Pope," yelled a boy throwing more wood on a fire, and his cry was echoed by the crowd as though it were a football cheer.

Listening to the rising scream of the bagpipes, Reilly made his way through the crowds for hours, letting the celebrators' emotions flow over him, dazed by the purity and the intensity of the hate. He spoke to no one, fearing he might utter an Americanism that would instantly draw questions: Who are you?

Then, rounding a corner, Reilly came face-to-face with a British Army lieutenant wearing full combat gear. His face was even blackened by grease for camouflage. What in God's name are they doing here, wondered Reilly, as he watched the patrol push past while men and women reached out to pat the soldiers on the back. "Brave lads, brave lads!" cried one woman. "Kill the bloody harps," yelled a man on the curb.

With a rumble of its siren, a fire truck began easing its way through the crowd. Reilly guessed that the soldiers had been called out to protect the firemen from snipers, who might be on rooftops along the way. The truck stopped about fifty yards from a bonfire that was rocketing showers of sparks over the neighborhood. The front of a candy store was beginning to blacken with heat. Only one man got out of the truck—a tall man wearing a white helmet. Reilly guessed he was the chief, but he wondered why the others were staying on the vehicle. The man began to walk slowly through the crowd, talking to groups here and there, while the other men on the truck observed him closely. In his white helmet and black boots and waterproof gear, the fireman looked grotesquely out of place—a death's head at the feast—among the celebrating drunks and flag wavers and pipers. Twice he was offered a drink, and twice he gently pushed it aside. He seemed to be looking for someone. After a moment, he walked over to a group of six men about Reilly's age who were standing on a corner, somewhat removed from the crowd. Reilly recognized them immediately for what they were: street fighters, gunmen, perhaps, the Protestants' answer to the IRA. They had the same air of sullen hostility, of incipient violence, that Reilly had seen often enough in his own neighborhood when the men who ran things gathered to talk.

The fireman began pointing at the buildings around the intersection, concentrating mainly on the endangered candy store. Reilly sidled closer until he picked up the last of what the man was saying: ". . . spray the store and let the fire die down a bit, what do you say to that?" One or two of the men nodded and the fireman turned to go back to the truck.

The truck moved slowly through the crowd. The men hitched a hose to a hydrant and began playing a stream on the storefront while the onlookers cheered. The wooden door began to crackle and steam. The firemen made no attempt to put out the bonfire, but they waited until it had died down a bit before they left.

Reilly could not believe what he had just heard and seen. The Fire Brigade of Belfast negotiating with the Prods to get permission to put out a lousy fire! Otherwise, the bully-boys on the corner might have driven the firemen away. That was it; that was clearly it. Christ, Sandy Row might just as well be in bloody Africa. It was another country.

He was turning to go home when he saw Sean Connors pushing his way through the crowd. Connors, one of his mates at the shop, caught sight of him at the same instant and came running.

"You've got to hurry," Connors said. "They sent me after you. I've been looking for hours. . . ."

"Jesus, what is it man?" Reilly said.

"Your father. It's your father. Someone threw a bomb into the pub on the corner."

Reilly began to run. He fought his way through the holiday crowd, plowing into people, knocking them aside. The hour was so late and the spirits so high that no one took offense. Men whacked him on the back and offered him a glass, and when Reilly began to swear at them with rage and frustration they only laughed.

"Bloody Prods!" Reilly yelled, shoving an amiable drunk out of his way. "Bloody fucking Prods!" That made one or two heads turn in puzzlement, but by the time they realized what the wild man had really said, Reilly was swallowed up in another part of the throng, struggling to get around another bonfire, running so close to the flames that he thought his hair was blazing. He felt a hatred so cold that it wiped out all other feeling, even the sense of physical exhaustion. For a frantic half-hour Reilly struggled through the crowds until he broke into the clear around the railroad station and hailed a cab.

The surgeon was talking to Reilly's mother outside the emergency room when Reilly came running down the long corridor, slipping on the polished linoleum. He could see his mother's tears.

"Is he all right?" he asked.

"It was his legs," said the surgeon.

"Is he alive?"

"Yes. Yes, he's alive," said the surgeon. He put a hand on Reilly's arm. "It was his legs. We had to take them both off."

An hour later, after he had settled his mother at home, Reilly plunged outside to walk the dark streets. Faintly, borne gently on the wind, the screech of Protestant bagpipes reached his ears. It was dawn when Reilly stopped at a phone box and dialed a number.

"Jesus," said Cassidy, when he finally answered, "do you know what time it is?"

"No," said Reilly. "I thought you wanted me to keep in

touch. I thought you'd be interested. The bombs—I'd like to design the bombs."

10

THE SESSION TOOK a few days for Cassidy to arrange. On the night of July 14, three days after his father lost his legs, Reilly was a member of the angry crowd that watched Thomas and his squad of experts drive out of their base on their way to the airport and London. On July 20, Reilly was directed to appear at Cassidy's shop that evening.

He never did learn their names. Cassidy did not introduce them ("The less you all know about each other, the better"), and they obviously preferred to stand apart. Reilly wondered why at first, and then realized that they did not trust him. He was the newcomer. He had never been tested. All right, thought Reilly, and tried to ignore the appraising gazes of the two stocky young men (could they be brothers?) who leaned against the workbench and listened without showing any sign of approval or disapproval at anything they heard.

Heavy black curtains covered the two windows so that no British patrol would see light and wonder why anyone was working late. Reilly knew there were lookouts waiting down the block in both directions; there would be plenty of warning at the first glimpse of a paratrooper nosing his way into the neighborhood.

Still, Cassidy lowered his voice as he began the meeting. "I will not try to be delicate," he said. "I have neither the time nor the inclination to be diplomatic. There is a job to be done, and we need all four of us to do it. None of us can do it alone. I can provide only the money and the plan." He nodded at the pair of men. "You and those who work with you can make and plant the devices—you've shown us that—but you need help. You need new techniques, new ideas, new approaches."

Why doesn't he just come out and say they're thick, wondered Reilly.

Cassidy was turning to him. "We hope you have the knowledge we need."

There was a pause while the three men looked at Reilly, Cassidy smiling faintly from his place at the cluttered desk beside the workbench, the other two squinting through the rising smoke from their cigarettes, which hung miraculously from their lower lips. There was an air of unreality about the scene for Reilly—shut off with this trio in the workshop behind Cassidy's shop, being asked to suggest ways of blasting the British out of Ireland. How in God's name had he fetched up here? "Maybe I can help, maybe not." He shrugged. "What's the problem?"

Cassidy explained that they were beginning to find it hard to obtain the dynamite and gelignite that they once acquired by simply raiding construction sites. The British had rounded up the explosives, put them under lock and key, and were rationing them, day by day, to work crews. Explosives could be imported, of course, but that was an inconvenience at best and dangerous at worst—what with the navy patrolling the ports and seacoasts. Then there was the problem he had alluded to earlier, said Cassidy, nodding at the pair of silent onlookers—the problem of helping our lads devise better weapons. Cassidy summed up his lecture like a professor: "We need to be able to do more with what we can get our hands on."

Reilly glanced around the workroom. All he could see was electrical equipment. "You got anything here?" he said. "Any chemicals? Anything like that?"

"We intentionally don't store much," said Cassidy. "When there's a job to be done, we bring supplies in that night, build the bomb, and then get rid of it."

Reilly shrugged again. "So I guess I just talk," he said.

"And draw," said Cassidy. He had a notepad in front of him. "We could use diagrams," he said, and handed Reilly some sheets of paper.

"Right," said Reilly and started in. For the next two

hours, he talked and drew on the sheets of paper that Cassidy handed him. He told them how they could use bags of agricultural chemicals as explosives. "Put them in a car," he said. "Haul them right up to your target building, park the car, and walk away." He told them how they could make low-yield explosives that incorporated such commonplace substances as mothballs, saltpeter, baking soda, lye, and salt. He recommended mining the milk urns he saw standing beside the roads patrolled by the army.

When Cassidy said they needed a timing device that could be set for longer than twelve hours—the limit for any standard clock—Reilly sorted through a number of ideas before he came up with the notion of using a spring-operated clothespin. "American 'know-how,'" said Cassidy, as he scribbled down notes, "Ain't it wonderful."

Pressed by Cassidy to think up a simple incendiary bomb, Reilly tried out a few sketches and then suggested using a cigarette box and a condom filled with acid. That made even the two IRA bombers grin, and for the only time that evening Cassidy laughed. "Marvelous," he said. "Delicious. But the Pope! The Pope will be livid!"

It was 2:00 a.m. on July 21 when Reilly put down his pencil.

"I think you've done it," Cassidy said. "I'm impressed, I really am."

Before leaving, the two young men came up to Reilly with their hands held out. "Bloody good," said one, and the other whacked him on the shoulder. Reilly was enormously pleased, as though he had just done well on an examination. He was also relieved in a way, for he knew that he had made a commitment to help the IRA. There could be no waffling now. He was in it with the others.

Cassidy stayed behind and brewed them some tea on a battered hot plate. "You'll want to help out, of course," he said.

Reilly did not understand. "I thought I just did," he said.

"I mean by setting out a bomb or two yourself," said Cassidy.

"Jesus, no!" said Reilly. He thumped his cup down on the table so hard that some tea sloshed over the drawings he had made. "That's not my thing, remember?" he said. "No hurting women and children."

"Never that," said Cassidy quietly. "No fear of that. But if you put out a bomb or two, you'll learn to appreciate the problems facing the likes of that pair I had in here this evening."

Reilly was pulling on his coat. "You've got the wrong man," he said.

"Have I?" said Cassidy. "I'm surprised. Say hello to your father for me when you get home."

His father. Plant bombs to avenge your father. Risk your life in honor of your father. There was no way Reilly could answer that. Every morning he carried his father downstairs, feeling the scrape of whiskers on his neck, and smelling the sour scent of the old gray bathrobe. Every night he gently lifted his father out of the sagging armchair in front of the television set and carried him back upstairs. The daily routine became a constant rebuke to Reilly: he should be doing more. He could feel the frustration building in him as he looked at Cassidy, resenting the quiet smile on the other's face. It was too much. Without a word, Reilly spun and walked out the door.

He got as far as the first telephone booth down the street. Cassidy was using his father as a hostage, and there was nothing he could do. The ransom had to be paid, and in full.

"All right," Reilly said, when Cassidy came on the line. "I'll put out the bombs. But no killing—understand?"

"I understand," said Cassidy.

True to his word, Cassidy gave him an easy target to hit three nights later: a Protestant-owned grocery store in an area just outside of town. Reilly did not even have to make the bomb; as directed, he simply picked up a cardboard soup carton from the loading dock at Cassidy's shop. Feeling the heft of the hidden wooden box, Reilly wondered if the device had been made by one of the men he had met in

Cassidy's shop. "You have plenty of time," Cassidy had said, "the clock will be set for three." It was only eleven when Reilly set out for the site, driving in a car mysteriously procured by Cassidy, but that did not help much. The worry that the bomb would go off in the car—that it had been put together badly—was far worse than the fear that he would be caught at the store. He almost ran up to the rear of the building carrying the box at arm's length—knowing how little help that would be if it went off. Then he slammed back into the car and sped off.

The papers the next morning said that the store was destroyed by an explosion at about three o'clock, but that fact did not soothe Reilly either. "Never again," he told Cassidy.

"Why?" asked Cassidy, misreading him. "You had no problems at all. Why not plant one or two more for the experience of it?"

"Fine," said Reilly. "But next time I make my own."

He built three bombs in Cassidy's shop—all employing an alarm clock—and set them out safely. To his surprise, Reilly found that even that action was not enough. It was not Cassidy who badgered him to do more; it was his own conscience. The bombing of Protestant property did not make up for what the British had done to his father.

"You want it both ways," Cassidy had said, when Reilly blurted out his frustrations. "You don't want to hurt anyone, yet you want to strike back for your father. You'll have to make up your mind."

Two days later, on August 11, Cassidy called Reilly to his apartment.

When they were seated, much as during their first conversation, the old man began very directly: "I have a proposition that I think will solve your dilemma."

"How?"

Quickly, Cassidy sketched out the idea: Reilly would go to London for a few months to help the movement there— carry the fight right to the enemy. And the whole point of the operation would be not to kill anyone but to destroy property: the great monuments and buildings of the city. "There's nothing like demolishing a bit of English history to stir the emotions of an Englishman," Cassidy said. "They live in the past, the English. Deprive them of the past and you have proved your—what is the American word?—your 'credibility.' You've proven you are serious."

It was ideal, just as Cassidy had said, and Reilly said yes before he left the apartment. On August 18, Reilly moved to London. A week later, the IRA began planting bombs made of fertilizer in Belfast. By that time, Reilly was working as a salesman in Cassidy's branch operation in London—an electrical-supply house in Fulham—and renting a nearby bed-sit. The neighborhood was not far from the area that a retired British major had chosen when he, too, was ordered by his superiors to move to London from Belfast.

Making simple bombs in the shop or his room, Reilly operated completely on his own. He set the charge that damaged Marble Arch—a task even easier, he discovered to his relief, than the missions in Belfast. There were no army patrols in the streets of London. Reilly merely left a parcel in the shadows timed to go off early in the morning when no tourists would be nosing about. During this period Reilly also set out the bomb that shook—but did not topple—the statue of Queen Victoria in front of Buckingham Palace and, without incident, planted another in Victoria Station that was discovered and defused by Scotland Yard.

Ironically, it was not what Reilly was doing that bothered him: it was what he was *not* doing. In the days after his arrival in London, someone else put out four bombs, both of which were dismantled by army experts. (Thomas was not mentioned in the press accounts of either incident, although his unit was involved.) Who was planting bombs in London for the IRA beside himself? More important, did the other men know about him? And, most important—the question that began gnawing at him right away: Would they inform on him if they were captured?

Then, on August 24, someone put the bomb in Westminster Abbey that killed Osgood. Reilly could imagine all too vividly how the army would react to that episode. Putting the screws on every IRA prisoner—trying to find out who did it, who was planting bombs in London. Trying to discover who Reilly was. On September 10, the situation got worse. Reilly read how army experts had taken apart a car bomb, on Tower Bridge, that was made of fertilizer—the technique he had taught the two men in Cassidy's shop.

Reilly was not reassured by what Cassidy had told him before he left Belfast: that none of the IRA bombing units knew anything about the others. There was no way, Cassidy had said with a smile, that anyone could betray anyone else. Even he did not know who might be operating in London. But Reilly remembered the two IRA men who had watched him draw the diagrams for the bombs during that long evening in Cassidy's shop. *They* knew who he was. And they would talk, if the British got their hands on them. Anyone would talk, Reilly's friends warned him. Every IRA man could tell you stories about the torture in Long Kesh.

And there was more, much more. Reilly had heard rumors—and believed them all—that the British Army would take a man, blindfold him, shove him into a helicopter, and then fly off. Once in the air, they would try to break him down with questions. If he resisted, the British would slide open the door and throw the prisoner out—when the helicopter was hovering only a foot or two off the ground. Jesus, thought Reilly, they'd stoop to that. They surely would. And then how could a man be expected to keep his wits about him? So Reilly spent some sleepless nights waiting for the stamp of feet in the hallway and the sharp rap of the police on his door. Who would betray him?

In his concern, Reilly stopped planting bombs altogether. Then, on the night of September 21, Reilly snapped the top off a bottle of ale and flicked on the television set to catch the news. He was instantly confronted by an announcer describing in measured tones how a man—whose name he did not catch—had taken apart a bomb in the Albert Hall.

Jesus, they've done it again! Who in God's name would take on the Albert Hall? A place like that, swarming with police night and day. Anyone daft enough to do that would crack if he was caught—tell everything he knew.

At that point, Major Thomas came on the scene. At first, Reilly was dumbfounded. Could it be a joke? Very slowly, he put down his ale and inched his wooden kitchen chair closer to the set. He studied the lean face of Thomas, so self-assured that he might have been discussing the weather, and he listened to the accent that he could not quite place—it was not "right" somehow—but that had clear overtones of the hated upper class.

Thomas was holding out the dismantled bomb for the camera to see. It filled Reilly's screen—a confusion of wires and splintered wood. He could tell that it was the standard IRA design. Thomas was saying how there was no trick to it, really; how he could take apart any bombs the IRA put together.

"You could disarm them yourself, Major?" the announcer asked.

"Yes of course I can deal with them myself. No problem whatsoever," said Thomas.

Reilly jumped to his feet. "You son of a bitch!" he shouted.

All of the frustration and fear that had been slowly building up erupted in an instant. What enraged Reilly was not so much what Thomas said—that he could defuse any IRA bomb—but by the *way* he said it. He did not raise his voice; he did not even change its tone. And Reilly saw the contempt in that, the contempt for the Irish. In a flash, Thomas became for Reilly the symbol of the British disdain for his people. Reilly did not think it through. There was no time for that, and no need to. Thomas's bland air of superiority crystallized Reilly's hatred of everything that had happened to Ireland and to him: the centuries of oppression, the bright orange sash the Prods had tied to his wrists when he was a boy, and, most particularly, the night they blew off his father's legs.

Thomas's picture left the tube and someone began to talk about economics, but Reilly was still raging, only this time his voice was very soft, very controlled. The finger he pointed at the set did not quiver. "You arrogant bastard," he said. "I'm going to blow your fucking head off: So help me Christ."

Two hours later Reilly was on a flight back to Belfast.

"You've changed, then," said Cassidy, after hearing his story.

"Changed?" asked Reilly.

"Thomas. You don't mind killing this man Thomas?"

It was the question Reilly had kept asking himself on the flight from London. "No," he said, without any hesitation. "He's a son of a bitch. Someone to be destroyed."

Cassidy mused for a moment. "Yes," he said, "I can understand that." A pause, then slowly and quietly: "And there's another point. Kill Thomas and we intimidate the whole lot. Who's going to dare touch a bomb after one has blown up the great man himself?"

"Right," said Reilly eagerly. "Right. That's what I was thinking, too."

Cassidy was fiddling with a letter opener that looked like a sword in his tiny hands. "I wonder if they see it the same way," he said.

Reilly tried to divine what the other man had seen, or thought he'd seen, behind Thomas's appearance on the telly. "If you've got something to say," he said, "spit it out."

"I'm not sure I do," Cassidy said. "Perhaps I'm trying to play chess with the Home Secretary, only there's no game, no game at all."

Reilly waited for more. "The Home Secretary?" he said. "How does he fit in?"

Cassidy put down the letter opener and took up his cup of tea. "I'm sure he doesn't," he replied. His enormously magnified eyes stared at Reilly over the brim.

In that instant, Reilly sensed that he was in over his head. He realized that what he had originally seen as a crusade simply to avenge his father was evolving into a wholly different kind of struggle, one that he could not even begin to understand.

Reilly stood up, looming over the little man. "What do you want from me?" he asked.

"What you want from yourself," said Cassidy. "Courage. Skill. A desire to drive the British out of Ireland." The resonant voice spoke so softly that Reilly had to cock his head to hear. "A desire for revenge."

Cassidy had him, and Reilly knew it. He had to go on. He was committed to act by the facts of the case. It was a matter of blood.

Reilly sat down and pulled his chair up close to Cassidy's. While the other listened intently, nodding with increasing approval, Reilly proceeded to explain the design for a totally new bomb that he had been thinking about for weeks—a bomb that could be used to kill Major Thomas.

On October 4, Reilly disguised himself as an artist, faked an American accent, and walked into the Tate Gallery. Hidden in his paintbox was the new bomb he had described to Cassidy.

11

ONLY A FEW hours before the bomb exploded at the Tate, Major Thomas had been trying to assure himself of getting the good night's sleep he so desperately needed. Ever since his appearance on television, he had felt like a bloody fool, and while he avoided some of the discomfiture by keeping away from his men as much as possible, he could not escape the knowledge that he had played the role of the supercilious ass. It did not much help that he knew it was an act; the others thought it was real. For most of his adult life, Thomas had fought the pompous and the patronizingly overconfident who typified the very worst in British life, and now he had joined them.

There was another reason for Thomas's restlessness: the challenge had been made and he knew it would be taken up. He had no doubt at all that sometime during the next few days the bomber would try to kill him. It was the question of how that kept him awake far into the night, drawing diagrams of bomb circuitry, trying to think with the mind—and the talent—of this enemy who undoubtedly was somewhere in London, perhaps at that moment working with strange combinations of wires and flashlight batteries and a little light that flashed on to symbolize an explosion.

The night of the Tate explosion, Thomas went to a public bath. The pool was virtually empty, and for half an hour he swam back and forth, pushing himself until he was nearly exhausted and the tension had begun to seep away. Then he had a steak and kidney pie in the Jolyon's cafeteria around the corner.

On the way back he had stopped off at his local on the corner where he occasionally dropped in for a pint of bitter. He expected someone to mention his television appearance outside the Albert Hall, which had occurred almost two weeks before, but there was no one at the bar whom he had seen before. After a few minutes Thomas realized that he actually had wanted someone to recognize him—was waiting for it, in fact. The irony made him grin. He knew how vulnerable he was to praise, how much he craved recognition. God knows what he would do when a bomb lay waiting and the TV reporters told the nation that Major Thomas was going to take this one on himself.

Normally the thought would have been enough to put him off sleep for hours, but the swimming followed by the food and drink had such a soporific effect that he had barely climbed into the narrow bed before falling dead asleep.

Thomas was roused by the insistent ringing of the phone. The clock read 11:45. He picked up the receiver and listened. "Who told him to touch it?" he snapped.

"No one, sir." The head guard at the Tate sounded close to breaking. "We all knew that we weren't supposed to touch anything like that. I don't know what got into Harry."

"Has anyone called his family?"

"No," said the guard, "not yet. I thought I'd go round to tell them—if that's all right with you, sir. Rather than ringing up, I mean."

Thomas was already reaching for his shoes with his free hand. "That's very thoughful of you," he said. "By all means, tell them yourself. I'll be there as soon as I can. Did you contact Phillips at Scotland Yard?"

"Yes, sir. He told me to ring you."

"Very good." Thomas was about to hang up when he had a sudden thought: "You haven't called the press, have you?"

"No, sir. Nothing on the list about that, sir."

"Yes, well let's not invite them in until we've had a chance to think things over a bit."

The instant that Thomas hung up and began to consider the explosion, the fear began. The bomb had been meant for him, of course, not for the guard named Johnson. It would be a long night.

The sergeant was waiting for him at the front entrance. "All right," said Thomas. "Let's take a look."

Phillips led the way down a long corridor to a side room. Two white-faced guards, hovering at the doorway, scrambled to get out of the way. Phillips's three men were hunting for bomb fragments. The air was still heavy with dust and fumes.

Thomas walked over to the blackened area where the explosion had occurred. "Where did he hit?" he asked Phillips.

"The wall over there," the sergeant said. "Where the blood is."

Thomas did not look. "Is there somewhere we can go to talk?"

Phillips led the way back to the empty guards' office. The two men pulled straight-back chairs up to the old wooden table. The top was stained with circles left by generations of tea mugs. Thomas realized that he and Phillips had automatically positioned themselves so that they did not have to look each other in the eye. Bloody ridiculous. His life might depend upon working closely with Phillips one day, and vice versa. Thomas groped for a way to apologize for his inexplicable arrogance in front of the television cameras outside of the Albert Hall.

"What did the old man think he was doing, playing the bloody hero?" Thomas asked.

Phillips shrugged.

Thomas went on: "That's what I'm supposed to be—the hero, right? Didn't Johnson own a telly?"

This time Phillips looked at him curiously. "I'm sure he must have heard about the show, sir," he said. "It was quite a performance."

"Yes, well, some day I hope it will all make sense to you—to *me*, for that matter." Thomas pulled a small notebook out of the right-hand pocket of his trench coat. "Right now we have a different problem to solve."

"Fair enough."

Thomas saw to his satisfaction that Phillips was beginning to relax. He said, "Johnson was bending over the thing?"

Phillips nodded. "He must have been. He took the full force in his chest and stomach. Pieces of the box were driven right into him."

"What time did the alarm clock show the exit door was opened?"

"At eleven thirty-seven, sir."

"Any marks on it from the outside? Was it jimmied or anything?"

"No, sir. It was clearly opened from the inside."

"Presumably by our friend?"

"Presumably by our friend."

"When did the bomb go off?"

"At eleven thirty-nine. Two guards looked at their watches when they heard the explosion. At the time they were on the run trying to get there after the alarm bell went off. It took some thought."

"Yes, well, we shall see that they are mentioned in the dispatches." Thomas was silent for a moment. The whole thing was already clear to him, and it was as bad as he had thought. But he would play out the scene with Phillips.

"So, whoever planted the bomb was obviously inside the gallery when it was closed. He or she remained hidden somewhere fairly nearby, I would think. Our friend did one of two things. He could have planted the device at, let's say, nine, and set the clock to go off at eleven thirty-nine, and then made his exit at eleven thirty-seven."

Thomas glanced at Phillips, whose face was noncommittal. "Not very likely, is it?" said Thomas. "Bloody *unlikely*, I would say. First of all, these friends of ours can't set their clocks all that accurately, as I'm afraid Osgood found out. No one in his right mind would hang about until two minutes before he *thought* the thing would explode."

"I shouldn't think so, sir," said Phillips.

Thomas continued. "By waiting until only two minutes before the explosion to leave, he accomplished only one thing: he got Johnson to come into the room just before the explosion went off. He managed to kill Johnson."

Phillips looked puzzled. "Why should he want to do that?"

"Exactly," said Thomas. "He wasn't trying to kill Johnson. That was an accident."

"An accident that it went off when it did?"

"No, an accident that it killed Johnson."

Phillips frowned. "I'm afraid I don't follow, sir," he said. "Who was supposed to be there?"

"You or me. Preferably me."

"Jesus Christ!"

Thomas began running his fingers around the outlines of the ancient tea stains on the table. "I said that badly," he went on. "You shouldn't worry. He's really not after you at all. He's after me." Thomas looked up. "That was the whole point of the program."

Phillips frowned. "No one paid any attention to that program," he said. "Why not just forget it?"

Thomas felt a surge of affection for the composed and sympathetic man sitting opposite him. "That's very good of you," he said. "Yes, let's try to forget it. We have enough to worry about."

Phillips was sipping his tea thoughtfully. "I still don't quite understand, sir," he said. "You think they're after you because of what you said on the program—about how you could handle any of their bombs?"

"Yes."

"And you think this bomb was meant for you?"

"Yes."

"And that it was different in some way from the one that killed Osgood?"

"Yes again."

"And you think there's someone new behind this bomb—someone who used a different design, something like that?"

Thomas nodded.

"But how can you be sure of all that?"

The major had to smile. "I can't—yet," he said. "But I will be when your men find the clue I need. And I have the greatest faith in them."

Thomas had returned to his bed-sit and was eating a bowl of cold cereal when the telephone rang.

"They've found something," said Phillips. "I've got it in my hand. It's a kind of metal cylinder, about two inches long, rounded at both ends. Quite heavy."

"Yes," said Thomas. "I thought so." He was so sure—had been anticipating the news so confidently—that he did not feel any fear.

"This is what you were expecting?" asked Phillips.

"I'm afraid so."

"What is it?"

Thomas described the nature of the device that he was sure Phillips was cradling in the palm of his hand. The major told how the bomber had used the capsule in the explosion that, quite by accident, had killed Johnson. And, as unemotionally as he could, Thomas told how he thought the bomber—whoever he was—would use the capsule again in the near future to try to kill him.

The sun disturbed Reilly. He was slumped in a worn, overstuffed chair, feet propped up on a stool that he had covered with a copy of *The News of the World*. For an instant, he blinked against the light and looked at his watch. Ten minutes after eight. Reilly lunged for the transistor radio on the bureau. The languid voice of the BBC announcer was discussing a riot in Lebanon. Reilly cursed and lashed out with a foot at a cushion lying on the floor. The domestic news was over. He would have to wait for the next broadcast.

Reilly bent to peer into the small refrigerator next to the stove and took out a bottle of milk. He got some Cornflakes from the shelf above the sink and settled into the big chair to have breakfast, suddenly realizing that he had not eaten in about eighteen hours.

He was sipping tea when the BBC announcer calmly launched into the national news. "An explosion last evening in the Tate Gallery took the life of a guard, Mr. Harry Johnson. Authorities stated that the explosion was caused by a bomb left by IRA terrorists. The bomb was the latest in a series to be detonated in London the past few weeks. Earlier, an officer of the Royal Ordnance Corps was killed while attempting to disarm a bomb in Westminster Abbey. . . ."

Reilly had stopped listening. He reached over, picked up the small radio and turned it off. Then he hurled the radio against the far wall. That bloody guard! Why did *he* touch it? For five minutes Reilly indulged his rage, and when his anger began to flag, he encouraged it further, trying to keep the emotion hot. The first thought that had leapt into Reilly's mind when he heard that Thomas had escaped was: Now I will have to do it again. Just when he hoped that he was free, he was trapped. And the next time he was even more likely to fail. By the next time, Thomas would know. He would know Reilly was trying to kill him—and how.

12

"HOW MANY DID you say?"

Phillips consulted his clipboard again. "Five hundred, at least. Maybe as many as a thousand. And that's just in this country, of course. Just here and in Northern Ireland. They're made in Sweden. We know that. We've talked to the manufacturer. But he doesn't know where they go. He just sends them out to wholesalers, and they go all over the place—to at least five hundred places, as I say."

"Damn the Swedes." Thomas was juggling the capsule in one hand. "Great help they are." He had been carrying the thing around since Phillips's men found it five days before in the debris at the Tate gallery. The major was trying to get the touch of the capsule. It was a matter of sensation in his fingertips. He *knew* how the capsule worked, all right; he had to *feel* how it worked. There was a difference.

When the lab at Scotland Yard reported there were no fingerprints on the capsule—no identifying marks except the manufacturer's symbol—he had begun carrying it in his left-hand pants pocket along with his prize Swiss Army pocketknife. Roaming the streets of London, Thomas would take out the capsule and hold it hidden in his hand, caressing it with his fingertips and wondering how clever the man was who had put it into a bomb. Bright enough, Thomas knew. Bright enough to make a bomb that was even a good deal more sophisticated than the one that had exploded at the Tate, and that one was bad enough.

Now, while Phillips dropped into a chair and stroked his mustache, Thomas peered at the capsule as though he had never seen it before. They were in Thomas's hideaway office in Scotland Yard, a room used by a succession of outsiders temporarily assigned, for one reason or another, to the organization. The place had the barren, impersonal air of a place for transients. A graying map of the London Underground System was thumbtacked to one wall. Someone had ripped out pages of the phone book that lay, gutted, on the metal-topped desk. Two of the four dusty fluorescent tubes in the light fixture in the ceiling blinked erratically. Maintenance thought it might be able to tend to the matter in a week or so.

"How long will it take them to trace where this thing came from?" Thomas asked.

Phillips shrugged. "They don't know. Three weeks, maybe. A month. Maybe not at all."

Thomas sat bolt upright and with elaborate care placed the capsule in front of Phillips. "Sergeant," he said slowly, "I need to know who sold or gave this little affair to our friend. Because if I do not find out where our friend got this thing, we may not be able to find our friend until it is too late. Three weeks or a month may be too fucking late. You and I and a lot of others may be dead by then. Do you grasp the importance of what I'm saying?"

Phillips did not take offense. He gave the impression of never taking offense. "I understand that, Major," he said. "Our specialists have been trying to trace that capsule for five days now. But even if we find the electrician or electrical supplier or radio manufacturer or whoever it was who got the capsule from the company, we may still be in the dark. Maybe someone in the shop made the bomb. If so, fine, we've got him. But maybe the capsule was stolen. The IRA steals parts all the time. Be practical, sir. We're practical men. We need another clue."

Thomas knew Phillips was right, but he could not admit it—not with the pressure that was building on him, the general on the phone every afternoon at three and the Home Secretary sending him articles clipped from the dailies about the bombings, with helpful little notes scribbled in the margins: "The Prime Minister was asking this morning how you were getting along."

Thomas retrieved the capsule and hefted it in his palm. "Clues are a luxury," he said. "We may not get any more. You'd better make the most of the one you've got."

"There'll be others."

"Don't count on it."

"He'll make a mistake."

"I wonder."

There was a pause, and Thomas and Phillips looked at each other with the calm respect of two tennis players—old friends and rivals—who had just completed a long rally in a set that was far from being decided. "I'm not a detective," said Thomas.

"I know that."

"I take bombs apart. I'm an engineer. But I need help."

"I know that."

"Christ," Thomas said, "how did we get involved in this blessed thing in the first place?"

Phillips got up to pour them each another cup of tea. "Patriotism, wasn't it?" he asked. "Weren't you being the bloody patriot?"

For the first time since the explosion at the Tate, Thomas began to relax, and he realized again the debt he owed to Phillips. There had been few men he had been comfortable with, let alone called his friends. He was tempted to tell the sergeant everything about the plan the Home Secretary had concocted, then fought off the impulse. It was too early for that. With all of the casualness he could muster, Thomas crossed one leg over the other and began to listen to himself talk to Phillips, not at all sure what he was saying until he actually heard the words.

"Patriotism," Thomas said, picking up Phillips's thought. "Patriotism is for heroes, isn't it? What was that line the Americans used during the war: 'There are no atheists in foxholes.' There are no heroes on bomb squads."

Phillips frowned. "Being a bit rough on yourself, aren't you, sir?" he asked.

"No, just realistic," said Thomas.

"Are we really that bad off?"

Thomas put down his teacup so that he could tick off the points on his lean fingers. "Look," he said, "we know there's somebody out there who's very good. We also know that he's trying to kill me—and that you or someone else could get blown up by mistake. But that's all we know. We don't know who he is—not the slightest clue. We don't know when he will try one of his little tricks again, or where he will do it. We don't know what new variations he will concoct for us next time, what new surprises. And to make things more interesting, there are some other thickheaded micks out there running around planting bombs that any two-year-old can take apart, only we don't know they're 'pieces of cake' until we work on each one. Each of which could blow us all to bloody hell, just as that one did Osgood."

Phillips considered all that for a moment. "Which is why they call you a hero on the telly," he said, deadpan.

Thomas could feel the tears of appreciation start in his eyes as he began to laugh. Phillips understood him so completely that he could go right up to the edge of presuming too much and then break the tension. Extraordinary man, sitting across the desk, natty and proper in his brown business suit with a modestly checkered vest, the very symbol of propriety, smiling over his teacup and waiting for the next move.

"You should be in public relations, Sergeant," he said. "I'd buy you lunch if I had the time."

Phillips was about to answer when the telephone rang. The sergeant listened to the receiver for a moment. Then he raised his eyebrows in mock horror and whispered, "It's for you."

The heavy voice of the Home Secretary thundered out of the phone as though it were a loudspeaker. Only afterward did Thomas realize that he had automatically risen to his feet when he heard who it was.

"What is your forecast, Major?" the Secretary began.

"Forecast, sir?"

"For the next bomb, my good fellow, the next special bomb like the one at the Tate."

God, the man really is a buffoon, thought Thomas. I've

got a buffoon running my life. "I'm afraid there's no way of telling that," he said.

"Do you have any idea yet who the bomber is?"

"None, I'm afraid."

"And Scotland Yard?"

"They're puzzled, too." Thomas cleared his throat. "There's not really much for us to go on at this stage."

"Lovely," said the Secretary. His voice grew a shade softer, which Thomas had learned to recognize as a danger signal. "What do you propose I tell the Prime Minister?"

"Tell him just that."

"I don't believe he'll accept 'just that.' "

Thomas said nothing.

"I think," said the Secretary, "that we should step up the publicity a bit. Have a few more newspaper and magazine stories about you and our little ploy. How you can take apart anything they put together. Challenge him again."

"Charming," said Thomas.

The Secretary seemed to be gathering his thoughts for a moment. "You are in charge of every dismantling?"

"Yes, sir."

"I mean, right there—on the scene, where the cameras will catch you. You don't stay back in some warren in Scotland Yard, do you?"

Thomas was beginning to flare. "No," he said. "I personally wave the flag over every bomb that's planted in London. I'm a bloody proper hero. The nation should be proud of me."

The Secretary's voice was very quiet: "Don't push your luck, Thomas," he said. "Just be there. Just be sure you don't quit on us."

Thomas heard himself shouting: "How could I quit now, for Christ's sake? The way you've got me tied up?"

The phone slammed down and Thomas was heading for the door before Phillips could say a word.

Seconds later Thomas plunged out of the nearest entrance of the Scotland Yard building. A man sitting on a nearby bench glanced at him casually, put down his copy of *The Guardian* and rose to his feet. He was a few years younger than Thomas—forty-seven or forty-eight, perhaps—and he was dressed informally but very well. His thick tweed jacket and heavy-soled shoes suggested that he was a countryman visiting London for the day. The only incongruous fact about his appearance was his pair of dark glasses. The sun had not been out for a week. Indeed, the day was so close to rain that the gray clouds hanging over the city seemed to ·be no higher than Nelson's column. Hurrying, the man began to follow Thomas.

With his escort trailing behind, the major walked the streets of London for an hour, trying not so much to get away from the memory of what the Home Secretary had said as to get away from himself—to get away from the obsessive thought of the bomb. As a lifelong bachelor, Thomas had never had the easy diversions of most men, who could always forget—or at least put off—one set of worries by substituting another. Thomas was alone, and so the sustaining thread of his life was a constant dialogue with his inner self, an entity far too sophisticated to be called a conscience and far too base to be called a soul. I'm married to my bloody self, Thomas would think, imagining the other nodding yes, yes, so it was.

When the bomb was there, Thomas knew that he would have to conquer the hidden side of himself. Or run. One of the two. Then there would be something concrete to work on, he liked to think, something to concentrate his thoughts. Then he would be able to gain control.

But not now. Now Thomas could not get away from himself, any more than he ever could whenever he blundered into a crisis. He refused to drink hard liquor, not because he was a Puritan but because he was afraid that alcohol would make his hand unsteady or weaken his resolve. Drugs were so alien to his character that he never even considered taking them.

So, just as he had for years during other crises, Thomas walked and walked, a slender, wraithlike figure whipping nervously through the crowds, his hands jammed into the sagging pockets of his trench coat, the collar up high to conceal part of his face (Christ, I don't want some fool woman recognizing me now), and the dark hollows under his eyes so pronounced that more than one person, looking up as he hurried by, wondered if he had a fever.

Striding through Trafalgar Square, Thomas scattered a flock of pigeons, spoiling a picture that a hefty German tourist was trying to compose as he stared into the depths of his Rolleiflex. Reaching the Haymarket, Thomas hesitated for a second, and then struck north. Outside the American Express office, some jeans-clad boys and girls were hanging about. Their backpacks were stacked on the sidewalk, blocking part of the way, but that was not what made Thomas mutter as he passed. He was infuriated—irrationally, he sensed immediately—by the casual laughter of the young Americans. They had no idea of what was happening around them.

Approaching Piccadilly Circus, Thomas could smell the sweet aroma of molasses popcorn floating out of a candy shop, and then the air turned foul with the exhausts of trucks and buses lumbering around the statue of Eros. Piccadilly belonged to the late-season tourists. Pushing his way through the crowd, Thomas indulged himself in a wallow of self-pity. What a farce—having to risk his life to save London's landmarks so that fat Germans would have something to photograph. It wasn't fair. Why him? Why not someone else—Phillips, say? How in Christ's name had he got involved in this thing to start with? "You're the best man for the job, and the country needs you badly, very badly indeed." Twaddle. He should have run the minute that general had begun to talk like that. Run the way the general himself had run later on.

The thought of the general's flight—he could hear the heavy clumping of his shoes on the bridge—made Thomas feel a little better. He began to consider his situation more rationally. The Secretary's the one, not the general. The Secretary's the one to watch out for. He's the clever boyo.

He'll put the spurs to you, given the chance. Thomas replayed the angry telephone conversation he had just completed with the Secretary; his memory recalled every exchange, every intonation, as though it were a tape recorder: *"Just be sure you don't quit on us!"* Fat chance of that. Fat chance of breaking free of the scheme the Secretary had spun round him like a spider's web.

"Quit," Thomas heard his other self say. "Quit. Don't be a fool. Quit and go home to Wales." Thomas answered silently, I'm not brave enough to run. "So you'll stick it out and get yourself killed. That will show them, right?" Yes, Thomas had to admit. That's about it. That will show them.

What an original idea, Thomas thought. Revenge from the grave. Disgusted with himself, Thomas glanced around and discovered that his headlong flight had carried him up Regent Street. He was standing in front of Hamleys toy store. Bobby Charlton, England's great soccer hero of the 1960s, smiled down at him from a poster in the front window. Fifty yards behind, the other man paused and began to leaf through a magazine on a vendor's stand.

Feeling the chill of evening, Thomas knew what he needed. For the most part, he had learned to live without sex. He was too shy to meet women easily, too demanding and irascible to keep them as friends after he had. Only two had ever agreed to live with him, the last stomping out of their basement flat without even bothering to pack. The screech of her voice came back to him, reverberating down through the years: "Next time, get yourself a bloody scullery maid!"

One of the benefits of advancing age, Thomas had discovered, was that he did not need women so often, and so was spared the ordeal of the hunt. He would have nothing to do with prostitutes; he was too proud and fastidious for that. On the rare occasions when the need was pressing, Thomas had developed a rather efficient routine that worked more often than not. He would go to an art gallery—the Tate, if he was in London—and stand about until the right woman walked by alone. He had learned to pick her out unerringly. She could not be too attractive. She should be dressed rather erratically, as if she did not care for clothes, and there should be about her an air of acute restlessness or barely controlled tension. *Something* had to be bothering her so that when he began a conversation about a picture—he really got quite good at it—she would soon pour out her emotions to him. It was the most extraordinary thing, and Thomas, mindful of his lack of charm or sex appeal, was at a loss to explain it. One of his most successful conquests had begun to cry on his shoulder five minutes after he said hello.

Thomas checked his watch and swore under his breath. Six o'clock. The museums were closed. There was nothing to do but try his other approach. He walked up to the underground station at Oxford Circus and caught a train going west (his pursuer just barely slipping into the next car), changed to a bus at Notting Hill Gate and rode down past the expensive little antique shops on Kensington Church Street. As the bus turned right at the bottom of the hill, Thomas glanced at the row of fashionable boutiques. He did not long for the casually chic girls and their breathless air of innocence and sophistication, and the reason was simple. He had no hope of getting one. Even in matters of sex, the major was a realist.

Thomas was heading for a quiet pub he knew near a couple of primary schools just off North End Road. At night the schools were used for adult-education classes. When the sessions were over, a few women usually came into the place for drinks before heading home to their small flats in Richmond or Putney. They came for the same reason that they took courses at night year after year—they were lonely.

Just after arriving from Belfast, Thomas had stopped off at the pub quite by chance and discovered this neglected gathering place for women. He felt rather like an explorer who had stumbled across a remarkable find. Most of the women seemed to have good enough jobs—teaching school or working at a bank. They were quite different from the ones he met at the Tate. Not only were they surprisingly good-looking and well dressed but far from seeming repressed there was about them an air of bittersweet good fellowship, as though they were cheerfully resigned to being over forty and alone. The first time there, Thomas had gone home with the hearty manager of a floor at Barker's department store. She had actually leaned over to say hello.

Now Thomas wondered if his luck would hold as he settled at the far end of the bar, away from the thunk of darts into the cork board, and ordered an ale. The place was almost empty. A yellow Labrador lying on the worn rug in front of the coal fire lifted his head, blandly inspected the major, and promptly went back to sleep.

Thomas nursed a series of ales for two hours, observing the patterns of the women, eavesdropping on their showers of gossip about their instructors in night school and their complaints about their landladies, until he sensed the right one had come in. She sat two stools away—a stocky woman wearing a long red woolen skirt. A single, thick braid of black hair hung straight down her back, giving her a sensual, earthy look. She laughed a lot with her friends—that was reassuring.

"May I buy the next round?" Thomas began, leaning awkwardly into the conversation of the woman and two of her friends. "Why, yes, that would be very kind," she said, with no attempt to feign surprise or play the coquette, or show her dismay at such an obvious approach.

It turned out that she was an artist of some kind—Thomas never did quite understand exactly what she did. After a few minutes her friends politely excused themselves, and Thomas was left to find something to say to the woman who introduced herself right off as Jessica. But Thomas soon found to his enormous relief that conversation was no problem. Jessica was interested in talking about herself—about her classes, and job, and elderly mother—and made it quite clear that she did not care if Thomas said anything at all. She was at ease in his company, she said at one point. She hoped that wasn't too forward to say. She liked quiet men. Thomas smiled and nodded and said he was flattered, wondering if that meant it was all settled.

At closing time Thomas and Jessica brushed against each other as they went through the narrow doorway. "Can I take you home?" he asked.

"Why, yes," she said. "I think that makes sense. My place is probably better, don't you feel?"

And Thomas, thinking first of his single room with the pile of newspapers in the corner and the unwashed dishes in the sink, said yes, that was perfectly true. The discussion was so matter-of-fact that it took him an instant to realize that she had said she would go to bed with him.

She had enormous breasts. She let Thomas undress her and unclasp her brassiere that hooked in front so that they seemed to jump out before his eyes, overflowing his hands. "My God," said Thomas, then was instantly afraid he had put her off. But she was warmed by his spontaneous reaction. She kissed him full on the mouth and tugged him down on the bed beside her.

What need Thomas was fulfilling for Jessica she did not say, and of course he said nothing. In the end, he forgot himself completely, just as he had hoped, forgot everything that had happened and that lay ahead. He reduced his life to the dimensions of Jessica's bed with its faintly scented, flowered sheets.

They awoke the next morning still cradled together. Thomas knew enough not to say thank you when he left. Instead, he squeezed her hand at the door, and she stood on tiptoe to kiss his cheek.

Thomas walked rapidly down the stairs and out into the mild morning sunshine. He was so relaxed that he felt positively lazy. Should he send her flowers? No, that would not be quite right. She was as much a realist as he. It was what they had done for each other that counted, and while the gift had been profoundly personal, it had not been romantic. Flowers would be all wrong.

Thomas got his bearings and headed for the Earl's Court tube station a few blocks away. As he stepped out, a man sit-

ting in a Morris Minor by the curb noted his jaunty depar-
ture with amusement. The observer had been filled in on
the details of the assignation by the man that he had relieved at six, who had in turn gotten them from the man
with the dark glasses. God, if Thomas could get himself
laid, there was hope for everyone. The driver of the Morris
made a note or two on his pad. Then he got out of the car
to follow the major.

13

THOMAS SLOWLY MADE his way through the throng on Earl's
Court Road, basking in the deep languor of a man who had
just spent the night in the arms of a warm woman. He
looked peacefully on tall Africans in dashikis walking arm-
in-arm with husky Australian girls, and bearded American
students with travel-stained packs who emerged from the
Underground and, consulting addresses scribbled on small
bits of paper, tried to get their bearings.

Thomas was feeling unusually mellow, thanks to his evening with Jessica, and he had the luxury of a Saturday afternoon to spend on his own. There was nothing he could
do but wait for the bomber to try again to kill him. That was
putting the point as succinctly as he could, and the neatness
and honesty of the idea struck him as being droll. He
strolled into a newspaper store and paused for a moment
before a bulletin board carrying hand-painted notices that
were being carefully studied by a few intent and silent men.
"Swedish stewardess specializes in rubber goods," Thomas
read. Not his thing, actually. "Craftswoman with delicate
old world touch interested in restoring old pieces." "Bottom
caning done with painstaking care." The major smiled and
let his eyes drift on to the next card: "American co-ed with
driver's license looking for stick shift to handle."

What to do? Turning, Thomas caught sight of a headline
on the *Mirror:* Arsenal v. Tottenham in Derby Match, and

his mood changed instantly. Of course. A soccer game.

The other man watched Thomas eying the *Mirror,* and then pause and glance at his watch. Moments later, as the major queued up for an Underground ticket, the shadow turned away from the crowd and spoke into a walkie-talkie he had concealed in the inner pocket of his raincoat. "I think he's going to the Arsenal match. Better staff it. I'm after him now."

Thomas's step was quick again as he moved through the long, cool shed of the station. The boyhood memories were all coming back, and the meanings he could not escape. He just managed to catch the huge elevator to the lower level, not noticing the little man in the black raincoat and dark glasses who scrambled aboard with a desperate lunge while the alarm bell was clanging and the door swinging shut.

When Thomas got off at Arsenal after the long ride, the other stayed close behind as the surge carried them up the stairs. The passageways were filled with Arsenal fans—teen-age boys and workingmen in their early twenties, all with red-and-white woolen scarfs tied around their necks, or carefully knotted to their belts, so that they could not be yanked away by Tottenham rooters.

With a rush, the mob emerged above ground and into a street scene that was beginning to crackle with the visceral kind of excitement that begins to grow outside a soccer stadium just before a big match. The vague menace, the threat of violence and the promise of poetry, all blended into one. Already Thomas could hear the Arsenal fans chanting their defiance of the Tottenham Hotspurs.

Instantly, the major felt at home. He was indifferent to classical music, and contemptuous of ballet, but the knowledge that a soccer match was going to start within the hour, and that he was going to be there to see it—and to *feel* it, to absorb it so completely that it became a part of himself— was for Thomas a profoundly stirring and exciting emotion. He had never fully understood the sensation, but he accepted it gratefully.

At a half-trot, Thomas hurried down the bleak streets of

north London. The stadium was only a few blocks from where he had once lain flat on his belly, embracing a German blockbuster while delicately unscrewing the detonator in its nose. It all looked much the same—the old two-story houses, the façades of small shops, the whole scene done in dull grays and reds, a soft, cold rain turning the streets black and slick, and the flat, penetrating, slightly sickening smell of cheap frankfurters being boiled in a peddler's cart by the curb.

The crowd swept on toward the stadium, completely filling the street and sidewalks, flowing in ripples around a line of mounted policemen looking down on the scene with benign boredom from the backs of huge horses. Thomas could already hear the chants of the Arsenal fans—Ah-sen-al!—short, staccato and somehow ominous. Suddenly there was a whirl of action off to the right, three quick shouts and then a surge as a dozen teen-agers began to run toward the melee. Thomas managed to catch only a glimpse of the struggle before he was carried on. He saw a flash of a Tottenham scarf held high in triumph, and then he was in a queue before a ticket booth, shoving his money at a shivering attendant and jostling his way through the narrow turnstile that caught him with a thump on the back.

Thomas had a ticket to stand on the terraces. They always had stood; only the posh and the poufs sat down. Growing up, going to matches with his father all over Britain before they settled in Wales, Thomas had never met anyone who actually sat down. It was not just the matter of the price of the ticket, although that was a factor—about four times as much. The thing of it was, you had to stand to get the proper feel of the game, had to be jammed in on all sides with the others, become a physical part of the emotion, with the great bulk of your father behind you for protection. You could lean back and feel safe when the hysteria erupted all around you and the shoving began.

But even on the terraces, there was one place they had always gone: right down behind the goal. Right down where they could watch the goalkeeper, *feel* for the goalkeeper and his problems. "He's a loner," his father would say. "Nobody behind him if he makes a mistake. Just like us. He's the one to watch."

The terraces were already so filled that Thomas had to squeeze down an aisle, drawing mutterings as he went, smelling the yeasty fumes of beer already beginning to rise. Behind him, teetering on tiptoe to watch his progress, the other spoke softly again into his walkie-talkie. In the glass-plated observation box over the main grandstand, one man received the message and passed it on to another, who had his binoculars trained on the terraces. "Yes," he said after a moment, "there's our friend. I have him now."

Thomas felt a surge of affection for the men packed in around him, buffeting him as they changed position, shouting over his head: young workers, mainly, a couple young enough to be his son. They were talking about fooking Tottenham and the fooking Jews that used to play for them—that fooking Chivers, though, give the bahstud credit, he could hit that fing, drive the fooking ball right through the fooking goalie's chest, he could—and genially making plans to get warm after the game by getting laid. Thomas admired their youth: that, and the fact that their lives seemed so marvelously simple. He was pleasantly surprised that life could still be so simple.

A man in a black uniform began running on the sidelines toward a spot near Thomas. Craning his neck, the major saw what he suspected. A young woman had fainted after standing for an hour or so. Since there was no way to get help to her through the crowd, the men nearby simply picked her up and began handing her, over their heads, to the rows in front. Slowly, carefully, the woman was passed along until the black uniforms of the St. John's Ambulance Brigade could reach into the stands and get their hands on her.

The referee and the two linesmen appeared, doing little sprints on the sidelines to warm up their legs, and Thomas joined in the song that started as though some invisible conductor had raised his baton:

Who's your father, who's your father, who's your fa-ther,
      referee?
You ain't got one, you ain't got one, you're a bah-stud,
      referee.

High up in the stands, the one with the binoculars said: "I don't believe it. He's singing."

"What?" said the other, dialing the phone.

"Thomas. Singing like a damn skinhead. I thought he was the quiet kind."

Waiting for someone to answer, the other said, "Maybe he's gone bonkers."

The first nodded. "Maybe, knowing what he has to do." A pause, and then: "What's he doing here anyway?"

"Likes the game maybe."

"Why not stay with that curvy bit of crumpet?"

"Had to come up for air, I suspect."

The man with the phone suddenly stood a little more erect and changed the tone of his voice to one of crisp authority. "This is Elliott of Scotland Yard," he said. "Please put me through to the Home Secretary. He's expecting a call."

Far down below, the game began and everything sharpened for Thomas, as he knew it would, in ways he both welcomed and dreaded. The field was wet, of course, just the way it should have been—the way it always seemed to have been. The players' shorts and jerseys were soon slick with mud, the drizzle dampening their long hair so that it hung in strands over their eyes. He remembered the eyes—the glaring intensity, the focused hate or disdain and, occasionally, the fear that was communicated on the field. Lean, gaunt-cheeked, acne-scarred men, with oddly thick and powerful legs, revealing themselves with their eyes as eloquently as actors.

We hate Nottingham Forest. . .

The familiar song began in the rows around Thomas and spread in an instant to the entire stadium. As always, the major noted with amusement the irony of the words the football fans set to one of the great celebrations of British imperialism: "Land of Hope and Glory." Working-class chums turning a bit of the Empire to their own uses. Tucked deep into the crowd, Thomas raised his voice as the second line began:

> We hate Liverpool, too.
> We hate Manchester U-nited,
> But Ah-senal, we-ee love you.

They had sung that refrain all over England, Thomas and his father, for it was used by every team, the only difference being to change the last line to celebrate the home club. When he had complained about the family moving so often, his father had simply said that he had to go where the work was. He was a demolitions expert, a man called to work on tricky jobs all over the country, including blasting slate out of the great quarries in Wales, where Thomas spent his teen-age years. Across the decades, a brief incident at his father's wake returned to Thomas: a mining engineer with an old powder burn on his cheek bending low late in the evening to rumble his thoughts into his ear about the man who lay in the sealed coffin: "Crack an egg with a stick of dynamite, your father could."

A rising scream snapped Thomas out of his reveries. The ball was floating in a graceful arc, drifting down out of a leaden sky toward a spot a few feet in front of the goal. Men were hurtling for the point, running and leaping into the air with their heads thrust out on elongated necks, hoping to meet the ball with their foreheads and drive it home. At the same instant, the Arsenal goalie dashed out of his net and jumped, swinging a fist like a heavyweight. He managed to punch the ball back toward mid-field.

The bellow of the crowd was a deep, hoarse shout of appreciation. In homage, the skinheads at the back of the terraces pushed the rows of spectators in front of them, so that sections of the packed crowd tottered forward, like toppling dominoes, until their momentum was brought up short by a crowd-control barrier, an iron bar set up about four feet high on a parallel line with the terraces. Another football song began, this one nicked from "Rule Britannia":

> Dear old Ahsnel,
> We're proud to say your name,
> While we sing this song,
> We'll win the game.

This time Thomas did not sing. He was lost for a moment in the death of his father, the death that he knew underlay the fear that seized him when he thought of the bomb that his unseen and unknown enemy would someday skilfully set out for him.

The Home Secretary took the call at his desk. "A football match," he said after a moment. "Why in the name of God would he go to that?"

"Don't know, sir."

He glanced at the other man in the room, but got no re-action at all.

"Where did you say it was?"

"Arsenal, sir."

"What do you propose to do?"

"Keep up the surveillance as ordered, sir, and await further instructions."

He winced. The man was a born bureaucrat. "You have him well covered?"

"One man behind him, and two others about twenty feet away. And us up in the booth."

"Well, there must be some way we can use the situation, but at the moment I confess I don't see just how."

He put down the phone and turned to the other man. "Extraordinary conduct."

"Sir?"

"He lives like a bloody monk for months at a time. Then he goes out and gets himself a woman and the next afternoon he goes gallivanting off to a football match. I thought we were dealing with a stable character."

"He's stable enough."

"Really? Strikes me he's behaving very erratically."

"Maybe he's just trying to relax."

"Maybe he should be concentrating a little more on the job."

"Maybe he's as ready as he can get."

The Home Secretary sat back in his leather-covered chair and coolly appraised the man sitting opposite his desk. A little too dapper, with that ridiculous mustache. And too cheeky by far for his own good. But he's got spunk. Spunk and loyalty. He's loyal enough to old Thomas.

"You don't much like this, do you?" said the Home Secretary.

Sergeant Phillips carefully adjusted his cuffs. He was sitting up very straight. "No, sir," he said.

"Why not?"

"I feel you're asking me to inform on Major Thomas."

"That's putting it a bit bluntly, isn't it?"

"I'm sorry, sir. That's the way it appears to me."

The Secretary nodded. "I can understand that," he said. "Informing is a dirty business. Against the code, yours and mine. We know that. We accept that."

Phillips waited.

"All right," said the Secretary. "Let me put you in the picture. You deserve to know." Swearing Phillips to secrecy, he told how the entire plan had been built around Thomas—how the television interview outside the Albert Hall had been a setup, how they were trying to get the IRA's bomb designer to concentrate on trying to kill Thomas, how everything depended upon the major disarming the best bomb that the terrorist could devise. "Then maybe we'll at least have a psychological edge," said the Secretary. "We'll certainly know for sure how the bomb works, and maybe we'll even get a lead as to who the bomber is."

As he listened to the account, Phillips relaxed visibly, and he nodded once or twice. "I suspected it was something like that," he said at the end.

"So we need your help."

"To do what?"

"To suggest ways of putting pressure on Thomas so that, when the chips are down, he *will* walk up to that bloody bomb. I'm afraid he's beginning to waver."

"I see no signs of that."

"You're too loyal to say if you did."

Phillips did not reply.

Suddenly anger flashed across the Home Secretary's face. He picked up a marble paperweight and slammed it down on his desk. "Do you want this to go on?" he shouted. "Next time you can sort out the bodies. I can arrange for that very easily."

The circumspect ticking of the dignified clock in the corner, the muffled sound of a door closing in the next office, while the sergeant looked the Secretary squarely in the eye. "All right," Phillips said. "What do you want to know?"

The Secretary moved around the desk, a surprisingly nimble man despite his bulk and age, conjuring up images of what he must have been like, years before, battling for the throw-ins at Twickenham. A massive hand gripped Phillips's shoulder. "Jolly good, Sergeant! Very good, indeed." He began stalking the office. "What do we want to know? Anything that will help us strengthen Thomas's resolve."

"Using the football match?"

"That's where he happens to be right now. If we can develop something there, so much the better. He's on the terraces."

"Probably the North Bank."

"The where?"

"The North Bank is the section used by the real Arsenal fans. It can be rather rough in there."

"Then why in Heaven's name would he go there?"

Phillips smiled for the first time since entering the room. "To be part of the crowd. He'd feel at home there."

"Really?"

"They're his kind of people—or at least he'd like to think they were."

The Secretary found that his pacing had brought him to a spot behind his desk, and he abruptly sat down. "So what do we do?"

Phillips leaned forward. "He rather liked the publicity, you know—the TV interview and all that. Maybe it scared him in one way, knowing what was behind it all, but he still liked the fuss. I could tell."

"So?"

"So I think it might pay if you had the public-address announcer say that he was at the game, and point out where he was standing so that the crowd could give him a cheer."

The Secretary nodded briskly. "Good, good—I can see the aim of that. We can do that."

Then Phillips snapped his fingers. "Yes," he said. "Yes, it might work."

"What might work?"

"It will take some explaining," said Phillips. For the next ten minutes, he tried to make the Home Secretary understand the importance of football to a person of Thomas's background, and how one of the great symbols of the game might be exploited to make the major feel a sense of obligation to country that could, in turn, bolster his will to go to the bomb.

Thomas was unaware of the Scotland Yard agent who squeezed his way down the terrace behind him, politely excusing himself as he went, and stopped a few feet from his shoulder. The major was thinking again about his father's funeral and the closed coffin. They had not even let him see the body. His mother had insisted upon having the lid opened after everyone was cleared out, despite the cajoling of the minister and the funeral director. He remembered her quiet sobs—that and the fact that the Welsh hillside where they buried his father (the face of the slate quarry looming on the far side of the valley) had been swept with a cold rain. "May I suggest the gentlemen leave their hats on," said the minister, trying to be kind, "and just touch the rim." Thomas had taken his cap off and stood, bareheaded, with the water running down his face and blending with his tears.

Rain, football, the great solid strength of his father—and demolitions. They were all mingled together for Thomas. They and the veneration of the goalie. (Around Thomas, the crowd went up on tiptoes, craning for a look, and he could remember the feeling of strong hands under his arms as his father hoisted him high into the air so he could see the play in Carlisle, Stoke, Liverpool, Cardiff.)

Be a loner. And that was just the point—the reason why he was afraid. The great flaw in his father's reasoning was that you could never rely on your own skill alone. Not while handling explosives. Things could go wrong, things no one could explain. Osgood had found that out. Something had gone wrong that day in the slate quarry when his father, trusting his own skill, lowered himself on a rope to inspect a charge that he had planted and that had not gone off. The six sticks of dynamite exploded when he was about five feet away, blowing him off the rope, so that his body not only bore the markings of the blast, but the effects of the two hundred-foot fall onto a pile of shale.

That was the realization that underlay Thomas's fear: *you never could be sure.* That was the fact that he had to assimilate and hide and ignore, and that he had succeeded in suppressing for so many years. Why was it bothering him now? Was it because he was now the same age as his father when he died? Perhaps. It made as much sense as anything else.

Thomas became aware that the tension of the crowd had suddenly broken and looked up to see the two teams trotting slowly off the field. "Good match," said the man at his elbow, offering Thomas a cigarette. "No thanks. Bloody Tottenham," said the major. "Bloody lucky—always have been. Should be two, three goals down by now, Armstrong get his bloody foot into it. He's carrying his ruddy handbag out there. They should call him 'Mary'—know what I mean?"

While the two men were talking, a Scotland Yard agent

up in the booth watched through binoculars and said to the public-address announcer, "Right. Do it just the way we said."

The announcer took off the record of rock music he had been playing to fill in the interval between the halves. "Ladies and gentlemen," he said, his amplified voice filling the entire stadium, "we have with us this afternoon a man whom I'm sure you all have read about and seen on television recently—a man who is performing what is surely one of the most difficult and patriotic jobs in Britain today, and who is working for us all. Just behind the goal in the North Bank, enjoying the match with the rest of the fans, is Major David Thomas, the leader of the demolitions experts who are taking apart the bombs that the IRA have been planting in London. Would you give us all a wave, Major, so that we can spot you down there in the crowd, and I suggest we all give him a cheer."

Thomas did not have time to wonder how they had found him. There was no time to think about anything, for the cheering had already begun and the sound swept him along. The cheers were coming not only from the seats up in the stadium but from the terraces, and he was conscious of pale faces turning his way and men pointing at him. He raised a hand to wave back, and the cheers increased.

"Good," said the agent in the booth. "That's just right." He spoke into his walkie-talkie: "Now let's try the other—as loud as you can."

The three agents near Thomas began to sing. Almost immediately, the men standing on the terraces nearby picked up the words. As the volume rose, other sections joined in until, within twenty seconds, the entire stadium was singing "You'll Never Walk Alone."

Just as Phillips had guessed, the song had an immediate and profound effect on Thomas. For the football fan, it was a pledge of solidarity with the team. The song tied the two together, the fans and the players, into one community. It was this fierce sense of identification that made football such an emotional sport, and that rooted its appeal in the working class, which has never been reluctant to hide its feelings. The laborer felt a blood tie with football; the game was part of his life. Others could watch, but it was *his* game. He sang "You'll Never Walk Alone" as though it were a hymn.

Thomas felt the emotion of the crowd flow over him. He knew that the people were telling him, in the most eloquent way they knew how, that they were with him.

The agent with the binoculars adjusted his focus slightly, and stared again. "I'll be damned," he said.

"What?" asked one of the others.

"Thomas."

"What about him?"

"He looks like he's ready to cry."

Listening on his phone, the Home Secretary bent his head as he got a full report of what was happening at the stadium. "I don't suppose he actually *was* crying, do you?" the Secretary asked when he finished relaying the news.

"Perhaps," said Phillips.

"Do you really think so? What an extraordinary man, changing like that so swiftly."

"Not so extraordinary, really. Quite ordinary, in fact. It's the pressures that are extraordinary."

The Secretary sat down at his desk with an air of great satisfaction and began to shuffle through a pile of papers. "It really doesn't make much difference, does it, so long as he gets the job done," he said.

"He'll get the job done."

"He'd better."

Phillips stood up. "May I go now, sir?" he asked.

The Secretary held out his hand without rising. "By all means," he said. "And thank you for your help. You were dead on about Thomas."

"I'm afraid I was."

The Secretary shot Phillips a quick look. "That doesn't bother you, does it, Sergeant?" he asked.

"It bothers me a good deal."

The big hand came up and pointed a finger at Phillips. "Don't let it," said the Secretary. "Compassion is a luxury you can't afford. None of us can afford. We have a job to do."

"Yes, sir."

"The job is to get Thomas to take those bombs apart," said the Secretary. "Nothing more."

"Lovely," said Phillips.

Now the Home Secretary stood up. "Go easy, Sergeant," he said. "You don't have to like your job. Just do it."

"Yes, sir," said Phillips, and turned to go.

The Secretary sat down and resumed his consideration of another problem.

In the North Bank, Thomas began edging his way down his terrace, unable to bring himself to stay to watch the second half, knowing that whatever happened would be an anticlimax to what had already occurred. The afternoon with its swirl of emotions and memories had completely overwhelmed him. As he moved along, Thomas could feel the strong hands patting him on the back, and he slowed his steps to prolong the sensation, the physical assurance of understanding and support. "Thank you," said the major to the men around him. "Thank you very much."

14

"A CAPSULE, GENTLEMEN. A capsule and a man."

The First Sea Lord still did not understand. He studied the small weighted object that he held in his hand. Around the great oval table, his juniors waited politely for him to say something, their faces betraying no emotion whatsoever. "Just what is it, John, that you would like us to do?" the admiral finally asked.

At the far end of the table, the Home Secretary smiled. "Find it," he said. "Find him."

"Just like that?" asked the First Sea Lord.

The Secretary blew lightly on his fingertips and rubbed them together, a lingering habit from his rugby days and a gesture that the First Sea Lord and one or two other of the admirals recognized. Their distinguished guest was plotting something.

Curious, suspicious, mildly hostile, the five men with the heavy, dull bands of gold on their sleeves waited and stared at the Secretary as he planted his elbows on their table, the only civilian in the room, a slouching intruder in their midst.

It was October 11. The members of the Admiralty Board and the Home Secretary were sitting in the ornate meeting room that the commanders of Britain's navy had been using since 1725. The predecessors of the admirals had sent orders to Nelson at Trafalgar from this room and, in this century, followed the Battle of Jutland, directed the destruction of the *Bismarck* and twice battled German submarines to the death. The room itself embodied the traditions of the navy. On the south wall was a limewood carving that included representations of the navigational instruments of the sixteenth and seventeenth centuries. The carving framed a wind dial that still worked, a gilded pointer showing the direction of the wind. Generations ago, that information had been vitally important to the men sitting at the table: Could the French fleet get out of Brest? Could the British fleet clear Plymouth by nightfall?

Suddenly the Secretary began to talk—rapidly, energetically, thumping the table with a thick knuckle to emphasize his points. He played his trump card first. "The Prime Minister wants you to give every assistance," he said. (Deferential nods around the table.) "From what I've said—from what you've seen yourselves—you know the scope of the problem. We have to put this IRA fellow out of business now, right now, by any means we can. We are trying everything. Even" (he winked to signal a joke) "the navy."

The First Sea Lord managed a thin smile. "How flattering," he said, and waited.

"We have the Yard, of course, trying to trace the capsule and find the man, but they have precious little to go on. We know the capsule is made in Sweden. We know the distributors in Britain and Ireland—the Republic as well as Northern Ireland—and the Yard is keeping close track of every capsule they get and where it goes. The Irish have been very cooperative, I must say. God knows how many capsules the IRA already has stolen or acquired in some way or other. We can't do much about those. But we want to cut off flow into England from illicit channels, and we are desperate to find any clue that would lead us to the bomber. We are trying everything, even" (the wink again) "the navy."

"You're surely watching the ports as well as the airports," said the First Sea Lord. "Aren't the customs people on this?"

"Of course, but we want more. We want a blockade."

Now the admiral leaned forward. "That's precisely what I don't understand. A blockade to find something as small as this?" He tossed the capsule in his hand. "You could hide this in a tube of toothpaste."

"We are desperate," said the Secretary. "The Prime Minister is desperate."

The admiral considered the problem. "We know something about blockading," he said, "but we don't have the manpower these days to stop everything."

"We understand that, Arthur," said the Secretary. "Do your best. We can't afford to miss any chance."

"Yes. Well, we'll try."

The Secretary reached into the inside pocket of his coat and produced a long, thin cigar, which he lit with great deliberation. No one else in the room was smoking. As the first clouds billowed across the table the admiral pressed a button beneath the table and an orderly appeared at a side door. The admiral inclined his head toward the Secretary. The orderly disappeared for an instant, then reappeared with a large glass ashtray, which he placed at the elbow of the Secretary, who was unaware of the disapproving glances he was receiving from around the table. The sharp smell of the cigar began to fill the room.

"I must be frank with you," the Secretary said. "We know how little chance there is to find a capsule. The Prime Minister knows that. But the search itself is the thing, you see. The very fact that it is going on. Because we can publicize that, photograph that—encounters on the high seas—show it all on the telly."

Baffled stares around the table, and then the exasperated voice of the First Sea Lord. "Why in God's name would you want to do that?"

The Secretary puffed deeply and studied the tip of his cigar. "To scare our man. To make him think we are on his trail. To force him, finally, to move fast. I don't think he'll go to ground. I think he'll try to get on with it and perhaps blunder into a little trap that we've laid for him."

The First Sea Lord broke in: "If I understand what you're getting at, John, you don't care if we find a capsule, so long as we can be photographed doing it—stopping boats and all that."

The Secretary smiled again. "We'd be delighted if you found a capsule, but I must admit we'd also be surprised." He nodded. "Right, we want the pictures for the telly." He looked around the table at each man. "Gentlemen, the Royal Navy is about to take part in a media event."

The silence that followed lasted for fully ten seconds. Then the First Sea Lord bowed slightly toward the Secretary. "Would you please," he said, "give our thanks to the Prime Minister for the faith he has placed in us."

The Secretary shrugged his enormous shoulders to acknowledge the point. "We must be frank," he said. "But there's something else—something entirely legitimate—that the navy can genuinely contribute to. If our friend escapes our trap, or simply decides to run now, he may try to go by sea in a small boat. I'm suggesting that you blockade this island, as best you can, and search everything leaving these shores from a rowboat on up."

The new development interested the First Sea Lord. "Who are we looking for?"

For the first time, the Secretary relaxed and threw an arm across the back of his chair. He smiled at his old friend at the end of the table. "On that," he said, "I think we can help you. We believe he is in his mid-twenties, quite tall—over six feet. And, unless we are very much mistaken, he is an American."

15

A CURL OF white at the bow, the Union Jack snapping in the wind, a roiling wake behind. At twenty-five knots, bright as a recruiting poster, the sleek patrol craft easily overhauled the fishing smack and made it heave to. The young commander shouted some orders. A four-man boarding party jumped over the rail and down onto the *Darling of Kerry,* two days out of Cork. Wiping grease from his hand, an astonished captain came forward to talk to the intruders, armed with carbines, who had suddenly appeared on his foredeck.

"This time the search produced nothing," intoned the BBC reporter who was standing on the bridge of the cutter. He was wearing a trench coat buttoned to his throat, and the collar was up around his ears. "It's a hard, thankless chore, hunting for contraband materials—the explosives and detonators and fuses used by the IRA. But it is a necessary job, one that must be done, the Government is convinced, if the IRA campaign of terror in London is to be brought to a close. . . ."

"Fuck off, mate," muttered Pat Reilly, and yanked the TV plug out of the wall. He was lying on the couch that doubled as his bed in his small apartment. It was the early evening of October 14, three days after the Home Secretary had made his visit to the Admiralty, ten days after Harry Johnson picked up the bomb in the Tate—and Reilly was beginning to feel fresh anxiety.

He was not concerned about the navy's blockade of Britain. A small wooden box in his dresser contained ten capsules. He had carried them into Britain concealed in the false bottom of a suitcase; the bored customs agent at Heathrow had not even asked him to open the case for inspection. Nor was Reilly worried that the British would be able to trace the capsules to Cassidy and then to him: Cassidy's electrical-supply shop did not stock the item. After Reilly told his mentor about the capsule and what it would do, Cassidy produced a dozen within a week—"Don't ask from whence these cometh, my boy," he had said. "I have forgotten the source myself."

For that matter, Reilly was not much worried that they would be able to find him by tracing any of his gear. He already had more than enough gelignite and detonators to make a dozen or more bombs. The materials suddenly appeared in a large carton left by his door one night. Cassidy had arranged for the delivery, of course, but he would say nothing about the source when Reilly had asked him during a telephone conversation. "The less you know, the better," declared Cassidy, leaving unsaid the other thought: The less you know, the less you have to tell if they catch you.

Reilly understood all that, and it was not what he knew that worried him; it was what he did not know.

He was still worried that someone in the IRA might be captured by the British, break under interrogation, and turn him in. And he was worried about other schemes the British might be concocting—besides the blockade.

Reilly had compressed his plans: Get Thomas and get out. He needed to plant one perfect bomb in a place where Thomas could not avoid it—not after his scene on the telly saying how great he was—and the major was finished the minute he placed his hand on it. Then he would quit the whole bloody business. Go hide with Cassidy's contacts in Dublin. Go back to the States, maybe.

But he had to hurry, had to bring it all off before the

something happened that he did not know about—could not guess—and there came the knock on his door. That was just the point: he had no time to lose, and he could not decide where was the surest place to put the bomb for Thomas.

At nine that evening Reilly put into effect a plan he had worked out with Cassidy to make sure they could talk on the phone without the risk of the line being tapped. He went to a pay phone and placed a call to Cassidy's flat in Belfast. The instant that Cassidy's voice came on the wire, he hung up without saying a word. Exactly thirty minutes later, calling from another coin box, he dialed the number of a pay phone near Cassidy's housing development. The old man answered immediately: "What's the matter?"

"It's getting a bit sticky," said Reilly.

"The blockade? The mighty navy's mighty blockade? Is that what's worrying you—getting me out of bed?" Cassidy's angry voice roared out of the receiver. "What if I was followed? What if they caught on to this little phone trick?"

Reilly felt a tingle of fear. "Why should they follow you?"

There was a pause, and when Cassidy spoke again his voice was patient and calm: "No reason at all, of course. None at all, my boy. What is worrying you?"

"How much time do I have?"

"What do you mean?"

"Before they get too close."

Across the Irish Sea, Cassidy sighed softly. "They aren't close at all. They've got nothing to get 'close' on; you know that."

"They've got a capsule."

"They can't trace that to me—let alone you. You know our firm doesn't carry it."

"I don't like the feeling."

Again the sigh, but this time drawn out and exaggerated. Theatrical, almost. He's putting me on, thought Reilly. He's faking it.

"Yes," said Cassidy. "I can imagine. Lonesome, is it?"

"You might say."

"Do you know the next target?"

"No. Not really. I can't get it right. I can't decide on the right one."

"You will."

"I'd bloody better."

Cassidy coughed, and Reilly could imagine the cold damp of the Belfast night seeping into the distant phone booth. "There is one thing," said Cassidy. "You'd better not call me again, just to be safe. You're on your own. You know what to do."

"Great."

"You don't have doubts, do you?"

Reilly shook his head at the receiver in his hand. "Not bloody likely," he said.

"When you have doubts, remember your father," said Cassidy. "Remember what they did to him."

"I know."

"You'll be fine."

"Yes."

Cassidy's voice became hearty and Reilly knew he was about to ring off. Building me up, he is. Trying to make it all seem grand.

"We've got immense faith in you, son," said Cassidy. "You must remember that. You can do it. Good luck—and remember, no more calls."

The phone clicked in Reilly's ear. He stood for a moment with the dead phone in his hand.

"Jesus, what a screwup," he said aloud, and stepped out of the comforting isolation of the phone booth. The interview left him more edgy than ever. He was afraid to examine his feelings too closely; he was not sure what they were, and he was not sure he wanted to find out. He wondered vaguely if he would be trying to kill Thomas if his father had lost only one leg. An eye? An arm?

For want of anything else to do, he began to walk, moving slowly through Fulham and on to Kensington, and then up to Notting Hill Gate. Looking for a pub, he walked a block or two until he found one that seemed quiet enough. For a moment he listened outside to be sure there was no distracting music or singing. He wanted to brood in peace for a while. Satisfied, he walked through the door.

She was sitting in a booth against the far wall and, in the darkness, he did not see her. In fact, he actually heard her first. She was laughing and the men on either side of Reilly at the bar smiled and turned their heads to see who was having such a pleasant time, who could laugh so warmly on Thursday night with another day of work to go. "It was your laugh," he would tell her later, when she would ask him what had first attracted him to her, watching carefully for his reaction, gently brushing out her long brown hair with sweeping strokes and frowning slightly to keep the count—one hundred strokes a night, every night. She was sitting on the rug in front of the gas fire. "Honest," he would say, marveling at her shadowy beauty in the soft light, "it was your laugh. Did you think it was your lovely lips or your lovely hips—is that why I should want to play with a girl like you?"

"Why not?" she answered, and swung around to face the warmth. And then, mocking: "My laugh!" He likes me for my perfect laugh. Bloody Irishmen. Bloody poufs, the lot."

But then she could not prevent herself from laughing, and she was already turning back toward him, her arms beginning to open wide when he reached her.

But all that was much later, and it was not even true, for what had attracted Reilly to her was not her laugh— although that made a fine story—but her accent. Before he had heard her say a full sentence, he was turning to seek her out. An American, he thought. She must be American. When he saw her, there was no doubt—there was something about the self-assurance, the casual way she shook her head to let her hair flow down over her shoulders, her unaffected delight in what she or her companions said that stamped her immediately.

Suddenly Reilly felt homesick for Boston and the girls he used to meet in the smoky student hangouts around Boston University and in Cambridge, where the Radcliffe girls used to be amused by his Belfast accent and his stories and who, from time to time, would invite him back to their dorms. He turned on his stool and watched her for a moment. She was seated with two girl friends, both English, Reilly decided at a glance. All three were dressed in long Laura Ashley skirts.

Reilly walked over to the darts game that was going on about ten feet away from the girls. "Do you mind if I have a try?" he said to one of the players. Everyone glanced at him and she began to smile. "Let the Yank have a go," said a player, and handed him the three darts. "Thanks," said Reilly. "What do I do?"

" 'What do I do?' " she would say later, and laugh. "Playing the helpless American, the polite American. Fooling everybody."

"Fooling you."

"That's everybody."

And he had fooled her, at least for a while—at least long enough for him to be invited to sit down. There had been a quick huddle and then one of the English girls—Chloe was it?—beckoned him over. They had not known what to say at first. Finally Chloe blurted out, "Your money. We were worried that you'd lose all your money" (nodding toward the men by the dartboard) "playing with them."

"That's very kind of you," said Reilly, drawing up a chair. "I don't even know the rules."

She said her name was Kate Rochford, and he told her his real name and said he was from Boston, Somerville, really—just a way outside the city. Did she know it? No, she was from Washington, D.C., had never even been in Boston. He'd gone to Boston University himself, he said. Marketing, business, things like that. Spending a few months in London for the fun of it before settling down.

She tried to include her two friends in the conversation, but he did not—he could not have cared less about them—and they were content to sit and listen. He could tell before they got up from the table that it was going to be all right, but he put his hand under her elbow anyway and squeezed it gently, and she pressed his hand against her side.

"Can I walk you home?" he said to her, and Chloe and the other smiled at each other. "They sound like an American movie," one said. That made them feel even closer. The others were outsiders.

"This way," she said, starting down Holland Park Avenue. "We can walk."

"I knew you were American the moment you stood up," she said, glancing at him. She came to his shoulder. "You're so tall. I'm so tired of looking men in the eye—isn't that terrible?"

"I could tell you were, too," he said. "English girls don't laugh like that. They don't know how."

She pulled him by the hand to peer into the darkened window of a secondhand bookshop, trying to make out the titles on the expensive leather bindings in the window. He liked the special intimacy of being alone with her, of being strangers together on Holland Park Avenue—the two of them separate from all the others. Reilly let her tug him along, content to let her push aside his problems, wondering, idly, if she was as rich as she sounded, wondering how soon he could get her in bed. Not whether, but when. Her hand was very warm in his.

After a half-hour's stroll, she stopped in front of a row of houses on Elgin Crescent that had just been freshly painted. Very well-to-do indeed, Reilly decided, looking up at the remodeled façade. He glanced around and could tell, even in the darkness, that some of the neighboring houses were also being done over.

"Yes," she said, noticing his look, "it's very posh."

He took both of her hands and tried to draw her to him, but she managed to push him back with one hand on his chest. She was surprisingly strong. "I've got to go," she said. "School tomorrow, believe it or not."

School? How old *was* she? "What school?" he asked.

"Holland Park."

"I'll see you after school tomorrow."

She was already heading up the walk toward the door, leaving him by the iron gate. "Of course," she said. She paused, blew him a kiss, and disappeared.

16

AT TWO-THIRTY THE next afternoon, he was waiting outside the front entrance of Holland Park School. Again, he heard her first, her laughter rising over the hubbub as a crowd of students burst through the doors. She waved good-by to some of her friends and walked over to him. "Wha'cha, mate," she said, brushing a hand over his denim leisure jacket. "Tysty—that's tasty to you, Yank."

"You're putting me on," said Reilly, taking her arm and heading her toward the park. "You're really a bleeding Cockney, s'truth?"

"S'truth," she said. "Buy me some tea, mister."

They got steaming cups at a stand and walked to a nearby rose garden to sit and sip slowly as the drinks grew cold. Then they window-shopped down Kensington High Street, he carrying her books ("Lord, just like back at Walter Johnson High School," she quipped), and stopped in a coffee shop. They sat back in a corner and touched knees under the table.

"Are you really just bumming around?" she asked.

"Don't you believe that?"

"You're kind of *intense* for that," she said.

"I'm a bum, pure and simple."

"The hell you are."

"Well, I do some looking around at businesses and things, or at least I'm supposed to. Or at least that's what they think back in Boston, back at the firm."

Reilly sipped his coffee, waggled his bushy eyebrows at her over the cup. "And are you really just going to Holland Park?"

"S'truth."

He did not understand why she should go to a comprehensive school like Holland Park, a state institution with a wide assortment of students.

"Why?" he asked.

"What do you mean, *why*?"

"A girl like you, why aren't you in one of those grand schools. . . ."

She shook her head. "Never happen, mate," she said.

"Why not?"

She put down her cup. "What you're really saying is: 'How come a girl like you goes to a school with all those Pakis and West Indians and assorted wogs?' Right?"

Reilly stirred uneasily. He did not like the way the conversation was veering. "Let's drop the whole thing."

"No, really, let's not, because we really better get this straight, right off, right now. It's important to me."

"What is, for God's sake?"

"That you think it's odd that I go to school with wogs and I don't."

Reilly started to get up. "I couldn't care less."

"Now *that* makes me mad," she said, pulling him back down. "Because *you* wouldn't, would you?"

"What?"

"Go to school with wogs."

"No, I guess not."

"Because you don't like wogs."

"I guess I don't. Who does?"

"Me."

"Horseshit."

"Right, horseshit It's a problem for me, even me, but I try."

"Why?"

They were drawn back from each other across the table, talking in fierce, hissing whispers so that the others in the room would not hear, but a few people were turning, curiously, to see what the commotion was all about.

"Why bother?" he repeated.

"It's what I can do over here—what little I can do. To try to help. To do some good."

He still did not understand. It was incomprehensible to him that anyone would go out of his way to help a Paki. "What's so good about going to school with them?"

"Brotherhood," she said. There was a taunting gleam in her eye. "We're all brothers under the skin."

"Jesus save me," said Reilly. He nodded at a West Indian sitting at the next table. "Why don't you try getting under his skin?"

She laughed at that, suddenly, naturally, and the mood changed back again. "Because it's more fun getting under your skin. I did, too, right?"

Reilly relaxed. "Be a wiseass, will you?" he said. "Pay for your own coffee, you will."

She leaned over toward him again. "I really wasn't teasing, but I shouldn't have done that. It's too early for that. You wouldn't understand."

"I'll say—I just wanted a nice talk and some coffee."

"And a roll in the hay?"

"It's too early for that," he echoed.

This time she laughed and elbowed him in the ribs so hard that he yelped. Heads turned to stare. She raised her hands, palms-up, in innocence.

"Jesus," he said, "what a show-off." He moved his chair to hide her from the gaze of the others.

"No," she said. "Wrong. I'm not a show-off. I'm a rebel. Every inch a rebel."

"Rebel, *sheeeit*," he said, drawling the word out as long as he could in imitation of the men he used to work with around Boston.

"That's why I don't go to one of those nice schools you're so fond of where the nice little girls wear those nice little straw hats."

"Screw the straw hats," he said amiably.

"Because what I can't stand, mister," she said, "is the kind of little proper little girl who wears those little straw hats, and I especially can't stand their proper mommies and daddies."

"Why not?" he asked, enjoying her performance.

"Because I don't like the upper-class Britishers who are so veddy veddy up tight. Especially in their assholes."

"Why not?"

"Because I'm a bleeding rebel, mate," she went on. "Back home in the good old U.S. of A. I used to be quite the thing. Thirteen years old, and marching around the White House with the rest of them, old Nixon inside hiding in a closet, and we'd be carrying signs and shouting about stopping the fucking war. I went with my big sister, but I went. Oh my, very impressive it was, very fierce."

"So what has that to do—" he started to ask.

"It has a lot to do with all this—because they're all the same, Nixon and this lot over here what runs things. They're not my dish of tea. So I go to Holland Park and neck with the wogs in the hallways. Understand?"

"No," he said.

"That's all right," she said, and now she was laughing. "No one ever does. Especially Daddy. Never Daddy."

"Christ, what about *him*?"

But she ignored the question. She was looking up at the clock on the wall that said five-thirty. "Is it that late?" she cried. "God, I'll miss dinner." She began sweeping up her coat and books and heading for the door. Then she paused to look back over her shoulder at him. She was outlined against the soft glow of late afternoon, and some men at a front table stared at her. Reilly broke the silence by pushing back his chair with a screech.

"Watch out for her daddy," someone said as he hurried to catch up with the girl.

"Daddy, hell," said someone else. "Watch out for *her*."

She was already standing by the stop, signaling a bus that was laboring up the hill.

"You're a nutter," Reilly said. "You know that, don't you?"

She swung herself aboard, grabbed the white pole on the landing with one hand and looked back at him. "Come up and see me some time," she called as the vehicle pulled away. She was still waving when the bus turned a corner and disappeared.

Reilly stood there for a moment before he shrugged and started to walk away. He had never met anyone like her before—not even in the States. Was she worth the trouble? Was she going to be good enough in bed to justify all the nonsense he would have to go through to get her there? He knew the answer to that one even as he posed the question. There was fire there. But what the hell was she all about? He did not have the slightest idea. A rebel? And afraid to miss supper with the old folks at home? Rebel, hell. But she had the right idea about the British. She was right about them. That was something, thought Reilly. It was a good start.

When she spotted him waiting by the entrance at Holland Park the next day, she did not show a glimmer of surprise that he was there. "I have a test for you," she said. "If you flunk, we're through, finished, washed up, even before we start." She was tugging him by the hand down toward Kensington High Street.

"What do I do, lady?" Reilly asked.

"That's part of the test," she said. "You won't know what the test is until it's all over."

But she broke down when they were seated on the top deck of a No. 73 bus headed toward the West End, riding in the first seat, far out over the driver, so that Reilly felt as though he were suspended in an airship above the traffic of London. "This is it," she said.

"What?"

"This. Just this. Riding on top of a bus."

"This is *it*?"

"Yes, sir."

"So what do I do?"

"You have to enjoy it," she said. "I'm a bus freak. Love

me, love my hang-ups. I'm hung up on buses."

"Good Christ," said Reilly. That was about what he expected—something as daffy as that. "So what do we do?"

"We ride all over town and you have a good time. Make believe we're on an ocean liner."

"I'll have a good time, honest," said Reilly. "And I'll make believe."

They rode back and forth across London all afternoon, stopping finally at her suggestion to browse through the Lacquer Chest Antique Shop on Kensington Church Street, which Kate said was her favorite—"taste, imagination and not too pricey, you know?"

He took her to dinner at the Lee Yuan, a Chinese restaurant on Earl's Court Road, which he had seen favorably mentioned in a magazine, and he could tell that she was properly impressed. This time she was as quiet as she had been chatty the night before, and she rubbed her ankle against his under the table.

"All right," she said as they left.

That was all. He hailed a cab and took her back to his room, where he had been sure not only to make the day bed but to tidy up a bit that morning. She was shy, which surprised him. From the way she acted he had expected her to be uninhibited and aggressive. But Kate was almost passive at the start, and he had to coax her along, whispering into her ear, until she finally began to respond. She clasped her strong legs around his back and, fleetingly, he remembered other American legs and how they too had been sleek as well as strong.

Later they talked and smoked, she balancing the glass ashtray carefully on her bare stomach. "My parents would have a fit," she said.

"So?"

"I mean if they found out about you." She looked at him closely. "I'll bet you're twenty-four or twenty-five, right?"

"Twenty-five," he answered truthfully.

She giggled. "Too old. I'm eighteen. They want me to stick to teen-agers."

"They're the worst kind, don't they know that? Horny little bastards."

"I know."

"So you've tried some, have you?" There was a tease in Reilly's voice, but he realized as he asked the question that he was quite serious.

She slapped him on the chest. "Why are you guys all so obsessed about who gets there first? Only one of you can, you know."

"And it wasn't me?"

"I'm not bloody well saying."

"The way you went at it," he said, deadpan, "I thought I must have been the first."

"Ohhhh!" This time she was aiming at his face, but she started to laugh and he grabbed her by both wrists. "What a piggish crack!" she said. "What an absolute bastard you really are!"

"Let's drop it." said Reilly. "I don't think it's very funny."

She looked at him closely, but he avoided her eyes. "You're jealous," she said. "My Lord, you're really jealous." She rubbed her hand across his stomach. "I like that," she said. "It makes me feel nice."

He had to take her home that evening because she would not spend the night with him—her parents would disown her if she did. For a week he saw her every day after school and sometimes she could stay at his place for dinner, which they would cook together on his hot plate. Reilly was aware that he was using her as an excuse for not pushing on with the job of dealing with Thomas. He wondered if he was falling in love with her and, if he was, what he would do about it.

The facts about her father came out rather casually one evening while they happened to be washing up the dishes.

"That's one thing my father will do," she said. "Clean up. He cleans up very nicely."

"Really?"

"That's about it, though."

Reilly asked the question as a matter of course: "What exactly does your father do?"

"When he's not washing dishes?"

"Yes."

"He works in the Embassy."

"Doing what?"

"For the CIA . . ."

Reilly nearly dropped the bowl he was drying. He was terrified. In an instant his mind made two or three lightning leaps. The CIA—they were using her to get him. Scotland Yard was working with the CIA. They were coming at him that way. Through her. That was the unknown that he was afraid of, and here it was.

". . . which is really why I'm going to Holland Park."

"What is?"

She jammed an elbow into his ribs as she kept on washing. "I just told you," she said. "Because my father is in the CIA is really why I'm at Holland Park instead of some nice little proper school he'd like to send me to."

She turned and blew some soapsuds off her fingers at him. "Would you like me in a straw hat?"

He grabbed her roughly by both shoulders and turned her to face him.

Startled, she asked: "What's the matter?"

"Your father—he's really in the CIA. No bloody joke?"

"Yes, really." She wiggled her arms. "You're hurting me."

"And what's he got to do with you?"

"Not much—like I was trying to tell you. We don't exactly get along. What's eating *you?*"

Reilly looked at her very carefully and, slowly, was reassured. She was either an extraordinary actress or she was telling the truth. He thought the latter.

"What's *wrong?*" she asked again.

"Nothing," he said. "I'm sorry. I just don't like spooks."

"Neither do I," she said. Slowly she wiped her hands on the dish towel and then led Reilly over to the couch. "Look," she said, "I think we'd better get this straight."

"Yes?"

"This father thing—it goes pretty deep and it goes pretty far back, you know?"

For the next half-hour Reilly listened while Kate talked on about her father. "It's not just *him* that I'm against." She kept returning to the point. "It's him *and* the fact that he's with the fucking CIA, that he's been part of the whole mess for years—the shootings and the plots and the spying on Americans, and helping out in Watergate, and all the rest."

Reilly nodded. He had paid only the slightest attention to the CIA scandals in the press.

"Okay," said Kate, "so maybe I don't get along with my father in the first place. Maybe he's too strict, whatever. But the CIA thing became big, *very* big for me. We'd fight about it all the time. He'd be defending the thing, the *system*, and I'd be kicking at it. So he wins all the fights, right? I mean, he doesn't quit the CIA or anything, so he wins. Or at least, I always lose. You understand?"

"More or less," Reilly said. He could not grasp how the CIA could arouse such passion in the girl with the marvelous laugh. "The CIA thing really gets you that uptight?"

"Christ, yes." She moved closer to him. "The spying and the bribing and the shooting and everything else—I hate it."

"And you blame your father for all of that?"

"For his share, for his share. And like I said, it's all mixed up with other things. Like I'd probably be fighting with my father anyway"—she paused while trying to think of the right point—"if he worked for the phone company or something."

"So?"

"So I did what I could—all those marches around the White House I told you about, when I was a kid, scaring hell out of fucking Nixon—*trying* to scare the hell out of him, at least."

"And those riots."

"Sort of riots."

"But people got hurt?"

"Some. Yes. Not badly. Tear-gas burns, things like that."

He was puzzled. "You were against the country?"

"Oh no." She snapped her head around to look at him. "Not that. The *country* was fine. The *people* were fine. I was just against what they were doing to it."

" 'They'—Nixon and the rest?"

"Yes. Vietnam first, and then Watergate. Mostly Watergate at the end."

"And your father?"

"Yes. He was part of it."

There was a pause, and then she began to talk again: "I mean, I always felt the country was fine. We were very patriotic—we all were, even then. Saluting the flag, standing up and singing 'The Star Spangled Banner'—the whole bit."

"Proud to be an American."

"Yes, proud to be an American."

The idea began to form in the back of his mind, and he blurted it out before considering it (remembering even as he did Cassidy's warning that he was too impulsive and that it would cause him trouble someday). He trusted an instinct, a feeling about the girl. "And this lot over here," he said, "what about them?"

"You know that," she said. "I don't like them much. I don't like the high and mighty that run *any* country for themselves. The British people are fine. But screw the government."

"So you go to Holland Park."

"Yeah," she said. "And neck with the wogs in the hallways, remember? That'll show 'em, right?"

"Maybe there's something else," he said.

"What?"

"Something else you could do."

"What do you mean?"

Reilly did not know how to begin. He got up and put on the teakettle. "What if I told you I wasn't American?"

She grinned at him. "I know that."

"What?"

"You make too many little mistakes. I was going to ask you about it sometime. What are you—Irish?"

Again, Reilly nearly panicked. He could imagine her remarking to her CIA father that she was going out with someone who claimed he was American but who really was Irish. Daddy could have some fun with that one.

She saw he was withdrawing. "Come on," she said. "Don't be mad."

Reilly poured the water into the teapot and left the mixture to brew. "All right," he said, walking back to the day bed. "I'm Irish." He spoke in his Belfast accent, and she clapped her hands twice.

"That's unbelievable—I mean like gorgeous," she said. "I like that."

It's a mistake! The warning screamed in Reilly's mind. She's a nutter. She'll screw you up somehow. "Gorgeous, shit," he said. "Come on. I'm taking you home." He got up and tugged at her arm, but she would not move.

"Don't get mad," she said. "I didn't mean to tease you. You just sounded so great."

"Yeah."

"Honest." She pulled him down next to her.

Looking back later, he would remember the moment vividly—she having no glimmer of what he had in mind, let alone what lay ahead, leaning toward him, toying with his hands in her lap. A strand of hair had fallen over her face and she shook her head and blew at it impatiently.

He decided to go on. The act was a matter of instinct and of trust. And, he realized, of self-preservation. She could help him. She could go places he could not go, do things he could not do. She could throw them off his track.

"I'm from Belfast," he said.

"Yes?"

"And I'm Catholic."

"So?" He could see she was trying to read his face.

"So," he said, still not knowing how to get it out, "I don't much like the British"

Her hands tightened in his. "Good God," she said. "The IRA?"

"Yes."

She sat back and stared at him blankly. "I mean, the IRA. Jesus."

He could not tell whether she was pleased or shocked. "It's not all that bad," he said.

"Bad? No, it's *good*," she said. "I mean, I guess it's good, what they're trying to do—get the British out of Ireland. *That's* good."

He had to push her further. "And the bombings?" he asked.

Again, the quick flash of astonishment. "I don't know what to think about the bombings," she said. "That's something else."

"I know."

She asked the question quietly: "Is that what you do?"

"No," he said quickly, telling the first lie. "At least not yet."

"I mean," she said, "the guard at the Tate. That was pretty bad. I don't know if I could take that."

In the hushed room, he could clearly hear the hiss of the gas heater. The soft yellow halo around the grate was the only light. She shivered slightly and pulled up the collar of his old sweater that she always wore in the room.

Reilly was still not sure of her—still not sure how she was reacting. He knew he had to persuade her somehow that the bombings were justified—that there was a motivation strong enough in him to explain why he would want to risk killing by planting a bomb. There was no need to talk about Thomas; Thomas could wait. First he had to tell how it was. He began to talk about the night the Prods blew the legs off his father, telling the story very unemotionally and softly, watching with satisfaction as tears came to her eyes when he talked about fighting through the crowds to reach the hospital.

He drove the point home: "I can carry him around like a baby," he said. "He's very light now, very light. You'd be surprised, the weight in a man's legs . . . How do you think that makes me feel?"

When he was done, she did not wipe away the tears. "I

understand," she said. "I can imagine what that must be like."

"Can you imagine what it does to me?"

"Yes."

Reilly sensed it would be all right. "So just don't take on so about the bombs," he said.

"I'll try."

"Try harder."

"I will."

She shivered again. "I have to go."

"You can't stay?"

"No. Not tonight."

"Why not?"

"I've got to think about all this. Alone."

"All right." He watched her get her things, moving quietly around the room, very composed, very much her own person. She was as strong as he had thought. Good. He counted on that.

At the door she turned to look at him. "You want me to help, don't you?" she said.

"Yes."

"I thought so."

"Will you?"

She shrugged. "I want to think about it. Like I said."

That was all he could hope for. "All right," he said.

"I'll see you." And then she was gone.

During the next two days, Reilly vacillated between elation and fear. He sensed that she would help, but he was enough of a skeptic to doubt his instincts, to imagine her—even the girl who had shared his bed—going to her father, going to *someone*, and letting his secret out.

When she finally appeared at his door on the night of October 27, he practically pulled her into the room. She came right to the point—she always had. "All right," she said. "I'll help."

He was still not convinced—it was too easy. "Are you sure?"

"Yes."

"Even with the bombings?"

"Even that."

Reilly felt a surge of relief. "Right," he said "That's my girl."

"It's not just that."

"What?"

"Not just that I'm your girl," she said. They were sitting on the old day bed, turning to face each other. "It's the whole thing—what happened to your father, everything. Mainly your father, I guess. I have to do *something*. They can't *treat* people like that."

At first he was surprised and hurt that she was not doing it because of him, but he saw what she meant. It made no difference; the effect was the same. "The fucking British," he said to encourage her.

"Yes," she said firmly. "So I'll help."

"When?"

"Today, tomorrow—whenever." And then she told him the news that shaped their scheme.

With other U.S. Embassy wives and daughters, she had been invited to go on a special tour the next day, Thursday, October 28. When Reilly learned the destination, he was flabbergasted by his good luck. For weeks he had been trying to find a way to roam that historic building. The British had mounted guards at the doors and insisted that everyone who entered register by name and show some kind of identification. And even if he got inside he knew that he would not be able to wander off on his own; he would have to stay with the tourists.

"What should I look for?" she asked.

Reilly told her precisely what it was about the building he wanted to learn. And he told her how to look for the right spot for him to plant the bomb. He still did not tell her about Thomas.

17

"SO WE THINK, you see, that there's an American connection."

"Why?"

"I just told you—because the man we believe planted the bomb at the Tate tried to fool the guards by affecting an English accent, but they spotted him straightaway for an American. . . ."

There was a sigh of infinite boredom. The huge man behind the desk piled high with reports and a collection of exotic potted plants looked down at his plump, pink hands. He was paring his nails with a daggerlike letter opener, oblivious to the irritated glances of the Home Secretary. It was four-thirty on the afternoon of Friday, October 29.

"What nonsense," he said finally. The voice was an unhurried rumble, weary and slow. He slurred words together carelessly, and the Home Secretary cocked his head slightly to try to follow the uneven cadences. "Since when does a guard at the Tate have the ear of Professor Henry Higgins?" He chuckled at that and the sounds erupted in small explosions, as though somewhere in his vast bulk a volcano was stirring to life. "By God, I don't think he's got it. You *do* catch the allusion, John."

"I do."

"You don't always."

"Good God, I understand!"

"Then why aren't you laughing?"

"Because I don't find any of this amusing—particularly your feeble attempts at humor."

The other pursed his lips and went to work on his right thumb. "Your chap could have been French, you know, for all the guards at the Tate could tell." He mused for a moment. "He could have been someone wanting to make the guards think he was American."

"Now why would he want to do that?"

"Damned if I know."

The Secretary stirred impatiently in the straight-backed wooden chair that, uninvited, he had pulled up to the desk. "You scoff too much, Richard," he said. "You always did."

"Even at school, John?" the other asked. "You always say at some point, during this recurring dialogue of ours, that I scoffed too much even at school."

"And then what do I always say, pray tell?"

"You say, 'It's been the ruin of your career.'" The other looked up at the Home Secretary and smiled. He had a massive head with a great mane of hair that straggled down over his ears. "And then, rather sadly, John, you customarily bring up rugger."

"I do?"

"Oh my yes. You recall how well I played at school and how I might have done well at Oxford and how I could have ended up playing for England like you—*beside* you—if I hadn't lacked team spirit. If I hadn't been such a loner. You usually make me feel quite unpatriotic."

"Yes, a great pity."

The two men regarded each other frankly across the scarred desk, thinking about the years they had spent together that went back to the September afternoon in 1930 when, aged eight, they had met at Euston Station. Each had been with his mother and governess who were delivering him into the hands of a young master for the trip to school in Scotland. The two boys had liked each other instantly; each was cradling a worn teddy bear under his arm— a point that they had mentioned only once in the past twenty years, and then only after a number of whiskies at the Secretary's club.

"So," said the other, resuming his work on his nails, "I suppose you've been around to my superiors at the Yard before" (he gestured at the small jumble of an office) "before you fetched up here."

The Secretary nodded. "Yes," he said. "I worked my way down through the chain of command until I came to you. Did it all very properly."

"No one objected?"

"No, they thought you could interrupt your work on—what is it? . . ."

"Communications techniques within the department, I think that's the point of the thing. Sometimes I forget myself. Wildly exciting, it is."

"But at least you get to do it on your own."

"Yes, there is that."

"Yes, but now, of course, we want you to be part of a team."

"And to be patriotic, too, I expect."

"That too, Richard."

"And work with that chap of yours, Thomas."

"Of course."

"Is he really as painfully dull as he seems on the telly?"

"Not at all. He's a good man, I think. I hope."

"We'll soon see. But why not just get someone to order me to help? Why the state visit?"

"To be quite frank, I thought it would help to speak to you—to get your interest up."

"But why me?"

The Secretary's fist slammed down on the desk so hard that an ashtray jumped. "Good Christ, Richard, stop fishing for compliments. Stop playing me like a bloody trout. I know you far too well." An exasperated pause. "All right, you shall have your bloody blackmail. I want you because I think you're the most brilliant man in the department."

The other smiled and bowed. "How generous of you, John," he said. "What a pity my superiors do not see with your vision."

"You're the pity, and you know it."

The other brushed away the idea with a swing of a newly manicured hand. "Let's not start that twaddle again," he said. "What can I do to help? How do I start?"

"Good," said the Home Secretary. "That's fine." Then, leaning forward across the desk so they almost touched heads, the Secretary began to go over the whole case with Richard Palmer, age fifty-five, Winchester, New College,

Oxford (a double first in classics and Arabic), whose career at Scotland Yard had languished almost to the point of extinction. The two old friends talked on until the shadows of early evening thickened in the small office far down the hall in a neglected byway of Scotland Yard.

"It will work."

"Do you think?"

"I *know* it will." He was immensely pleased with her. They were kneeling on the thin red carpet in his room, peering down at the building on a tourist's map that she had carefully spread out before them as though it were a picnic cloth. The spot she had chosen for the bomb was perfect. Thomas couldn't possibly ignore the challenge.

Reilly could see that she was pleased with her success, but she was all business. There was nothing of the schoolgirl about her. "How do I get there?" he asked.

"Not on a weekday," she said. "There's no way on a weekday. Too many people. It will have to be on a weekend. A Sunday, probably, or a holiday."

He had known that, of course, but still he did not like to hear it. It would be easier for the guards to spot him on a weekend. "How do I get in?" he asked.

Kate pointed to an entrance that was seldom used. "We walked by here on our little tour," she said. "There's just one guard there. If we can figure a way to get past him, you're home free."

With a slender forefinger, she traced the route from the entrance, down the long corridors, and through the swinging doors. She finished by lightly touching the target.

Perfect. It was perfect. Reilly was amazed at her insight. He started to hug her but she moved away.

"Can you do it?" She was serious.

"If I can think of a way of getting in," he said. "It's bloody marvelous."

"It's pretty dangerous—there, of all places."

"I know."

"You *sure* you want to try it there?"

"Very sure."

She looked at him appraisingly. "Don't take this wrong," she said. "You're not afraid?"

Reilly flared. "Watch yourself."

"Don't get mad," she said evenly. "You can be afraid. I just don't want you taking on anything you think is too risky. That doesn't make sense."

He saw what she meant. He also saw that he would have to tell her about Thomas—how he *had* to get Thomas. Then she would understand. "You need to know something," he said, then proceeded to lay out for her the whole story—how Thomas's taunts on television goaded him so sharply, how the claim that he, Reilly, could not make a bomb that Thomas could not take apart struck not only at his worth as a man but at the worth of his people. Thomas was scoffing at the dignity of the Irish. "I can't let him do that," Reilly concluded. "I've got to get him. That's why it's worth the risk."

She had listened intently and now she nodded. "All right," she said. "I understand that."

Reilly was surprised. "The Thomas thing doesn't bother you—trying to kill him?" he asked.

"He brought it on himself," she answered.

She's a cool one. Reilly studied the calm face of the girl, wondering how she could be so matter-of-fact, and realizing he did not really know her at all. What was more, he could see that their relationship had changed in a subtle but important fashion. She was treating him as though she was his equal. It was as plain and open as that. She was in it with him, and thus felt justified in asking if he was afraid. Reilly did not know if he liked that or not, and he tried to dodge the issue for the time being by joking it away. "So you're a partner now," he said. "Moving into the firm, are you?"

"Yes." She was beginning to relax.

"So you should be moving in here with me, share and share alike," said Reilly.

Kate was smiling as she sat back on her heels. "My, what a lovely proposition," she said. "Best I've had in weeks."

"Best I can do," said Reilly.

"I'll take it," she said.

"What?"

"Just for tonight," she said, laughing now. "As a reward."

"What do you mean by *that*?"

"I wasn't sure I wanted to stay," she said.

"Why not?"

"It depended."

"On what?"

"On how you reacted to my little plan."

"If it scared me or not?"

"Something like that."

"And if it did, you weren't going to stay?"

"No. I was going to think it over."

"But if it did not scare me off, you were planning to stay?"

"Yes."

"What a charming creature."

"Whoever said I was nice?"

Reilly could not sort it all out. He looked at her for a moment, trying to decide what to do, and knowing all along that he wanted her, that probably he needed her, and that that was as deep as he cared to go. "You're daft," he said, "and I'm probably daft to keep you."

She got up to put on the teakettle. "You forget," she said, "I'm a partner now."

When they were settled, cups in hand, Reilly said, "So we're partners, are we?"

"Right on," she said firmly.

Then Reilly began to tell her how he thought she could help him some more, the idea he had been mulling over in his mind for days. He told her what he would need to be sure to get past the airport guards when the operation was all over and he would have to get out of Britain that very day.

Visitors to the room usually detected it at once and stood, puzzled, as they tried to recall the childhood association—what it was that triggered the memories of Christmas. To ease the boredom, Sergeant Phillips had made a little game out of the situation. From his seat at the desk, he would watch the newcomers trying to identify the smell and then throw out a hint: "It's something you used to eat," he would say, and if that produced no response he would add: "Sweets."

That almost always did it. "Of course! Marzipan!" But then the visitors naturally would want to know what the smell of marzipan was doing in the squad room of the British Army's bomb experts, and Phillips or whoever else was manning the phones and radios would explain that it really wasn't a sweet at all—it was gelignite, which had the same penetrating smell of almonds. On a workbench were fragments of two or three dismantled bombs that still bore particles of the explosive. Phillips would hand over a pinch of the stuff for inspection. It looked like light-brown sugar.

On Sunday, October 31, two days after Kate reported to Reilly about her scouting expedition, Major Thomas walked briskly into the squad room and tried not to wince at the odor. He had considered ordering Phillips to get the smell of that stuff out of the area immediately, but realized that would simply exacerbate his anxiety.

"Nothing new, of course," Thomas said to Phillips.

"No, sir. It's very quiet."

"Damn. I wish he'd get on with it."

Thomas looked around the office in Scotland Yard that the army sergeants had made into a replica of one of the ready rooms in Belfast. Someone had scrounged some old cots, which were used by the men on night duty. One wall was papered over with huge nude pinups that were, Thomas noted, considerably more graphic and gynecological than the ones that he remembered from World War II. A pile of flak jackets was in one corner beside a gunrack filled with automatic rifles. On the desk in front of Phillips were radios that connected him to the networks run by Scotland Yard and the Metropolitan Police. There were two regular telephones and, on the wall, a newly installed red phone that was a direct line from the Home Secretary.

Thomas noticed something new on Phillips's desk. "What's this?" he asked, picking it up.

Phillips grinned. "One or two of the lads fixed it up from some pictures they got in Belfast," he said. "Quite clever, really."

As he turned the pages, Thomas saw that it was a scrapbook of photos taken after some explosions in which IRA members had been blown apart while assembling bombs. The details were shown with clinical clarity: the bodies were usually half-covered with debris, but he could see the stumps of arms and legs. The clothes had been blown off the bodies, and the skin was charred black.

"You're a football fan, I believe, sir," said Phillips. "You'll fancy the one on page ten, I think it is."

Thomas remembered the picture. Four men had been killed while building a bomb above a Belfast pub. Someone had written a caption on the bottom of the photograph: "Own Goal"—the football term for the disaster that ensues when a player inadvertently kicks the ball into his own net.

"Good Lord," Thomas said, and quickly turned the page without commenting on the football reference. Thomas next found himself staring at the decapitated torso of what had once been another IRA man who had blown himself up. "Let's see," ran the long caption, "does the red wire get attached to the yellow wire or the green. . . .?"

Thomas did his best to smile as he handed the book back to Phillips.

"Gives the lads something to chuckle about," said Phillips.

"I dare say," said Thomas, and disappeared into his small room adjoining the office.

He had to wait for five minutes until the tremor left his hands. The pictures brought it all back. He could even feel the sweat on his forehead. Jesus, let him get on with it, he thought. It was the delays that Thomas couldn't stand. The waiting around, the wondering where it would be, when it would come. Thomas knew he was losing his edge. The euphoria generated by the football match was wearing off. His fear was still there. The pictures of the mutilated bodies showed that.

Thomas forced himself to start working on a model of the bomb he had been constructing on his desk. The wooden box was exactly the same, except that one side was glass so that he could see the works. The layout included a battery and a capsule like the one that was found after the Tate explosion. The major was trying to guess how the wiring circuit was laid out, reasoning from the more elementary bombs he had taken apart. The only thing that was missing from the real thing was the gelignite. A light bulb substituted for the explosives. Every time he made a mistake, electricity flowed through the whole circuit and the light went on to tell him he had just been killed.

Time and again, the light flashed for Major Thomas. Before Phillips left at six, he stuck his head round the door and asked if there was anything he could do—bring in some tea, perhaps? The major said no. He was fascinated by the problem. It was like playing chess by mail against a grand master. The light flashed again, and Thomas swore softly to himself. He did not give up until midnight.

18

RICHARD PALMER HAD not been so angry or moved so fast in years. At nine o'clock on Monday morning, November 8, he labored up the broad stone steps of the American Embassy and into the main entrance under the giant gold-tinted eagle that glowers over Grosvenor Square. A fountain murmured quietly in the background. The guard at the desk in the spacious lobby was on the lookout for him. "You can go right up, sir," he said to Palmer as the man from Scotland Yard bustled past. He stomped into the first elevator and stood glaring out at a startled mailgirl who chanced by until the doors closed silently and he vanished from view.

Paul Anderson, the embassy officer in charge of security, was waiting for his visitor—had been waiting, in fact, for the ten minutes since their phone conversation had ended with Palmer slamming down his receiver. "Good Lord," Anderson had said to his secretary; "He hung up on me." He thought a moment. "The last time someone did that was in high school. I didn't like her much anyway."

"What's his problem?" the secretary asked.

"Damned if I know," Anderson replied. "He didn't say. He just spluttered." With that, the doorway to Anderson's office quite literally darkened with Palmer's bulk, but only for an instant, since the Scotland Yard official did not pause to be invited in. His rumpled raincoat flapping, Palmer strode up to Anderson's desk and sat down, folding his big hands over the handle of his umbrella, which he planted in the rug before him as though it were a battle sword. Anderson half-rose to greet his visitor but, finding himself alone on his feet, slowly sat down again, withdrawing the hand that he had automatically stuck out.

"Mr. Palmer, I presume," Anderson said.

Palmer did not reply, apparently because he could not. He was breathing so audibly that Anderson's secretary turned to look at him anxiously. After a moment the heaves and shudders that were passing through Palmer's great torso began to subside. He whipped off his horn-rimmed glasses and used his tie to wipe away the sweat that marred them. Palmer began to talk while still occupied with the task, peering down at his glasses, so that his deep, sleepy voice seemed to emanate from his enormous chest. "You're very astute, Mister . . ." (he put on his glasses and looked at the name plate on the desk in front of him) ". . . Anderson, isn't it, yes. Very astute indeed."

"We try," said the American. Palmer shifted an inch closer. "Do you? That's the very reason that I'm here," he said. "You don't try bloody hard enough."

Anderson's voice began to rise. "Now just what the hell

do you mean by that?" he asked, "if I may speak as diplomatically as you."

"Diplomacy, hell. There's nothing diplomatic about this at all."

"Look," said Anderson, "why don't you just try to explain what's on your mind."

Palmer searched wildly in his suit coat pockets for a moment and then produced a crumpled package of cigarettes, which he did not offer to Anderson. Soon the air in the room was blue with the pungent smoke of a Gauloise. Anderson's secretary silently got up and left, raising a tissue to her nose as she went out the door.

"You have heard," Palmer said, "of the special arrangements that have existed for years, decades, between this embassy and the British Government, have you not?" he asked.

"Yes, I've heard reports of the like."

"Indeed, I think it fair to say that we often live in each other's pockets. The word 'symbiosis' comes to mind."

"I've heard of it."

"I wouldn't have thought so—from the way you acted."

"Oh, shit!" Anderson was on his feet and pointing toward the door. "Why don't you come back some other time and we'll talk this thing over—whatever it is."

Palmer did not stir. He continued to address the empty desk until Anderson shrugged and wearily resumed his seat. "Because if you fully understood these informal protocols that had developed over the years you, as the embassy's security officer, would surely have let the Yard know immediately when such a thing occurred—"

Anderson interrupted loudly. "*What* thing?"

"The passport, my dear fellow, the stolen passport."

Anderson remembered a report a few days ago from the office downstairs: the inventory of passport forms had been one shy when the routine check was made at the end of the day. "First of all," said the American, "it wasn't a 'passport' that had been issued to anyone—it was an unassigned passport, simply the booklet itself. Second, I wouldn't characterize it as 'stolen.' I'd say it was 'missing.' "

"That's just what you did," said Palmer. "You called it 'missing' and you were bloody wrong."

"Why?"

"Have you ever had a passport disappear like that—be 'missing' for a while and then turn up later?"

"I can't recall ever having one disappear."

"Trust me," said Palmer, "no clerk is going to find it under a filing cabinet. It's been stolen."

"Your instincts tell you this?"

"Yes, if you want to put it that way."

"Do they tell you who stole it, then?"

Palmer lit another cigarette with the butt of the first. "Someone who worked in the office or who had access to it. That's fairly obvious, I would think. That's *your* problem. What interests us is not so much who stole it but who it was stolen *for*—who is going to get it and make use of it. It most likely will not be the person who stole it. The Americans, of course, already have their own passports, and the British nationals who work in your office are hardly likely to forge an American passport. No, someone else is going to do the forging."

"Assuming it was stolen," said Anderson, "who do you think would end up with the passport?"

Palmer passed a hand across his forehead and glanced disapprovingly at the sweat he had wiped away. "You Americans will kill us all with heat," he said. "My Lord, it's still early November." Rising to his feet, he struggled to take off his raincoat and threw it into a far chair. Then he took off the coat of his worn gray sharkskin suit and hung it daintily over the back of his chair. Anderson was too startled to offer any assistance. He had never seen a British official with his coat off except during country weekends when he was playing cricket on the village green.

Fumbling with thick fingers, Palmer loosened his tie. "I must put you in the picture," he said. "*My* picture." As he began to talk about the case Palmer lost all of his brusque and imperious air. He spoke earnestly and confidingly, slowly tapping Anderson's desk to tick off his points.

"You are aware," he said, "of the bombings of London and of my government's concern to stop them immediately. We think that the man who bombed the Tate is the man we are after, and there is a theory that he is an American."

"But why should someone take the risk of stealing an American passport to give to another American?"

"Precisely. I don't believe our chap is an American. I dropped past to talk to the guards who called the man an American, and they thought I was a Scot. A Scot! Do I sound Scottish to you?"

Anderson smiled. Palmer's accent was so slurred that he might have been born a Bulgarian. "Go on," said Anderson.

"The more I talked to the guards, just as I suspected, the less sure they were that the fellow *was* an American. But that's what he claimed, that's what he let on."

"So?"

"So I am very interested in any curious thing that might bear on Americans. I'm collecting Americana. Which is why I'm interested in a missing American passport that could be forged to help someone pretending to be an American get out of the country. Which is why I'm interested in this report of yours that came across my desk this morning saying that a passport has been missing since November second, six days ago. Six bloody days. That lead may be too long— far too long. If there is some kind of American connection here, our clever chap may be figuring on planting the bloody bomb tonight and getting out tomorrow morning with his brand-new American passport—"

Anderson interrupted: "We know the number on the passport, you know. You could have all your people looking for the number as Americans come through the ports and air terminals."

"I've already done that, of course. We have to take every precaution, no matter how unlikely. But if the bomber does get the passport, he could get the number changed by a good forger.

Anderson leaned back in his black leather chair. "So what

would you like from us?" he asked.

"To be told instantly if you find out who stole the passport," Palmer replied. "And, in the interim, to get a list of every person, American or British, either a visitor or an employee, who conceivably could have had access to the area where the passports were kept."

"Fine," said Anderson as Palmer rose slowly from his chair and began to dress himself again, retrieving his garments from around the room and adjusting his tie.

"You wouldn't like a cup of tea?" asked the American.

Palmer shot him a sharp glance. "Bags?" he said.

"I'm afraid so. Yes."

"No, thank you very much indeed," said Palmer. With that, he turned—rather nimbly, Anderson noted, for a man of his bulk—and disappeared through the door as quickly as he had come.

19

"I TOLD YOU, 'never again!' "

"I know, I put off calling, but I need—"

"Much too dangerous. You're putting me in danger, you're jeopardizing the entire operation."

"There's a reason—"

"What, for God's sake?"

Shouting into the pay phone on Earl's Court Road, Pat Reilly tried to explain to Cassidy why he needed someone to forge a blank passport, the document that Kate had stolen. "I figured you'd know someone," said Reilly.

"Why do you want to be an American?" Cassidy demanded.

"As a backup" said Reilly. "In case they get close. Americans can go anywhere. No one ever checks them. You know that."

"Yes," Cassidy admitted. "All right. But why so jumpy?

What makes you think they suspect you?"

"Nothing," said Reilly. "I just want a second out if things get sticky."

There was a pause, and then Cassidy gave Reilly the name and address of a photographer in Soho. "Tell him I sent you," Cassidy said. "It will be all right. And then I don't want to talk to you again until you're back here in Belfast and Thomas is dead. Do you understand that?"

Reilly did not even have time to say yes before Cassidy hung up.

At the instant that Palmer was beginning to belabor Anderson in the American Embassy, Reilly was ringing the bell at the address Cassidy had given him. A pleasant young man let him in and showed him to a seat near an old-fashioned bellows-type portrait camera.

"A Mr. Cassidy suggested I drop by," said Reilly.

"Oh, yes?" asked the young man casually.

"He thought you could do something with this." Reilly produced the blank passport booklet and placed it on the table before him.

"Yes," said the other, "I believe we can help you."

Reilly was impressed by the aplomb of the photographer. Was he Irish? Reilly thought he could detect the faintest vestige of Belfast in the other's speech. Reilly produced a picture of himself taken fifteen minutes before in a coin-operated photo booth on Oxford Street.

"A few details, please," said the photographer. "The eyes are blue, the hair is red, the height is—"

"Six feet two," Reilly interjected.

"And the name and address is? . . ."

Three days later, on Thursday, November 11, Reilly picked up the finished passport, which showed that he had been on a tour of Europe for the last three weeks, traveling from France to Germany and Belgium before flying into Heathrow. The name of the lean, red-haired tourist was Martin O'Rourke, and he lived in Somerville, Massachusetts.

As Reilly was picking up his forged passport, Richard Palmer was again going over the names on the list that Anderson had sent over that morning. There were thirty-three in all: twenty who worked in the section, and thirteen visitors who had registered at the desk outside before being allowed into the passport office. Palmer had learned that the documents were kept in a cabinet in a part of the room that was inaccessible to visitors. It seemed unlikely that one of them could have reached it unnoticed. Still, every possibility had to be checked out. He was wondering if he had the manpower to interrogate everyone on the list—wondering, in fact, if the whole exercise was worth it—when the phone rang and the Home Secretary's voice boomed in his ear.

"Have you found anything yet?" the Secretary asked.

"Nothing. What did you expect—"

"Nothing? No leads at all?"

"A vague idea that might be something and probably isn't."

"Tell me."

When Palmer was through, there was a pause, and then the exasperated voice of the Secretary: "Is that all, Richard?"

"Bloody all."

"Good Lord. Well, pursue it by all means. If you can't get the manpower, I will. Let me know."

"All right," said Palmer, and was about to hang up forthwith when he had a thought: "Any luck on tracing that capsule?"

"None. They're so common I suspect Boots carries them by now."

"Still, put out the word through your television friends that we're onto something—that we've been able to trace an important 'component' of the bomb to a source in London. Let's put more pressure on our friend. Let's make him edgy to get on with it."

"All right," said the Secretary, but Palmer had already

hung up and was on his way out of his rabbit's warren of an office to organize an interrogation of all thirty-three persons on the list, staffers as well as visitors.

There were problems with the Americans. Ultimately, the Home Secretary had to call the U.S. Ambassador before permission was given for Scotland Yard to question American employees about an event that had occurred in a building flying the American flag. Even then the Ambassador insisted that a representative from the embassy's security force sit in on the questioning.

Palmer conducted the interrogations himself, starting on the morning of Friday, November 12, in a back room in the embassy and continuing into the late afternoon. The man from Scotland Yard flipped through the witnesses as though they were playing cards, letting a number of people go quickly and then holding someone who interested him for twenty minutes or longer. He took down the names of people mentioned by the employees that would need further checking. Palmer had about given up on the last embassy employee on the list—a twenty-three-year-old clerk named Nancy Clark—when she mentioned almost in passing that she knew the cabinet had been locked because she had checked just before going out on a lunch date.

Diverted for the first time in an hour, Palmer asked if the man she had gone out with had worked in the embassy as well.

"It wasn't a he," she said. "It was a she."

"Oh?"

"Yes. She's a friend of mine. Her father works in the embassy."

Palmer stirred. "Where did you meet her?"

"Right there—in the office. She just wandered through. Everybody knows her."

"And did you leave her alone at all?"

"Just while I got my coat."

The room was very quiet. "And then you checked the cabinet and it was locked?"

"Yes."

"Was it normally open during the morning?"

"Yes."

"And how does one lock the cabinet? With a special key?"

"No. You just push the door closed."

"I see."

The girl glanced from one man to the other. She was beginning to twist the handbag she held in her lap. "There's nothing wrong, is there?" she said. "She wouldn't do anything wrong."

Both men had picked up their pencils. "What is her name?" asked Palmer.

The girl looked at the American officer. He nodded.

She said, "Her name is Kate Rochford."

Twenty minutes later Palmer was again beginning to lose his temper, this time in the office of the chief inspector at Scotland Yard who controlled the assignment of detectives. "To repeat," said Palmer, "I need background checks on every one of the thirty-three persons on this list, and I want particular attention paid to Kate Rochford. No, I'll do her myself."

The inspector ran a nervous finger down the list. "We're rather hard put, you know, Palmer," he said. "I can't say when we could get around to covering thirty-two suspects."

"I suggest tonight."

The inspector leaned back in his seat and looked at Palmer warily. He clearly was not at all sure how to handle this figure out of the back corridors—and legends—of the Yard. "Who's in such a hurry?" he asked.

"The Home Secretary," said Palmer.

"Oh, I see."

"Well?"

The inspector cleared his throat. "You have no real clues, of course, nothing that would definitely link any of these thirty-three persons to the bombings?"

"Nothing whatsoever."

"Just the business about the passport."

"Just that."

"Rather vague, isn't it? I mean, what if somebody stole the thing to send it back to America for a friend or something?"

Palmer reached over and pushed the inspector's telephone next to his elbow. "Why don't you ring up the Home Secretary and tell him that you think this is all foolish."

The inspector moved slightly away from the phone. "That won't be necessary," he said pleasantly.

"I'm quite aware of the problematical nature of all this," said Palmer. "Much more aware than you, in fact. But when you have nothing but slim leads to follow, you follow slim leads, right?"

"Right."

"Particularly with the Home Secretary prodding you in the arse."

"Right."

"So I want each of these thirty-two others checked out. I want to know who they are, who their friends are, and I particularly want to know if any of them is hanging about with an American, or someone who claims he is an American, or someone who even looks like an American."

With that Palmer abruptly left the room, only to reappear seconds later. "And one more thing," he said. "I want to know if any of them has visited any public building or monument within the last month—whenever it was since we started making every visitor identify himself and register at the entrances. I want to know if any of our thirty-three has suddenly become an ardent tourist."

This time Palmer left for good, stopping only long enough to pick up a detective named Olson, who had recently been assigned to his office. At their first meeting Palmer had told the young man, "I don't want you following me around like a puppy. Speak up, speak up—I want to know what you're thinking." But after a moment's reflection, Palmer had reappeared in the small office assigned to Olson and added: "Mind you, I don't want you spouting drivel. I don't want you chattering away."

All of which had so intimidated and inhibited Olson that he said very little at all, and nothing, in fact, as the two men drove silently together later that evening to a large, brick row house on Elgin Crescent. A ten-speed girl's bicycle was leaning up against the pillar. Someone—a younger sister? —was practicing the piano.

The door swung open and Palmer found himself looking down at an attractive, dark-haired woman who was wearing an apron. The conversation went badly. Palmer stammered as he tried to explain to the woman that he and Olson were from Scotland Yard and that they would like to talk to Kate for a moment or two.

Mrs. Rochford studied Palmer coolly. "What's this all about?" she asked.

"I'm afraid I can't really explain it to you," Palmer said.

"Then I suggest you go through the American Embassy," she said. The woman began to close the door.

"Madam," said Palmer, "I assure you we have every legal right to speak with your daughter, whether or not the American Embassy approves."

"I wonder," said Mrs. Rochford. "I will call the Embassy's legal office in the morning to check on that." The door shut.

Palmer found himself staring at the brass knocker.

"My pleasure, madam," he said, before turning and striding down the walk. Olson was one step behind.

At the corner Palmer began talking without slowing down: "Keep an eye on that house," he told Olson. "Work it out, shifts around the clock. I want to know when that girl comes back. "We'll start checking on her school. If she comes back, and leaves, follow her. Damn well follow her."

With that Palmer squeezed into the driver's seat of the car and pulled away from the curb, leaving Olson standing alone. After a moment the detective flicked on his walkie-talkie, told headquarters what he was doing, and asked for another car to use as a blind.

It was a long night. Kate Rochford did not come home.

When Olson phoned Palmer with the news at eight-thirty on Saturday morning, the Scotland Yard official came awake in an instant. "I don't like it," he said. "I don't like it at all." He hung up, then quickly phoned the duty officer at the Yard. "Put out a general alarm," he said. "I want her found today." But Kate Rochford had disappeared.

20

THE RASPING SCRATCH of the needle on the record woke him. He stirred in the narrow bed and found his arm trapped beneath her. Slowly, trying to let her sleep, he eased away, but she was looking up at him when he came back from turning off the old phonograph.

"What's the time?"

"About twelve."

"We almost slept through," she said.

"Yes."

"That would have been a lovely pickle—sleeping right through the night."

"Mmm."

"Waking up tomorrow—no, *this* morning, Sunday, *the* day, with nothing done, nothing ready. Bloody marvelous, what?"

"Bloody marvelous."

Naked, she swung out of bed. He looked away. There was enough on his mind already. He did not want to be distracted further.

She dressed hurriedly and put the kettle on. He was sitting in the old green chair, thumbing through yesterday's paper.

"Anything wrong?" she asked.

There was no use pretending, not with her. "You know what's wrong," he said.

"Edgy?"

He flared. "Edgy, shit."

"You can do it."

"Sure."

She walked over and sat on the floor beside him. "We've planned it all—what you'll do, what I'll do. It's all perfect."

"If it works."

"It will work."

Reilly did not answer. He thought for a moment of saying he was afraid because of her—because of what might happen to her—but he knew she would not buy that. *She* certainly wasn't afraid.

He said, "I always get this way before."

It was not true. He had been perfectly confident at the Tate. Everything had been fine at the Tate. But now it was different. Maybe it was the build-up of the publicity, the appearance of Thomas again on the telly just the other night, talking so calmly again about how he would cope.

"The plan's too complicated," he said.

He waited for the bite in her voice, and it was there.

"We worked it out together," she said. "I found the spot, you figured out the rest. It's more your plan than mine."

That was not it, and he knew it. He was worried about the bomb, worried that something unexpected would go wrong when he made it, when he planted it. Something inexplicable. You never knew what might happen. Three nights before, a car had exploded in Belfast as it was being driven toward the downtown area. The BBC explained that the bomb was being carried in the lap of the IRA man sitting next to the driver. Something had gone wrong, and two men were dead. An own goal. Two own goals.

"Remember your father," she said suddenly.

"Yes." He had expected that.

"You've *got* to do it."

"I know."

"Remember Thomas."

"Fuck Thomas."

Thomas didn't matter. Thomas wasn't pulling him into this. He was being pushed from the rear by this cool bitch

of a girl and the sense of guilt over his father. He knew
there was no escape, and he was goddamned if he was
going to give her the satisfaction of seeing him hesitate any
longer. "Right," he said. "Let's get on with it."

"I've got my own problems, you know," she said.

"What?"

"Doing what I have to do. I'm not so damned pleased
about that."

Her confession somehow made him feel better. "Not
much we can do about it now, is there?" he said.

"Not really."

He put his hand on hers and found it very warm.
"Right," he said. "Let's pull up our socks and get on with it."

For a while Kate watched, saying nothing, but before long
Reilly heard her sigh deeply and saw that she was asleep
in the bed. By that time, working on the floor, he had
the box all made—two feet long, one foot wide, and one
foot deep. The air smelled of fresh pine shavings and sawdust. The lid needed more care. Reilly drilled a quarter-
inch hole close to each edge and corresponding holes down
into the top edges of each of the four sides. Next he fitted
the plywood lid over the box, matching the holes perfectly,
and screwing the top down carefully. He then removed the
screws and rubbed them with a wet cake of soap to make
sure they would go in even more easily the next time.

Reilly worked swiftly. He was so absorbed by his task that
he did not think of Thomas at all. One night in Belfast Cassidy had watched him at work and had said that he should
be a cabinetmaker, his hands were that strong and sure. It
was a compliment that Reilly remembered, one that made
him try harder to do the job well.

With quick, deft taps of his hammer, Reilly began nailing
heavy wire staples to three of the interior walls of the box—
the two long sides and one of the narrow. He was careful to
leave about a quarter of an inch clearance between the hoop
and the wood. When he finished, each of the three sides
was festooned with six to eight staples placed in what ap-

peared to be a random pattern. None was closer to the bottom than four inches.

Reilly unlocked the strongbox that he kept under the bed. The sticks of gelignite were lying in neat bunches, like stalks of asparagus. Reilly took out six sticks, each fourteen inches long and an inch thick. Reilly knew that the gelignite was harmless, but still he handled each piece as though it were brittle glass. Piling the sticks on top of each other, he braced them against the sides and ends with crumpled newspaper. He might have been packing a very valuable and fragile gift.

Reaching again into his strongbox, Reilly took out a capsule identical to the one that Phillips's men had found in the Tate after the explosion. He taped it to one of the wide sides, about one inch from and parallel to the top.

That done, Reilly consulted a diagram that he had drawn the previous evening. When he was finally satisfied, he took down a role of wire from a shelf above the stove and cut off six pieces ranging in length from six inches to two feet.

Next he took out a marine clock that had a twenty-four-hour dial. With a tap of his hammer, Reilly broke the glass. Taking his pliers, he twisted off the minute hand. Then he plugged in a small soldering iron and waited, lighting a cigarette to help pass the time. The only sound was Kate's breathing. When the iron was hot Reilly took a piece of soldering wire in his left hand and held it an inch above the dot marking eighteen hundred—6:00 p.m. He touched the soldering iron to the tip of the wire and drops of molten metal began to fall onto the dial. They cooled and formed a tiny cone about a quarter of an inch high. Reilly tested the metal with a finger to make sure that it was solidly attached, and moved the hour hand around. It just touched the top of the cone. Reilly added three more drops of metal to the contact to be sure. Then he wound the clock and set the hour hand at 02:30—2:30 a.m.—the time showing on his watch. He placed the clock, face-up, on the gelignite.

Slowly, Reilly removed a detonator from the strongbox. He was more afraid of the detonator than he was of the

gelignite. The fear was illogical, he realized. The detonator
would not kill him, even if it did ignite. Blow off a finger,
perhaps, but not kill him, which a stick of exploding gelignite would certainly do. Still, Reilly hated the detonators,
which looked like machine-gun bullets to him, and he held
the one he had just selected as though it were the cigarette
belonging to a stranger.

Carefully, Reilly placed the detonator on the table. Beside
it he put a small, nine-volt battery that he had bought at
Boots. For the next hour Reilly painstakingly worked all of
these elements into his bomb. In the end, five of the criss-
crossing wires were wrapped around the hour hand of the
clock. The interior resembled a cat's cradle of string woven
on the hands of a little girl. But only one complete circuit
was connected to the battery, the switch, the detonator, the
hour hand of the clock—and the tiny pyramid at eighteen
hundred.

Cutting off more lengths of wire, Reilly began making a
separate circuit to connect the capsule to the battery and the
detonator. This time he bypassed the clock altogether, but
he added one refinement to the system: a standard European light switch, the kind that is attached directly to the
wire of a reading lamp. The button of the switch had been
removed. To keep the contacts of the switch apart—to keep
it "off"—Reilly had inserted a flat metal band into the
switch. The band was about twenty inches long.

Pleased with the job, Reilly began the last tricky step. He
took the band protruding from the switch and gently poked
it through the small hole in the piece of plywood that would
be the top of the box. With the band sticking straight up,
Reilly fastened the lid down firmly, using the previously
drilled holes and the soaped screws. It went easily, but
Reilly nonetheless moved cautiously. He knew that ten or
more IRA bombmakers had been killed at their work-
benches during the past two years.

There was one thing more to be done. Reilly retrieved
from a closet an object that he had made three nights before. It was a black box slightly larger than the one on the

bench. There was a handle on top. Reilly had painted a white cross on one narrow end.

The new box had one peculiarity: it had no bottom. Reilly lowered and raised the black shell over the bomb he had just constructed. The fit was perfect: tight, but not too tight. The metal band was bent flat as the top came down. One final time, Reilly eased the box over the bomb. Then he turned a few lugs near the bottom of the box so that the· locked with the grooves he had previously dug around the bottom of the bomb. Gingerly, Reilly lifted the whole affair by the handle. It held. He could carry the hidden bomb anywhere.

"Right," said Reilly aloud in the silent room. At the sound of his voice, the girl stirred in her sleep. The bell of the church down the way tolled four times.

Reilly set the alarm for seven-thirty and slipped into bed beside the sleeping girl. He lay still for a moment, his mind rehearsing what would happen in the morning. Reilly could see the whole sequence of action as clearly as though a movie were being played on the wall at the foot of the bed. He planted the bomb, just as he had planned during the previous week, and then here came Thomas, strolling up to the box, wearing that half-ass army trench coat. Reilly watched Thomas's hand reach out for the bomb. The explosion happened in a kind of slow-motion, so that there was an interval between the flash and the roar and the great swirling cloud of dust. Right, said Reilly to himself, and almost instantly went to sleep.

21

WHEN THE ALARM went off, they were both half-awake, dozing intermittently, not speaking to each other. They had a silent, quick breakfast, and then, for the third time, he showed her the device she was to operate, going through the procedure step by step and assuring her that no one, including herself, would get hurt. He put it in a small Harrods shopping bag, and she hefted it tentatively.

"It's very light," she said.

"A big firecracker," he said. "That's all it is, really."

"How do you feel?" she asked.

Now that it was beginning, he was less nervous. At least it would all be over soon. "Pretty good," he said. "Really."

She was trying to smile. "I wish I did," she said.

That made him feel better, made him feel superior. She was not as tough as she had let on. Gratified, he told her again that everything would go fine, there was nothing to worry about. "You'll be all right," he said.

She looked very young, somehow, dressed up in her American jeans and boots, a heavy tan cape over her shoulders. Her face was very pale and very solemn. She should be laughing, he thought, laughing and carrying some schoolbooks.

"I'll meet you later, where we planned," he said.

"Sure." She was watching him very closely. "There's no other way, is there?" she said.

God, was she going to fold? After coming this far—after urging him on? But he could detect only honest questioning in her eyes. "This is the best way, the quickest way," he said. "You know that—you helped plan it."

"I know," she said.

Reilly could see she still was hesitant. Christ, he was a fool to let her get him this far out on the limb. But he would not pull out. Not after he had come this far; not after Thomas was this close to being destroyed. Think of your father, he reminded himself as if by rote, and told the girl again: "You'll be fine—it will all work fine."

For another few seconds she stood there, hesitating, the Harrods bag hanging at her side, while he wondered what she would do. Then it was all decided. She walked to him quickly and kissed him on the cheek. "Be careful," she said.

At the door she turned and smiled at him. He had forgotten how dazzling she could be. For an instant he wondered if he were taking unfair advantage of her after all.

She must have read his mind. "It's all right," she said, and disappeared.

At that moment, on Sunday, November 14, Richard Palmer was sitting alone in his paper-strewn office, looking sourly at the report filed by Olson just an hour before. The Rochford girl had not come home for the second night in a row. Palmer was waiting for Scotland Yard's switchboard to locate Anderson. He wanted the American to pressure Mrs. Rochford into talking about her daughter, who was behaving so oddly. Or was it oddly? What was so odd about spending the night out—how was it the American put it?—"shacking up with someone." And there was no proof definitely linking her to the missing passport.

He needed some other clue, some other vector pointing in her direction, before he could be even half sure. Still, he had to cover every possible suspect, however unlikely the circumstances. He picked up the phone to ask one of his detectives to see what her headmaster had to say about her. Her school was British; the headmaster and his staff would talk. Anderson had told him that the girl was attending Holland Park. That was odd in itself: an American girl in with the Pakis and the skinheads and the products of trendy Kensington. Very odd indeed. Palmer began to drum his fingers as he waited for the detective to pick up his phone.

Smiling at the gray November morning, Patrick Reilly strode down Fulham Road, so confident that here and there a woman turned to grin at him as he bounced by. Overhead, the Boeing 747s arriving after all-night flights from New York seemed to hang motionless in the air as they began their descent to Heathrow.

In his right hand, Reilly carried the box he had made the night before, but it was hidden by wrapping paper held in place by a length of clothesline that also served as a handle. In his left hand, Reilly carried a small suitcase. He had on a business suit and a black raincoat like thousands of others in London. His only concession to disguise was a pair of metal-rimmed dark glasses with large, curved lenses that he felt made him look like a bit of a flash. Reilly resembled any number of slick young men in the area who were salesmen by day, drank beer by night in the crowded pubs on King's Road, and watched Chelsea play on Saturday afternoon.

Reilly switched to the District Line at Earl's Court and got off at Westminster. As he left the station, Reilly automatically glanced up at the clock in Big Ben's tower: 10:25. Plenty of time.

He turned right and immediately ran into the crowds gathered for the ceremony in Whitehall that he had been counting on to draw attention away from his mission. It was Remembrance Sunday, the day on which Britain honored the generations of men who had died in its wars. Reilly had the sensation of being in church. The people around him were reverentially quiet. They were standing there patiently, although they could see nothing of the ceremony and had no hope to. The crowds had already overflowed Whitehall and pushed back into Parliament Square. Far up ahead a band was playing a funeral march. When it was over an officer shouted a command, and there was a single, sharp crash of military boots on the pavement.

Reilly had heard the ceremony described on radio many times while he was growing up, and later watched it on television. Like the middle-aged men and women dressed in grays and blacks all around him, he could imagine the Queen, the Prime Minister, and the members of the Cabinet taking part in the ritual at the Cenotaph, the memorial to the dead in the middle of Whitehall, just down from Downing Street.

Earlier that week, as he worked out his final plans, Reilly had twice walked down Whitehall and, dodging traffic, crossed over to the Cenotaph to look at the flowers. The great monument was a national cemetery stone. There were huge sprays of flowers from veterans groups and a large wreath from the Queen, but what caught Reilly's eye were the small bouquets that came from families or individuals. Most of the messages referred to World War II ("In memory of Tom, lost at sea, 14 April 1944"). The most moving were a few from the relatives and widows of the men who had died sixty years before. The rain had begun to wash away the faded blue ink of one note written in a spidery hand: "We still remember Alfred Somers, husband and father, who died at Ypres, 24 October 1914."

Standing in the somber crowd, Reilly wondered who about him had lost sons or husbands in the war. He could hear two men talking about fighting the Japanese in Burma; they apparently had met by chance and were exchanging the names and numbers of units, trying to establish a connection. One praised a battalion of Ghurkas. "Oh my," said the other. "Didn't they love it, though. Bred for it, they were."

Then Reilly heard a puzzling new sound. He turned to see a group of veterans marching by. They were graying men, but their arms were swinging in unison and their backs were straight. With each stride the men took, the medals pinned to their coats rose and fell on their chests, causing the sound that had caught Reilly's ear: *chink . . chink . . . chink.*

It was the pride of the men that moved Reilly. For a moment he stood there, lingering, knowing he had to get on with it, but unwilling to leave until the marching men passed from view. Then the irony of the situation struck him: he was being impressed by the traditions of the nation that he hated. Jesus, he was being taken in by love of Queen and country.

He glanced at his watch. Twenty to eleven. No time to dawdle. She would be on her way there by now. Reilly picked up the sample case and the square parcel that he had gingerly placed down on the sidewalk and headed for the flight of steps that led to a tunnel under Whitehall. Halfway down the gaudily tiled passageway, he turned into the men's room and took a booth. He opened the suitcase and started to get undressed.

No one gave her a second glance. She was an American, obviously—her height, the confident way she carried her-

self, her elaborately casual grooming, and a dozen other details proclaimed that—and precisely because she was an
American she went unnoticed. Even in November, with the
tourist season drawing to an end, Americans were everywhere in London. They could go anywhere, do anything.
They were visitors of a special kind, and they were accepted, absorbed—the way the French, say, would never be.

Kate was going against the tide, moving through the
latecomers hurrying to the ceremony, heading straight toward the huge, ornate building just down and to the left of
Whitehall. She was walking toward Parliament. Strolling
along, she occasionally glanced up at the statues of kings
and queens and obscure heroes that festooned the gothic
walls of the great structure.

She made for the visitors' entrance, just across the
street from the rear of Westminster Abbey. A couple
walked by, burdened with guidebooks and maps, pointing
out the sights to each other in strong, clear German. Un-
smiling, one or two Britons turned briefly to stare. A tourist
bus packed with Japanese swung slowly around the square.
The passengers moved in unison to the side facing Parliament and dozens of huge camera lenses glinted at the windows. The shifting weight made the bus tilt toward the left.

Just as Reilly had expected, there was no crowd in the
Old Palace Yard in front of the entrance. Parliament, of
course, was not in session. Even so, there were two policemen on guard, and as Kate watched they stopped a very of-
ficial-looking man who searched angrily for some identification and then had to sign his name on a register before
being allowed in. While Kate waited out the last few minutes, a pair of tourists walked through the little square, but
they did not go near her destination: the trash can set back
against a stone wall. Reilly had said it would be clear of people, and it was.

Kate glanced at her watch a final time. A few seconds
before eleven o'clock, she reached into her shopping bag
and twisted an oven timer to fifteen minutes. She was about
to walk to the can when it happened. Big Ben started to toll,

and at almost the same instant an explosion sounded close by. *The bomb!* Pat was dead! She was beginning to run toward the Underground Station when she heard an icy command: "Stop right there!" In a panic, she whirled about, expecting to see a policeman advancing toward her, but the speaker was a young man. "Show some respect," he hissed. He was braced at attention. Confused, Kate looked around her and discovered that everyone was standing absolutely still, women and men alike. Then she remembered. Of course. The silence in honor of the dead. The explosion must have been the sound of a cannon firing, perhaps in Green Park. She had read about the tradition.

But as she faced toward Whitehall like the others, a second fear swept over her. Had she made herself conspicuous by starting to run like that? Would someone remember her later on? Then she suddenly realized something much worse: the timer was still ticking. Her bomb would go off in fifteen, no, about fourteen minutes. How much longer would she have to stand there? How long did the silence last? She could not recall.

To occupy her mind, she counted out the seconds to herself. Just as she reached fifty-eight, the crowd about her began to move again. Kate took two deep breaths and ran a hand quickly through her hair. Then she tossed her head and squared her shoulders and walked deliberately up to the trash can. Carefully, she placed the bag holding the timer, a detonator, a small battery, and a packet of black gunpowder into the receptacle and covered it with a copy of Saturday's *Times*. The job done, she walked rapidly away.

The message had been a long time in coming, delayed more by happenstance than inefficiency. Part of the fault was that the expedition had been organized by the wives of officials at the U.S. Embassy. They visited the House of Commons as a group and hence did not register separately. Kept in a separate folder, their roster was overlooked after the order came down from Scotland Yard to produce the names of visitors to Parliament for the previous month.

The mistake was discovered the previous afternoon and the list immediately sent to the Yard, where it was placed with pages from registers kept at all the shrines and great buildings of London. Working in six-hour relays, teams of men had been performing the laborious chore of going through all the names, hunting for one that was on the list of thirty-three people who had had access to the passports in the American Embassy. In four days of work, they had found two: an Embassy secretary who had visited the Tower of London with her two small sons; a file clerk who had taken her mother to St. Paul's. Both employees were English. As a precaution, Palmer had ordered the security strengthened at both sites and had the women's pictures posted in the guards' offices—not only at the places they had visited but at every other tourist attraction in London. In addition Palmer interrogated both women himself, looking for what he called "the vector" that would point him in the direction of the bomber. But both women were so obviously taken aback by the implications of his rather brusque line of questioning that he soon gave up. "If they aren't innocent," Palmer commented to Olson, "they belong in the Old Vic."

On Sunday morning, Olson was in the basement room of Scotland Yard when one of the young, bleary-eyed clerks looked over the list of women who had gone on the wives' tour of Parliament, searching for the name of one of the thirty-three. Suddenly, he whistled softly. "Here's one," he said and handed the sheet to the detective.

"Lovely," said Olson, and dashed for Palmer's office. It was 11:14.

While Kate was undergoing her ordeal, Reilly was finishing his change of clothes. When the cannon sounded at eleven, he was just starting to walk out of the men's room. The sound, heard very faintly, made him react exactly as she had. He raced up the stairs and was on the sidewalk, heading to her, when he noticed that everyone was standing still. Then he remembered—remembered all the times life had come to a halt in Belfast when a cannon sounded on the memorial day when he was a boy. She was safe, after all. Anxiously he glanced around to see if anyone was staring at him with curiosity, wondering why he had been running at such a time. But no one seemed to care about him. With the rest, he faced Whitehall for the remainder of the two minutes. When people began to stroll again, he returned to the Underground Station and stored his suitcase in a coin locker. Then he walked out of the station, slowly this time, and turned left toward the Thames Embankment. In his right hand he carried a large black box that bumped gently against his knee with each stride. He crossed Bridge Street and stopped at the corner of Parliament. Large crowds were still arriving to attend the memorial ceremonies.

A few couples paused to look at the river and Parliament. Reilly joined them, leaning as nonchalantly as he could against a stone wall. Blow, you bastard, Reilly said to himself, listening, listening for the blast. *Blow now!*

Nothing . . . nothing . . . and then, while two women nearby worried about where they should eat lunch, a clap of thunder. Startled, the people around Reilly stared at each other in bewilderment and then dawning fear. Moving at a trot, Reilly was on his way before the last echo died away. He ran up to a policeman on guard at an entrance far from the trash can that had just exploded. The guard was hunched over his walkie-talkie, trying to make out the words of a man whose excitement sounded plainly through the static. Reilly clearly caught the word "explosion" and then "blood on the sidewalk."

With his radio to his ear, the policeman turned to look at the person who had just hurried up to his door. He saw a rather tall, slender man wearing one of the most honored uniforms in the British Isles—the black garb of the St. John's Ambulance Brigade. The policeman glanced down at what the man was carrying in his right hand. It was a black wooden box. Painted on the front end was a white cross.

"Somewhere inside, was it?" Pat Reilly asked. "Can I cut through here?"

22

THE POLICEMAN PUT a hand on Reilly's chest and listened intently to a burst of garbled words. Someone was shouting orders. "I can't tell where it was," the policeman said. "Could be outside. I don't know." He looked at Reilly. "They tell you anything?"

Reilly shook his head. "They never do, do they?" he said. "And it's us that has to do the work."

The policeman did not seem suspicious. Reilly tried to appear anxious to be helpful. "If it was out in the street," he said, "I could still get there faster going straight through here instead of all the way around, right?"

The policeman inspected Reilly again. He was shorter than Reilly, a heavy-set, powerful man with a round, bearded face. Reilly had felt the man's strength when he braced him with his hand. "What's your name, then?" the guard asked.

"Thomas," said Reilly, blurting out the first thought that came into his mind.

A siren began to sound in the distance. The policeman looked around anxiously. "Right," he said. "You'd better hop to it."

As Reilly ducked through the door, another squawk of static sounded on the walkie-talkie. He did not wait to hear the message.

Once inside the Palace of Westminster, Reilly produced the map that Kate had given him and began to look for the landmarks she described. The building was honeycombed with long, dark corridors that seemed to intersect at random. Reilly recognized a crossing and turned left, heading for the House of Commons.

Because of the holiday there was no one in the passageways to note his appearance, just as he planned. The click of his footsteps on the stone floor was the only sound. Then

Reilly turned a corner and almost ran into an elderly woman who was trying to flutter into her raincoat as she hurried along.

"Thank God," she said when she saw Reilly. "You know where to go, do you?"

Reilly nodded.

"Good," she said. "I do so hope no one was hurt badly. But it's all right, now that you're here." She disappeared, still struggling with her coat.

Reilly turned another corner and saw the carved entrance that led to the House of Commons. There was no one in sight. Reilly could hear the hoarse shout of a man outside. He took a breath and pushed open the swinging doors.

The room was empty. Reilly stood in the aisle between the front benches and stared around him. It's so small, he thought. Could it really be so small and so green? The rows of benches that rose on both sides of the hall were covered in green leather. Or maybe the green was in the light that shone palely from the ceiling. Reilly felt as though he were standing in the bottom of a giant aquarium.

The other strange thing about the room that struck Reilly was its silence. It was a place meant for argument, sarcasm, jeers, eloquence. Now it was so quiet that Reilly could hear his shoes brush against the carpet.

He turned and put down his box on the wooden table just below the Speaker's chair. The top of the table was faintly marked where Prime Ministers and Cabinet Ministers had rested their feet during debates, and on the opposite edge, where members of the Queen's loyal opposition had done the same. On either side of the end of the table was a small lectern used by two opposing debaters as they leaned toward each other to press home their arguments. Below the end of the table rested the huge gold mace that would be brought out when the House went into session. If and when it goes into session, thought Reilly. He picked up his box in his right hand, walked the length of the table, and climbed two steps. Then, gently, he placed the bomb on the chair of the Speaker of the House.

At that instant Olson burst into Palmer's office with the news that Kate Rochford had visited Parliament on October 28. The inspector immediately picked up the phone and asked to be connected to the security office at the House of Commons. The holiday operator on duty at the switchboard in Parliament had trouble finding the right connection, and when she did the line was busy.

"Break in on the call," ordered Palmer.

The operator was shocked. "Oh I couldn't do that, sir," she said. "It's against regulations."

Palmer bit off every word. "Bugger the regulations," he said. "This is Scotland Yard."

"Yes, *sir*."

Within seconds Palmer was talking to a man who seemed close to panic. At first the guard refused to believe that Palmer actually was calling from the Yard, and then when that point was cleared up he did not want to listen, he wanted to talk. "Damn it, man," Palmer shouted, "what are you gibbering about?"

"An explosion, sir. Right outside the gate. Hurt a woman badly. Maybe she's dead by now. We've got everyone outside clearing the area. . . ."

Palmer saw the plan in a flash. "No!" he roared. "No, not *outside*! He's *inside*! Get your men inside! He's inside right now planting a bomb. Do you understand?"

"Yes, sir."

"Move then! I'm coming right down."

Palmer hung up. "Come on!" he yelled to Olson, "they've got him trapped!"

Carefully, Reilly unfastened the latches on the bottom of the black box and eased it off. There was a whiff of freshly cut pine wood. For a moment Reilly looked down at the bomb, then stroked the rough grain on the top. The metal band poked out of its hole about four inches. More than enough. Now that he was so close, Reilly was stalling for time, and he knew it. Another moment passed in the shaded room.

Suddenly there was another commotion outside—men raising their voices and the deep scream of a truck's engine laboring under some kind of strain. Reilly stirred. *Do it now*, he thought. Now, before someone comes.

He knelt, hesitated, and then pushed the box against the back of the Speaker's chair. His hands were completely steady. Reilly began talking to himself in a kind of soft whisper that was instantly swallowed up by the silence of the room. "Hold the box steady with your left hand. Take the band in your right hand and pull it out slowly. *Slowly*."

Reilly knew that he could die in the next ten seconds. IRA men had been blown apart while planting bombs a tenth as complicated as his. If he had mixed up the wiring, if something had gone wrong with a switch, if a spark unaccountably arced between two wires—he was dead.

Left hand on the box. Pull the band out slowly.

The metal was cold in Reilly's fingers. He pulled on it. Nothing happened. In an instant, all of the abstraction, all of the remoteness, disappeared. "Sweet Jesus," Reilly said aloud, and jerked on the band. It came out in his hand. Reilly braced for the explosion. One second, two seconds passed before he was sure he was still alive. He squeezed the hard metal in his hand to prove it.

Get out now! Scrambling to his feet, he dropped the band. Before it hit the carpet, he was already bending to pick it up. Thomas would be delighted to find that little piece of mischief. He had enough clues already.

Reilly stuffed the piece of metal into a pocket. He picked up the black box with the white cross on one end. Then he strode down the aisle between the opposing rows of benches and out of the room.

When he came to the octagonal Central Lobby, Reilly lost his bearings for a moment. Four doors opened off the passageway. There was a statue of Gladstone at Reilly's elbow. He went out of the door opposite the entrance he had used and found himself in the Peers' Lobby.

To avoid the House of Lords, he turned right to a long corridor, then left until he reached the Prince's Chamber, where he came face to face with a statue of Queen Victoria, and hurried on to the adjacent Royal Gallery. Reilly swept past the large frescoes of Nelson dying and Wellington meeting Blücher after Waterloo. He was twenty feet from the exit when the whistles began to blow.

Reilly began to react even before he heard the shouts outside and the thump·of boots on the square as men began to run. He was already behind a pillar when the first plain-clothes man dashed through the entranceway, a revolver in his hand. He ran right past Reilly. Within seconds the foyer was filled with scrambling men and a red-faced sergeant shouting orders. Pressed against the stone, Reilly tried to think. He was finished if he made his break too soon—or too late. He would have to wait until the first wave had swept through the passageway and then go before someone arrived to take charge.

Reilly inched around the pillar until he could see most of the foyer with one eye. It was empty. He fought off the impulse to make a run for it. *Come on, come on, where's the rest of the lot?* As if on cue, two older policemen wrestled a table through the door and set up what looked like a field telephone. Three army sergeants appeared and stood about hesitantly, apparently waiting for someone to tell them what to do. A pair of civilians walked briskly into view, one of them speaking into a walkie-talkie. *Now?* Reilly forced himself to wait a minute longer, and was rewarded by the sight he had been hoping for. A pair of St. John's ambulance men appeared carrying a folded stretcher.

Now. Reilly strolled from behind the pillar. He was in the middle of the group before anyone noticed him, and then no one did more than glance up. He could have come from anywhere. Reilly nodded at the other two St. John's men and kept on going, waiting for someone to call out, waiting for a hand to grab his elbow.

Nothing happened. He walked out the door just as two

armored cars drove up. There was an ambulance on the sidewalk and two attendants were bending over a figure on a stretcher. *It's her!*

Reilly was starting to run toward the stretcher when he saw that the girl was wearing a dress. It was someone else, someone about Kate's age. Her left leg was almost torn off.

Jesus! Reilly was swept with guilt for what he had made Kate do. He had to get away. He was beginning to walk toward Westminster Station when another siren sounded and a jeep screeched to a halt in front of the entrance. Reilly recognized the man on the passenger side. He turned and watched Major Thomas get out and begin to walk slowly into the building.

23

THE DEFERENCE THAT Thomas had been anticipating—dreading too—began inside the door. The policemen recognized him, and there was a pause in the activity and conversation as they turned to stare. The major nodded and smiled as he walked in. He was onstage already. They were all assuming he would go to the bomb. And just as he had expected, the attention produced a sense of euphoria in Thomas. He had the vague, heady sensation of starting down a roller coaster that he had never ridden before.

"This way, Major," said a young police lieutenant who suddenly appeared at Thomas's elbow.

Side by side, Thomas and Phillips followed the lieutenant through the same passageways that Reilly had walked no more than minutes before. Behind them a team of three sergeants and a corporal began unloading equipment from the jeep and another truck that had just pulled up. As they worked a BBC caravan arrived and a photographer, carrying a hand-held camera, jumped out and began to film the scene.

Across Britain, millions of people who had been drowsily

watching a panel discussion of the government's economic policies snapped awake as the façade of Parliament flashed onto their screens. An excited announcer reported that a bomb had been planted in the House of Commons.

At a weekend cottage in Essex, a teen-age girl who had just turned on her set ran down the hallway to the far bedroom and rapped on the door. "Daddy," she called, "you'd better come look. Something's happening."

Wearing his dressing gown, the Home Secretary hurried into the living room. The announcer was telling how Major Thomas had just arrived to cope with the bomb that had been left in the House. "Splendid," said the Secretary. "I knew he couldn't resist."

"Major Thomas?" asked his daughter.

"No. The bomber. The IRA chap. Make sure there's enough petrol in the Jaguar. We're driving up to London in fifteen minutes."

Thomas had never been in the House of Commons before. When he was a boy he lived too far away; when he reached manhood he wanted to have as little as possible to do with politicians.

"It's in the Speaker's chair, sir," said the police lieutenant.

"Where?"

"You can't really see it from here," said the lieutenant. "We'll have to go up into the galleries." He led the major and Phillips out of the chamber and up a flight of stone steps to the Strangers' Gallery, where visitors watched the House of Commons in action.

Thomas peered down into the dusky room and shrugged in disgust. "I still can't see the damn thing," he said. "We'll have to wait for our lights."

The lieutenant was already hurrying away to talk to the members of the crew, and within minutes they were wrestling three spotlights into place. Two were placed in the galleries on either side of the chamber, and one in the far end. Three switches were flipped simultaneously. The beams of light cut through the shadows and the white pine box miraculously appeared, perfectly defined and gleaming slightly in the glare.

"Jesus," Thomas murmured to himself. The shining white box held him transfixed. A phrase tugged at his memory: "a terrible beauty." What was it? A book title? A quote? He could not remember.

Thomas reached into the side pocket of his trench coat and pulled out his old binoculars. The worn brass felt reassuring in his hands. He lifted the glasses to his eyes and turned the focusing wheel until he could see traces of sawdust clinging to the upper edge of the box. He began searching the top for what he feared would be there.

"Can you see it?" Phillips asked.

Thomas did not have to ask what the "it" referred to. He and the sergeant had been talking for weeks about the telltale characteristic that they expected the next big bomb to have. "No," he said. "I can't make it out."

"Are you sure?"

"Bloody sure," Thomas snapped. "Let's go."

They clumped down the stone stairs to the lobby outside of the House of Commons. A small group had gathered while they had been on the balcony—some police officials, some men in plain clothes that Thomas instantly divined were from Scotland Yard. There was an air of expectation, of waiting. Thomas caught sight of two St. John's men standing rather apologetically off to one side and quickly looked away.

Heads were nodding in his direction. A huge man in the Scotland Yard group looked over his shoulder at the major, and then began walking toward him. Who is this bloody fool? Thomas thought. The major barely had time to notice that the shaggy bear of a man who was descending on him was wearing a university scarf wrapped carelessly around his neck. One end dangled down around his considerable waist.

"Are you quite prepared?" the stranger asked.

"Who are you?"

"Palmer. The Yard."

Thomas glanced at Phillips, who shrugged almost imperceptibly and raised his eyes to the ceiling.

The intruder spoke again, raising his voice: "I said, Are you quite prepared?"

"Quite."

"I may have some help for you."

"Really?" Thomas automatically folded his arms and stood with his feet wide apart. He was back in the army, dealing with an impertinent man he considered to be his inferior. "Would you like to take it apart yourself?"

Palmer ignored the jibe. He pulled a crumpled handkerchief from his raincoat pocket and swabbed his scarlet face. Something made the fat boy run, Thomas thought. Something made him sweat.

Palmer spoke again: "I may be able to help you."

"How?"

"We have a good lead on the ones who did it—who planted the bomb."

"Fine."

"I mean, would that help? If you found out who did it—what he knew about these things?"

"Maybe," Thomas said. It was a point he had wanted to know for months, but he did not want to give Palmer the satisfaction of acknowledging it.

This time the impatience showed clearly on Palmer's face. "You don't seem awfully interested, Major."

Bloody fool. Thomas had had enough. He began to walk away. "Let's get on with it," he said to Phillips. They walked up to the command center that the sergeants had set up outside the chamber's doors. "I'll do the first walk by."

A sergeant held up a flak jacket. The major took off his coat and struggled into the bulky garment. Thomas recalled the macabre chatter in Belfast when the sergeants would put on their jackets. "Keep yourself together, mate." And then, in a falsetto: "Yes, but I might lose my head."

Thomas looked through the door of the chamber at the Speaker's chair. He could not see the bomb at all. "Is the tape recorder ready?" he asked.

A sergeant nodded.

"Watch me, Phillips," he said, flicking on his walkie-talkie. "Here we go."

It was ridiculously easy. To his surprise and utter relief, it was easy. Why, he did not know, but he walked through the door so naturally that he almost sauntered. Thomas headed straight down the aisle between the two rows of benches rising up on both sides—the government's to his left, the opposition's to his right—until the box came into view. Keep it going, thought Thomas, play it out. He had planned just to walk past, as was customary the first time, but he felt so confident that he found himself actually approaching the chair—rising on tiptoe as he did.

"I'm nearing the bomb," he said into his radio. The box came into view, very white against the black chair, and then he saw it. Just as he expected, there it was: a small, rectangular hole in the top of the box. Now he knew what he had to deal with, and that was reassuring in a strange way. He reached down to brush a fingertip across the hole and then thought better of it.

Thomas bent low over the box and sniffed. Damn, the smell of the freshly sawed pine overpowered everything else. Was there the faintest whiff of marzipan? He could not be sure. In his fascination with the job, Thomas even forgot his fears. He took a stethoscope out of a pocket, fitted the plugs into his ears, and carefully applied the black listening disk to one side of the box. He changed the position of the disk once, twice, three times before he detected it: the faint, steady ticking of some kind of clock or timer.

Right. Of course. Thomas had so surely expected, and feared, finding a timer that the actual confirmation of his concern came as a kind of anticlimax.

He moved slightly to the side. Again, it was just what he expected to find. The back side of the box was pushed against the rear of the Speaker's chair. *Damn.*

"It's flush," he radioed back.

"Better come back, then," said Phillips.

Thomas turned slowly, being careful not to trip on the

steps—that might have been enough to do it then and there—and walked rapidly past the bench where the Prime Minister sat. The Home Secretary's voice came back to him: "The Prime Minister was asking this morning how you were getting along. . . . What do you propose I tell the Prime Minister?" Slightly breathless, he rejoined Phillips.

They stood alone by the command table the sergeants had set up, the others keeping back politely so as not to overhear the conversation.

"A timer," said Thomas. "Better than the kind he normally uses. Quieter."

"Yes."

"The hole is in the top," said Thomas matter-of-factly. He might have been delivering a report on the post commissary. "And the box is pushed back against the rear of the chair."

"We expected as much."

"There's a capsule in there."

"Unless the hole is a decoy."

"I doubt it." Suddenly Thomas craved a cigarette. He had not had one since he was a boy, but he could feel his lungs filling with soothing smoke. "I wonder what other surprises he has in store for us."

"None that we can't cope with, sir," said Phillips.

What bullshit; what loyal bullshit. "So let's get on with it, then," Thomas said. "Where is that thing?"

"Beside the table," Phillips replied.

Thomas walked over, stooped, and picked up the portable X-ray machine. The weight made him gasp and his right shoulder slumped forward. "Jesus," he muttered, and tried to straighten up. He nodded at Phillips. "Here we go," he said.

This time Phillips put his hand on the major's arm. "Good luck," he said.

As he walked, Thomas kept his eyes fixed on the top of the chair. The weight of the machine numbed his shoulder after a few steps. He tried to concentrate on the technical problem he faced, but an antic corner of his mind, working like a computer under its own control, was busily figuring out his chances of surviving the next ten minutes. The answer came clicking out: a tossup.

Thomas watched the chair grow larger as he trudged ahead. "I'm going up the steps," he said into his walkie-talkie. Slowly he eased the X-ray machine to the floor.

His hands did not quiver as he picked up an X-ray plate. Then, as he prepared to begin, he felt a kind of joy surge through his body. After all the weeks of worrying and waiting, the endless planning, the action was about to begin. It would be settled one way or the other, and soon.

Almost eagerly he began to set up the X-ray machine. The first step was easy. He moved the unit to the right side of the chair and adjusted it for height. "No problem so far," he radioed Phillips. "All going nicely."

Gently he attached the plate with tape to the far side of the box, and took the picture. Elapsed time: thirty seconds. "All right," said Thomas, "now the other one."

"Go easy," said Phillips. "It looks fine from here. I can see your hands clearly."

Indeed, the spotlights focused on the bomb caught Thomas in a fierce glare of white light. He took a second plate in his hands. To get a proper view of the complex circuitry that he suspected was inside the bomb, he needed to X-ray the box not only from side to side to side but from front to back, which would be a good deal more difficult.

The bomber had anticipated this and had pushed the box against the rear of the chair so tightly that Thomas would have a problem getting the plate in place on the back side without nudging the box.

For a moment, Thomas stood poised over the box, holding the plate in both hands. *Now,* he thought. He placed the plate in the tiny wedge of space between the rear top edge of the box and the back of the chair. Then gently, but with complete confidence, he pushed down. The plate slid easily into place. The box did not move.

Thomas backed away. "It's all right," he radioed Phillips. Even through the static, the major heard the relief in

Phillips's voice: "Take the bloody picture and get out of there."

The major grunted as he shifted the position of the X-ray. He needed only a few seconds to make the exposure. Then he faced a second problem: retrieving the plate. He put his right hand squarely on top of the box. The grain felt rough under his palm. With his left hand, he grasped the top of the plate, and he pulled it out. He was so confident that he did not turn his face away. It would not explode. He knew it.

Ten minutes later, with the plate under his arm and Phillips at his side, Thomas walked out of Parliament and into what looked like the set of a movie. For an instant Thomas stared around him. He had completely forgotten that he was onstage—that he had allowed himself to be put onstage. Five cameras on rolling platforms were set up in the little courtyard where Kate's bomb had exploded less than an hour before. Behind them waited four large vans that Thomas knew contained the transmitting equipment for the cameras. The whole area was roped off and guarded by a cordon of policemen. Thomas heard a faint patter of applause, and turned to see a crowd behind a line of barriers across the street near Westminster Abbey. A few white handkerchiefs were waving at him, and he saw the glint of light on binoculars and cameras. "Good God," he murmured to Phillips.

The announcer who had interviewed him outside the Royal Albert Hall was approaching with a microphone in his hand. "Major Thomas," he called, "could we please have a moment with you?"

His instinct was to brush on past, but he felt Phillips's restraining hand on his elbow. Thomas turned to face the interviewer and found himself smiling. "I'm afraid I can't spare much time," he said.

"Could you put us in the picture, please?"

He plunged ahead: "Yes, well, we're dealing with what we assume is a bomb that has been placed in the chair of the Speaker of the House of Commons."

Thomas began edging toward the nearby jeep and freedom.

"And do you know, yet, sir," the announcer asked, "just how you might be trying to disarm the bomb?"

"No, not yet. We've taken some X-rays and they may give us a clue."

"When will you know?"

"An hour, perhaps." Thomas nodded pleasantly and smiled into the camera with its implacably winking red eye. He might have been leaving for a holiday abroad. "And now I'm afraid we really must be off."

"Good luck, sir."

A bobby lifted a rope and Thomas and Phillips climbed into the jeep. Another burst of applause drifted across the street from some people standing in Parliament Square. As the jeep pulled away, Thomas waved a casual hand to the crowd.

24

"I DIDN'T THINK he'd have the guts," said Reilly.

He was seated with the girl in a Fulham pub, watching the television set that the proprietor had brought in so his customers could witness the drama at Parliament. Thomas and Phillips had just driven off in their jeep.

Kate had not spoken since the announcer had reported that a girl had been badly injured in the explosion outside of Parliament. She was slowly tearing her napkin apart and rolling it into tiny balls, which she meticulously laid out in the pattern of a circle on the table. "You never think of that," she said.

"What?"

"Hurting someone like that. Someone who just wanders by."

"Look," said Reilly irritably, "don't worry about her. She'll be all right. It was an accident. You didn't *mean* to do it.

Worry about Thomas. He may do us in yet."

"I hope she's all right."

Reilly lifted up Kate's chin and looked into her eyes.

"Are *you* all right?" he asked.

"Yes." She did not try to avoid his gaze.

Reilly took a sip of his ale and put the glass down hard. "I mean, you were so hot for this whole business—'Remember your father,' and all that."

"I know."

"So a girl was hurt. That's the price for getting Thomas."

She brushed back her hair with both hands and sat up straight. "You're worried about me, aren't you?" she said.

"Some," he admitted.

"Don't be. I knew something like this might happen, no matter what we said. It was just a jolt, that's all."

She looked completely composed now. Relieved, he reached across and gave her hand two quick, perfunctory pats. "Worry about this one, love," he said, nodding at the television screen, where Thomas's face had just appeared. The BBC was rerunning his interview.

"It's going to work out," Kate said calmly. This time she reached across the table and took Reilly's hand. She did not let go. They sat there quietly, holding hands and talking quietly, a pair of lovers watching the telly in the drowsing pub.

The X-ray laboratory at Westminster Hospital was ready for Thomas and Phillips when they arrived. A pair of respectful technicians took the two plates that the major was carrying under his arm and disappeared to develop them. The young doctor in charge of the lab made polite conversation while they waited.

In five minutes' time, the plates were flashed onto two screens, side by side, and Thomas confirmed at a glance that the bomb contained everything he was afraid of, and a good deal more.

"My God," said Phillips.

"Yes, my God," said Thomas quietly. "At least that."

The doctor looked anxiously back and forth between the two men, and then left. Thomas and Phillips walked up to the screens. Finally, Thomas said, "Lovely."

"At least that," said Phillips.

It was worse, far worse than Thomas had expected. That clever bastard. That *clever* bastard. "Well," he said, "let's get it all down on the record. Maybe it will look better in writing."

As Thomas began to talk, Phillips took notes on a clipboard. "First of all, the explosive appears to be gelignite from the length of the sticks, and there are, I would think, five—perhaps six—I can't quite tell. There is, of course, a timer, but whether or not it is attached to the bomb is another matter. I can't say right off—"

Phillips broke in: "What would be the point of that? Why wouldn't he hook the timer into the circuit?"

"Just to confuse us," said Thomas. "Just so we wouldn't know how much time we had—to make us hurry, perhaps, and make a mistake."

Phillips nodded to acknowledge the point, and Thomas went on: "There is a standard nine-volt battery, I should say, and a standard detonator. All these are quite clear." Thomas was pointing with his index finger to the items that he ticked off. He looked very official, very cool. "Now we come down to it. There is a capsule that appears to be the same size as the one we found at the Tate after the explosion there."

Thomas reached into his pocket and took out the capsule that Phillips's men had found. He placed it against the dark outline in an X-ray: the two matched perfectly.

Ah yes, Thomas said to himself. Yes, indeed. What was that fool's name—Palmer?—had thought it would be helpful if he knew more about the bomber. Looking at the outlines of the capsules, Thomas knew enough: whoever put the bomb together understood something about electronics. He was also a person who would "rise to the fly," as the Home Secretary put it. Thomas knew that the bomb waiting in the Speaker's chair was designed to kill him. The capsule was proof of that. It would set off the bomb the instant anyone began working on the box. A foolproof system.

The capsule was a supersensitive piece of electronic gear known as a "microswitch." Placed in an electrical circuit, it would stay "open"—and hence prevent the flow of electricity—until it was shaken. Just the movement of a few thousandths of an inch would be enough: tiny pieces of metal would swing on tiny pivot points, the minute switch would close, the electricity would flow, and in an instant the gelignite would evaporate in a deafening flash of blue light. Just as it had when Johnson tried to get his fingers under the box at the Tate.

The X-rays confirmed the presence of the microswitch, but Thomas had known that one was in the box from the moment he saw the small, rectangular hole in the lid. The reason went back to the nature of the capsule; the bomber could not even pick up the box himself without setting off the charge unless he had added a safety device to the wiring. Thinking the problem through during those long nights with his drawing board, Thomas had decided that the simplest solution would be to attach a lamp switch, the kind that goes right on the wire itself, to the main firing circuit. Then a long band of metal could be inserted into the switch's mechanism to keep it "off." Once the bomb was in place, the band would have to be removed—but how? Through a hole in the lid, Thomas reasoned. That would prime the switch, and the bomb would explode when the box was jiggled.

The X-rays showed that Thomas was right again. There, half-hidden by the gelignite sticks, was the shape of the light switch. "Here it is, right here," he said to Phillips. "The metal band went right up from here through the top of the box. Very simple."

Phillips nodded. "Must have been pleasant pulling that thing out and wondering if you were going to set the whole thing off," he said.

"Yes," said Thomas, "very pleasant. I would have liked to watch him do that."

"Give him credit, though. He's clever enough, and he's got some guts."

I know all that! "And he's trying to kill us," said the major. "Let's not leave out that little quirk of his character."

"That's a point," said Phillips.

"*They* don't know what this is all about," said Thomas. "The Secretary and all that lot. They haven't the slightest idea."

"I'll tell them."

"No," said Thomas. "Let's just get on with it."

Thomas looked again from one X-ray plate to the other. All of the wires that Reilly had painstakingly installed in the bomb showed up plainly, weaving back and forth, winding down around the gelignite and extending to the ticking clock. He knew I'd be using X-rays, thought Thomas, and look at the decoys he built in. Was the timer linked to the gelignite? Thomas could not tell. He could not even figure out which was the main circuit. "It looks like a goddamn bird's nest," said the major to Phillips.

For the next hour, while the BBC announcers tried to think of new things to say and the TV cameras swept constantly across the front of Parliament, Thomas and Phillips tried to decide which was the firing circuit. At first Thomas worked with pencil and paper, attempting to draw the various circuits by comparing the two plates back and forth. Then, using string and a cardboard box, he tried to make a model of the bomb. But each of the X-ray plates gave a flat, two-dimensional view of the interior of the box. He could not be sure exactly how the wires related to each other—which were in front, which behind.

For twenty minutes more Thomas worked on the model, trying to ignore the thought that was growing in his mind until it became a conviction, and even then he did not share his conclusion with Phillips right away. He wanted the sergeant to come to the same decision without any prompting from him. That might be important later on. Finally Phillips sat back and lit a cigarette and watched Thomas work on the model. He knows, thought the major. He did not feel any sense of relief or, for that matter, any anxiety at what might happen later on. He had done his best.

"We'd better talk about this thing," he said to Phillips. For the next five minutes Thomas outlined his thoughts and his plan to the sergeant, who nodded as he listened.

"It's as bad as that?" said Phillips when Thomas was done.

"Yes. And you know it."

Phillips frowned and picked up one of the X-ray plates. "Goddamn," he said. "There must be *something* we can do."

Was Phillips criticizing him? Suggesting he was afraid? "I do what I can," said Thomas quietly.

Phillips looked up quickly. "Of course," he said. "I know what you've done already—what that cost you—taking these X-rays. No one else would have done it, knowing what you knew."

It was the first real praise that anyone had given Thomas in a long time. "Thank you."

"What I meant," said Phillips, "was that I just wish we could figure out something to beat our ingenious friend, and I can't. That's bloody frustrating."

"I know."

Phillips put down the plates. "And I have to agree," he said, "there's nothing else to be done. We'll have to tell them."

When they left the hospital Thomas was prepared for the TV cameras and the reporter waiting anxiously on the steps. This time he did not even pause. He was damned if he was going to play the hero any longer for the Secretary's little scheme.

"I'm afraid I have nothing to say," said Thomas into the microphone that the reporter shoved in front of his face, and then they were safely into the jeep and heading back to Parliament, moving slowly as they drew nearer, through the crowds that were lingering around Whitehall after the ceremony at the Cenotaph.

So many women in black, Thomas thought, and began running the TV gauntlet again in front of Parliament, smiling and saying nothing, blushing at the rattle of applause that sounded across the street, finally waving a hand (he had to do *something*) before disappearing into the building. He passed quickly through some high-ranking police officers who stiffened to attention as he went by.

The Home Secretary was waiting, and beside him stood Palmer.

"Delighted to see you, Major," said the Secretary.

He doesn't trust you, boyo, thought Thomas feeling the limp handshake. Fuck him.

"Now then," said the Secretary when they were all seated in a nearby room, "what have we learned and what have you done?"

Briefly, Thomas went over the events of the past two hours, telling about the discovery of the capsules and what they meant, but leaving out any mention of the danger that he had faced.

Phillips followed the account with increasing agitation, and finally broke in: "I think you should know, sir," he said, "that Major Thomas X-rayed and inspected the bomb at considerable risk to himself."

Thomas shot Phillips a glowering glance.

"I dare say," said the Secretary. "But tell me, Major, just how do you propose to defuse the bomb?"

Thomas looked the Secretary squarely in the eye. "I don't, sir," he said. "I can't."

For an instant the Secretary did not react. Then his face began to redden before he could get a word out. He was rising from his chair when he finally managed to utter a sound: *"What?"*

Now that the moment had come, after all the weeks of worrying that it might occur, Thomas was amazed that he felt so relaxed. He was not embarrassed or ashamed. He had done what could be done—everything that could be done. Thomas felt utterly removed from the scene, as though he were watching it from a distance, as though the angry figure across the room was a character in a movie.

"No, sir," the major said. "It can't be done. Not with that capsule in the box. Not without exploding the charge."

The Secretary was standing now. He's going to have a go at me, Thomas thought, and began to rise himself.

"I knew I couldn't trust you," the Secretary shouted. "I knew you didn't have the—"

"*John!*"

The word exploded like a cannon shot in the small room. The sheer force alone might have stopped the Secretary cold—it left everyone else poised motionless—but there was more to it than that. There was an unmistakable tone of command and superiority in the voice. The Secretary turned to look at Palmer, who was pointing a plump finger at a chair.

"Do sit down, John," said Palmer, this time calmly. "Don't be such an ass."

The Secretary hesitated, glanced around uneasily, and then—to Thomas's astonishment—did as he was told.

"Now, then, Major," said Palmer. "How do you propose to handle this situation?"

Who is this man? Thomas looked to Phillips for help, but got only a bewildered shrug in return.

Palmer beckoned to a police captain who was hovering outside the door. "I think we could all use something to drink," he said. "Would you see if you could find us some tea?"

The captain disappeared and Thomas watched Palmer settle himself into his chair and cross one enormous leg over the other. He put his fingertips together and held them under one of his chins. Faded blue eyes fixed Thomas from across the room. What was the oddly familiar sensation? Thomas groped for a second and then got it: a head-master getting ready to ask questions. Jesus, he's going to run a seminar.

"What do you plan to do?" Palmer repeated.

Thomas could feel the glare of the Secretary. He concentrated on winning over the man from Scotland Yard. "The problem is the capsule," the major said. "No one can open that box without setting off the charge. I was afraid of this since the explosion at the Tate. . . ."

"Are you sure that's all you've been afraid of?" The Secretary's voice was low and insinuating.

Palmer brushed him aside with a wave of his hand. "So?" he asked Thomas.

"So all we can do is let the bomb go off, but under controlled circumstances. We can limit the damage."

"How?"

"By building a cocoon of sandbags around and over the chair."

Blowing gently on his fingertips, Palmer mulled the idea over for a moment. "The damage would be slight?" he asked.

"Negligible, I would say. Depending on how much time we have to work—to pile up the bags."

"I don't understand."

Thomas took out one of his diagrams from his briefcase and made an X on it. "That's a timer—a clock," he said to Palmer, handing him the paper. "It's ticking, but I don't know if it is hooked up to the explosives or not. If it isn't, the bomb won't go off until someone jolts it." The memory of his father's death flashed into Thomas's mind—the explosion in the slate quarry that should not have occurred. "At least, it's not likely to go off. It could sit there forever, laughing at us. Now then, if the timer is hooked up to the detonator and the gelignite on its own circuit, the whole thing could go up anytime. Right now. Five minutes from now. I have no idea when it—"

The Secretary broke in again: "Assuming what Thomas here says is right," he said, "why not try it? Build a fort of sandbags around the bloody thing and let it go. Then tell the BBC we've done it. We've cracked the best the IRA could build. We'd still win."

This time Palmer had listened respectfully. "Would it work?" he asked Thomas.

"No, sir."

"Why not?"

"Because we couldn't muffle the sound. Not completely. The people outside would hear it go off."

Palmer nodded. "Yes, I can see that," he said. "And then there would be all the people who knew it was a hoax—who carried in the sandbags, for instance. People talk. Even our own people. Word would get out." The chair creaked as Palmer turned laboriously to smile at the Secretary. "Clever idea, though, John," he said. The Secretary nodded with mock gravity.

What kind of a hold did Palmer have on the Secretary to treat him so? They were obviously old friends; the intimacy in their manner showed that. Could it be that the Secretary knew that Palmer was smarter than he was? Could it be that simple?

Palmer was silent for a moment, and then he asked Thomas, "If you knew more about the bomb—how it was put together—would that help?"

Now what did he have in mind? "It might," Thomas said cautiously.

"Yes," said Palmer after another silent interlude. He had been staring into the teacup that the police captain had miraculously produced. "Yes," he repeated, talking more to himself than the others.

"Yes, *what*, for God's sake?" interjected the Secretary.

"Yes, it could work," said Palmer. Then the man from Scotland Yard began to talk.

25

"SO YOU'RE SURE he knows by now."

"Of course."

The girl nursed her glass of shandy and watched the screen. The cameras were focused again on the façade of Parliament. Thomas was somewhere inside.

"The X-rays would show up the capsule?"

"You know that," Reilly said sharply. Glancing at her, he had no idea what she was thinking. He was becoming increasingly edgy. It was taking too long. He had expected it to be resolved by now. "Get your finger out," he said to the absent Thomas. "Get on with it."

The girl ignored him. "He's so damn *casual*," she said. "*They're* so damn casual. Always. Sauntering in there, knowing we're trying to kill him. Jesus!"

Reilly was not sure what she was driving at. She was talking more to herself than to him. "*That's* what pisses me off so. The la-de-da of it."

He began to smile. "Now you're getting it," he said.

The girl took another sip of her shandy. "It's funny," she said. "I don't care what happens to him. The girl bothered me, but not him. Maybe because it's all so remote, watching it on TV."

"It's real enough," said Reilly. "Look."

On the screen, the door to Parliament was swinging open.

The reporter's voice had taken on a slight edge of urgency. "We're going in," he announced. "Major Thomas is about to start work on the bomb. We're going in with a hand-held camera right now."

The image on the screen wavered badly. "Sorry about that," said the announcer. His accent and poise were impeccable; both tightly controlled despite the situation. For a moment his calm face filled the screen, projecting a mood of reassurance that infuriated Reilly all the more.

"Get on with it, you wanker," he said.

Now the camera was in the foyer, sweeping over the police and army officials who glanced up in surprise. Fascinated, Reilly watched as the changing images on the screen retraced his steps of a few hours before, nosing through the shadows of the long corridor, skirting the pillar where he had hidden. There were the two ambulance men that he had joined briefly before walking out of the building. There was the sergeant who had led the first dash of security men through the door.

"We are informed that Major Thomas has been working on the bomb for about ten minutes," said the reporter. The camera picked up the scene outside the House. Reilly caught sight of the table that was serving as the command post. Three sergeants standing nearby turned their heads away as the camera approached. They were wearing flak jackets. Where are your tin hats, lads? Reilly thought giddily. Very comforting, a tin hat.

He had the sensation of watching a play staged just for him, the one person who could fully understand all the nuances of the plot. Even Thomas could not fully appreciate the story, and besides, Thomas was not a spectator. Thomas was a participant; he was at work somewhere behind the closed door to the chamber. Reilly tried to imagine him approaching the bomb: Slowly? On tiptoe? Backward, you bastard?

"We've just been told that we will not be able to photograph the actual dismantling of the bomb," the reporter was saying. "It would be much too dangerous, no matter where we placed our equipment. We'll have to stay in the hallway here."

Thwarted, the eye of the camera began to roam the scene outside the doorway of the House. A civilian sitting at the table was holding what looked like a walkie-talkie to his ear. The man had a mustache that put Reilly off. Too neat, by half. For a moment, the camera focused on a tape recorder. Reilly could see the turning reels.

Something tugged at Reilly's memory, a scene that had the same feeling, and then it came to him: a drab waiting room in a Belfast hospital, and far away behind the doors some doctors working on his father, operating a second time on the legs that had been shattered by the bomb in the pub. Then, as now, the eye looked for detail—the faded roses in the wallpaper pattern—to ease the strain by occupying the mind. Staring at the tape recorder, the girl at his side forgotten, Reilly put his hands beneath the table and rhythmically began cracking his knuckles. He was minutes away, perhaps seconds away, from the end. Touch it, you bastard. *Touch it!*

For an instant, Reilly thought that the TV cameraman had stumbled: the picture blurred just as it had before.

Then the screen was filled with wildly swerving images—the distant ceiling, a far wall, the astonished face of the man with the mustache sitting at the table. Reilly was starting to rise to his feet even before he heard the blast, or at least before the sound actually registered in his mind. The noise was stunning: not a *whump* or the beat of a giant, distant drum, but a short, sharply defined BAM, as crisp as a pistol shot that somehow had been enormously amplified.

My God, said Reilly to himself. He was entranced by the explosion itself. For a second or two, he did not even relate it to Thomas.

At the bar, the conversation abruptly stopped. Three young women who had been gossiping in one corner twisted around to look anxiously at the screen. "Did you see that?" one called across to a man sitting alone. "What was that?"

The man kept looking at the screen. "It went off!" he said in amazement.

"Did it kill him—that fellow?"

"I don't know," said the man. "Watch."

A second man at the bar, also sitting alone, shook a fist at the screen. "Bloody IRA!" he yelled.

The three women hitched their stools around noisily. "Is he dead?" one asked.

Was he? Reilly had no way of telling—no way of knowing whether his fight was over.

The picture steadied on the screen, as the cameraman apparently got his footing. The reporter was standing in the middle of the foyer, partially obscured by a cloud of dust. He was looking around in confusion. Someone off-camera yelled, "Get the ambulance crew!" The man with the mustache was struggling to push away the table, which had jammed him up against a wall. When he got free, he dashed across the room and into the chamber.

The reporter finally managed to speak as the camera watched Phillips disappear. "Something terrible has happened," he said. "There's been an explosion. I don't know

. . . we'll try to get through. . . ." The doorway of the House of Commons grew larger as the cameraman moved across the room.

Then the screen was usurped by the angry face of a police officer.

"You can't go in there," he shouted.

"It's cleared—we're all cleared!" said the reporter.

"Show some common decency!" said the officer, putting out a hand that grew grotesquely large until the palm filled the entire screen. The reporter kept on objecting, but when the screen came alive again he was standing back on the opposite side of the room, and the panning camera showed two policemen standing on either side of him. "I really must protest this treatment," said the reporter, "but for the moment there's very little I can do. At the right time, of course, I am sure that the BBC will take up the matter with the proper authorities. . . ."

"You bloody pouf!" cried Reilly. *What about Thomas?*"

The screen was filled with running men. The trio of army sergeants appeared from somewhere. A contingent of police officers hurried past, glancing angrily at the camera.

"We still have no word about what happened to Major Thomas," said the reporter, "but the call went up a moment ago—perhaps you caught it—for the ambulance men. That would be the St. John's ambulance men, of course, and I'm afraid . . . here they are now—" The reporter broke off as three men in the familiar black uniforms trotted past. One was carrying a folded stretcher. They were followed by two men in civilian clothes who were carrying black bags. Reilly guessed they were doctors. He felt a hand on his arm.

"Is he dead?" Kate asked. She was absolutely white.

"How do I know?"

One minute passed, three, five. The reporter was filling in time again, recapping the story from the beginning. The camera focused steadily on the doorway to the House of Commons.

There was no warning—just the open door. Reilly saw the frowning face of a St. John's man. He was carrying the front end of a stretcher. As he and his teammate walked past the reporter, the camera swung down to the victim. It was Thomas. There was a bandage around his head, but his sharp features showed clearly. His eyes were closed. A blanket covered him up to his chin, but his right arm dangled over the side of the stretcher. The reporter seized the elbow of one of the doctors as he walked by. "How is he?"

The doctor paused and shook his head. "He's dead," he said.

Reilly sat down slowly. "Jesus God," he said. He felt no joy of triumph, no sense of relief. Everything had happened too quickly. And now that it was over, he was not thinking about Thomas's death. He was thinking about what Thomas had done: going to the bomb, knowing what awaited him. "I didn't think he'd do it," he said.

"The fucking IRA!"

Reilly glanced up to see the man at the bar shaking his fist again at the screen, where the cameras were watching Thomas being lifted carefully into an ambulance.

"We'd better go," Kate said.

Reilly had almost forgotten her. He looked at her sharply.

She read his mind and smiled. "I'm all right," she said. "Honest. It's what we expected."

"Good girl," said Reilly, already reaching for his suitcase. No one turned to see them leave. Everyone at the bar was watching the screen; the BBC was starting to replay the scene outside of the House of Commons during the explosion. The tape was being run in slow-motion, like the instant replay of a goal in a football match.

A passing cab slowed as the driver saw the suitcase. "The West London Air Terminal, on Cromwell Road," said Reilly, and they both got in. Only then did Reilly fully grasp what he had done: Thomas was dead. It was all over. Reilly was free of the lot—Thomas and Cassidy, the IRA and the British—free of them all.

He turned to say something to Kate, but she was looking out of the window. "*Now* what?" he asked.

"Nothing," she said. "I'm fine, really. I just can't celebrate. I'll be all right."

He could not leave her. God knows what she might say. "You've got your passport?" he asked.

"Yes."

"Good. You can come with me to Dublin," he said.

"I was planning to," she said.

He liked that—he liked the idea of her planning to stay with him. It made him feel very close to her, closer than at any time since their first night together.

At the terminal Reilly changed his mind about taking a bus out to Heathrow. There was an hour and a half until the plane, and he preferred to kill time out there over a beer rather than sitting on a bus. He'd treat himself to the extravagance of a cab ride. And a cigar. He'd get a cigar.

Kate waited for him while he stood in line at the Aer Lingus counter. He bought the cigar and headed down the stairs to the cab stand. They held hands standing in the short queue waiting for taxis. When their turn came, Reilly helped Kate in. They looked like a couple going away on a honeymoon, and two elderly ladies in the line behind them were smiling as they watched the cab pull away.

Then their smiles vanished. A screech started to echo through the passageway, reverberating off the concrete wall, growing louder the longer it endured. A policeman was running down the walk, blowing again and again on his whistle, but the cab had already pulled out of the drive and started down Cromwell Road.

The officer stopped, drew a deep breath, and flicked on the walkie-talkie strapped over his left breast. "It's her," he said, after identifying himself. He was keeping his voice calm, and he glanced down at a small photograph he held in his right-hand as he talked: "She's in a cab with a man heading west on Cromwell Road from the airline terminal. License number is five-six-nine-J-two."

Within seconds, the three squad cars that had been idling nearby took up the chase. Two others headed for the intersection of Earl's Court Road and Cromwell Road, about a quarter of a mile ahead, to set up a roadblock.

As the chase began, the crisp exchange of radio messages was monitored in a squad car cruising near Hyde Park Corner. The two huge men in the back seat suddenly leaned forward.

"We've got him," said the Home Secretary. "My God, it worked—we've got him."

"We've got *her*," said Palmer.

"If we've got her, we've got him."

"Yes, I think so. Let's hope so," said Palmer. He thumped the driver on the shoulder. "Get us to that roadblock."

As the car shot ahead, the officer at the wheel glanced up into his rearview mirror with astonishment. His two passengers—the men he'd been driving around London for more than an hour—were chortling and whacking each other like a couple of schoolboys.

"You're bloody brilliant!" cried the Secretary. He was pounding his fist into his left hand. "We've got him by the balls, and you know what you do then."

"I believe, sir, you squeeze," said Palmer, with exaggerated deference.

Reilly saw the roadblock starting to form, saw the first squad car swing across Earl's Court Road and a bus swerve to avoid a collision. He knew instinctively that they were after him. "Stop here!" he yelled at the driver, grabbing Kate and starting to pull her out the door while the taxi was still rolling. He began to run, knowing that the area would soon be swarming with police, knowing that they had only a few seconds to get out of sight. The cab driver was yelling for his fare and then he stopped. Reilly could not resist the temptation to look back over his shoulder just as they were going around a corner. A squad car was pulling up behind the taxi, and a policeman was halfway out of the door. Reilly could see the cabbie pointing at him and Kate.

She was asking what was wrong, where were they going, but at least she was keeping up with him, her long legs stretching out to cover ground. The pair flew through the warren of streets paralleling Earl's Court Road.

"The police," was all Reilly said, noting that she put on a burst of speed. She's afraid, he thought, she's as afraid as I am. She's on the run now, too.

They came out opposite the Earl's Court Underground Station. Catch a train, any train.

Two officers were standing in the entryway, but they had their arms folded across their chest as they surveyed the crowds. They weren't looking for anyone.

"Right," he said. "Let's go." But even as they crossed the street, one of the officers bent his head to listen to his walkie-talkie. When he looked up, he was scanning the faces of the people hurrying past.

Jesus God. Don't run. Reilly took Kate's elbow and steered her in the other direction. The sidewalk was filled with young people. We're safe here. Stay right here. Stay on the sidewalk forever.

"Where can we go?" Kate asked. She was pressing her side awkwardly as she walked. The pain of the cramp showed on her face.

He could hear a siren start to wail somewhere up toward Cromwell Road. "Just keep going," he said, and guided her down a side street.

"They won't shoot, will they?"

He hadn't thought of that. For an instant he resented her bringing it up. Leave her, turn her loose—she's trouble. Then she squeezed his hand, and he realized how afraid she was. "They don't shoot," he said. "You'll be all right."

The crowds were beginning to thin. They came to an intersection, and automatically turned their faces away as a police car shot past. Far down the street, Reilly saw the car stop. Three officers got out and stood in a huddle on a corner. Even at that distance he could see they were carrying automatic rifles. Another siren was sounding up the street in the other direction.

"This way," he said, and tugged her across the road, dodging cars as they ran. Ahead of them was the entrance to the Earl's Court Exhibition Hall, a huge indoor auditorium. The marquee announced a military tattoo. He could imagine the auditorium filled with people, thousands of them. Why not hide in there? Slip in and take a place in the audience. Sneak out with the crowd. Or stay hidden somewhere inside. He didn't know. All he knew was that they couldn't stay there on the sidewalk. The three policemen were starting to head their way.

"Come on, then," he said, pulling Kate into the entranceway.

The officer with the high-powered binoculars was standing on a corner two blocks away, but he could see the girl's face clearly as she disappeared into the building. Before he radioed in his finding, he checked the small picture that the sergeant had handed around the day before. Kate was smiling at the camera. She looked very young, but the officer was satisfied. "The suspect has entered the Earl's Court arena," he said into his walkie-talkie. "The man with her is tall, and very slender, and appears to have red hair."

Five minutes later a cordon of policemen circled the entire building. The Home Secretary and Palmer arrived just as a captain was preparing to take a group inside. The three men walked into the darkened auditorium and stood in one of the aisles. Two great banks of seats rose on either side of a rectangular arena, where the massed bands of the Guards' regiments were playing a funeral march. A spotlight played on the Union Jack at the end of the hall. The trio could hear the muffled coughs of the audience that rose above them.

"A full house?" asked Palmer.

"Jammed," said the captain.

The three men were standing close together and speaking in whispers. "What do you propose to do?" asked Palmer.

"Stop the performance and turn everybody out," said the captain. "Make everyone leave the building, and then pick up our pair at an exit."

Palmer immediately shook his head. "It won't do," he said. "It would take too long—twenty minutes, maybe, a half-hour. We can't wait that long. That bomb could go off any time. We need every minute."

The Secretary looked up into the blackness. "We need to flush them out," he said.

Palmer seemed fascinated by the spot-lit British flag. "Get me the man in charge of this performance," he told the captain. "Right away. Then get me every officer you can spare away from the exits."

A few minutes later the attentive members of the audience noted that there apparently had been a change in the program. Instead of the house lights coming up, as scheduled, and a young marine taking the microphone to sing a medley of World War I songs, the hall stayed darkened as the last funeral march crept to a mournful close. Then, suddenly, the drums began to roll, the rapid beat building up and continuing long past the normal point of release, until there was not a sound or stir of movement in the audience—everyone waiting to see what would happen.

"*Now!*" cried Palmer, who was standing on the floor of the arena beside the director of the massed bands. The fluorescent tip of the conductor's baton made a tiny white streak in the darkness as he lifted his hand to shoulder height, and then came down swiftly for the first note of "The Star Spangled Banner." At the same instant, spotlights mounted in different sections of the auditorium slashed through the blackness to illuminate a giant American flag at one end of the arena.

Palmer counted out the beat to himself—One, two, three, *four*! With a great flash, every light in the house went on. Blinking in the glare, scattered pairs of men and women were already standing or rising to their feet throughout the audience. Palmer scanned the seats above him, then turned his search to another section. Two dozen policemen up in the stands were doing the same thing, looking for the act that would distinguish the girl from all the other Americans who had automatically started to rise when they heard their national anthemn.

"There she is!" Palmer yelled, and pointed to one of the topmost rows in the auditorium. A girl who had been standing had just quickly resumed her seat. The policeman in the section spotted her at almost the same instant and grabbed her arm as she was turning in bewilderment to the man sitting next to her.

"Christ!" Reilly instantly bolted in the other direction. He flailed his way past the people still seated in his row and started to dash up the steep flight of concrete steps to the very top of the arena. There was no one there and for a wild instant he thought he was free. Then the crushing weight hit him in the back and he was flung forward onto his face by the tackle of a second policeman. They twisted his arms behind him and slammed on handcuffs that hurt his wrists. As they led him away he tried to turn to see what had happened to Kate.

"Straight ahead, Paddy," said the man who held his right arm.

"Fuck off," said Reilly, and tried to slam his heel down on the officer's instep.

They hustled Reilly down the cold passageways and out into the street where a squad car was waiting at the curb. They jammed Reilly in back, one man on either side of him. The officer sitting beside the driver turned halfway around in his seat. There was a revolver in his hand. "Mind yourself, Paddy," he said.

The captain stuck his head in through the window. "Don't take him down to the Yard," he told the driver. "They want him at Parliament."

"Parliament, sir?"

"Parliament," said the captain. He was still trying to catch his breath. "And keep a close eye on our friend."

As the car shot away, the driver asked, "Why do they want him there?"

The officer with the gun was looking the prisoner

squarely in the face, but Reilly was avoiding his eyes. He was trying to think: *Parliament?* "Maybe you'll get another chance to blow someone up, Paddy," said the man with the gun.

"Done enough already," said the officer on Reilly's left: "Done enough to be charged with murder already, haven't you, Paddy."

Reilly was thinking about Kate. They must have traced him somehow through her. But he felt no resentment. The rage that swept over him when she stood and attracted the police had disappeared. He hoped they were not frightening her.

"That really was the most extraordinary stroke of luck, you know, Richard," said the Home Secretary. The two men were riding in the Secretary's limousine, trailing the squad car that was carrying Reilly.

"I can't imagine what you mean, John," said Palmer. He was sitting with his hands cradled in front of his comfortable bulk, inspecting with mild interest the passing scenery of London's streets.

"You know very well what I mean—assuming that the girl would stand up when she heard 'The Star Spangled Banner' played like that."

Palmer was unperturbed. "Very chauvinistic, these Americans," he said. "They'll pop out of their seats like robots if you play that song—particularly if they're over here. Makes them feel very patriotic. Makes them feel different from us. They like that."

"And the rest?"

"The rest was simple. I assumed that once she stood up and the lights came on she would realize that she was exposing herself and then quickly sit down. She'd be the only one who would. That was crucial, of course."

"You relied purely on reflexes: stand up, sit down. Is that right?"

"Reflexes are safe, if you can use them. They're predictable. Never get a man to try to think his way out of a problem. Thinking is dangerous. Too erratic."

"You have such a sanguine view of mankind."

"A practical view."

The limousine glided noiselessly along. The Secretary looked out of his window, Palmer out of his. Each was grasping the strap that dangled on his side of the compartment. There was none of the elation that had made them elbow each other in the ribs after the girl was spotted at the airline terminal. The heavy faces of both men were blotched with fatigue, and they were talking unemotionally, almost idly. They might have been discussing a disappointing cricket match at Lord's.

"How do you propose to use our fellow?" said Palmer.

"I won't try to exploit his reflexes," said the Secretary. "And I won't try to get him to think."

"Oh? So what will you do?"

"I will make him sweat."

"And how will you do that?"

The Secretary turned his head and smiled at his old friend. "You forget, Richard," he said. "I have him by the balls. I will simply squeeze."

They drove Reilly right up to the entrance of Parliament, where he had emerged, four hours and forty-five minutes before, dressed in the uniform of a St. John's ambulance man. One TV cameraman managed to get a brief shot of his face as he was pulled out of the car, and then he was led into the building and being hustled down the long corridors past knots of policemen and soldiers who looked at him curiously as he was swept by.

The man with the mustache that Reilly had seen on TV was part of the small group just outside the doorway to the House of Commons. Then Reilly was through the entranceway and into the foyer, a policeman holding firmly to either arm.

"My Jesus," said Reilly. There, sitting at a table, a quiet smile on his face, was Major Thomas.

26

"LEAVE ME ALONE with him," said Thomas.

The two guards exchanged a glance and moved off to a side of the foyer. The handcuffed prisoner was not looking at Thomas. He was staring at a point a few feet above the head of the intense, sharp-featured man with the dark smudges of fatigue under his eyes who was leaning forward in his metal chair, one forefinger slowly tap-tapping the table before him. The chill of late afternoon was rapidly settling in, permeating the old stone walls of the structure, and Thomas pulled the collar of his ancient trench coat up around his neck.

"So you're the bloody bastard," he said.

"Up your arse," said Reilly.

Thomas let the remark pass. He had expected as much, and he did not care. He had his man. A hatred so intense that it was almost delicious swept over the major. For an instant he was on the point of rising from his chair to strike Reilly.

"So you're the clever bastard," said Thomas.

This time Reilly made no reply. His face looked blank, almost bored as he waited to see what would happen.

Around the walls of the foyer, the policemen and the soldiers were standing very still.

"Blown up any children lately? Killed any women?"

"Shit."

"Nobody killed recently? How disappointing. Anyone hurt, perhaps? Maybe an arm or a leg sent flying? *Look at me!*"

Reilly glanced contemptuously at Thomas and then looked away. "The fucking British," he said.

Thomas rose and slowly walked over to the prisoner. The major was holding his hands behind his back, and his pace, though slow and measured, had a slightly insolent swagger. He might have been about to work over a corporal who had just been caught going AWOL. "We have some interesting plans for you, Reilly," said Thomas.

"Oh?" Reilly wondered how tough Thomas really was.

"Yes. You're going to help us out; you're so clever."

"Make me," said Reilly.

"Precisely!" The third voice boomed so loudly that both Thomas and Reilly jumped. They turned to find the Home Secretary advancing on them, with Palmer one step behind. "Precisely," repeated the Secretary. "We will make you anxious to help—*eager* to help."

Thomas did not know exactly what the Secretary had in mind—only that it involved forcing Reilly to cooperate. Cabinet officers do not explain their plans to retired majors; Thomas knew that and accepted the fact. Curious, he stood back to see what would happen.

The Secretary beckoned to someone hidden down an adjoining passageway. "Bring her in," he said.

A husky policeman came into view, half-turned to the left, as though he was tugging something. "Come on, then," he said, and swung his left arm forward.

Stumbling, Kate entered the foyer. Her right wrist was chained to the left of the policeman. She pulled herself erect and slowly looked around. Reilly could tell she had not been crying. When she saw him she shook her head emphatically. He took that to mean she had told them nothing—not that it mattered much. They had them. But then they also had the bomb.

"Get her out of here!" yelled Reilly.

"I think not," said the Secretary.

"She had nothing to do with this."

"Oh, I think *so*," said the Secretary.

Thomas wondered what he was up to, what kind of secret he had.

"I think she had a good deal to do with the past of this little—" the Secretary paused dramatically, seeming to grope for the precise word "—this little 'enterprise,' and I think she'll have a great deal indeed to do with how it will all be resolved."

Reilly was shouting. "*How*, you bloody pouf?"

The Secretary seemed unperturbed. "Why, by encouraging you in your endeavors. By encouraging you to help Thomas here disarm your little packet."

"Get stuffed," said Reilly.

The Secretary beckoned again, and a policeman carrying a wooden chair and a length of rope came into the foyer. His voice hardened just enough for Thomas to sense his change of mood. "Shall we go?" he directed, and led the way through the big door into the House of Commons. The policeman carrying the chair and rope followed him, and last in the little procession came the policeman and Kate. Just before she disappeared, she turned and cried out: "I'm all right!"

Reilly tried to follow her, but the two guards were at his side, holding his arms. He looked at Thomas. "What the hell *is* this?" he asked.

Thomas was as bewildered as Reilly, but he recognized the Secretary's contrived air of nonchalance. He had seen it far too often before: colonels and generals prancing about before they unveiled a little scheme that they thought was oh so clever. But this man, thought Thomas, this one is a knife-fighter. This one is a killer. What in Christ is he doing?

The major got up and walked with Palmer into the House. The policeman had put down the chair within fifteen feet of the Speaker's chair and begun lashing it to a rail. The second policeman was leading Kate to the chair when she began to fight. "You bastards!" she screamed, swinging her free arm at the man who was holding her. "Take your Goddamn hands off me! Now!"

Her rage so startled everyone in the room that they froze in place for a moment. "I'm an American!" she yelled. "You've got no right!"

Palmer broke the silence. "She's right, you know, John," he said to the Secretary. He lowered his voice so the others would not hear and moved closer to his old friend. "I see well enough what you're up to," he said. "You want to use that girl as a hostage—to force that fellow to dismantle his own bomb. But you can't endanger anyone like that, let alone an American." Palmer was talking in a fierce whisper now. "It's not only immoral—it's illegal," he hissed. She's not even charged with anything, and you're punishing her—*torturing* her—already. With 'cruel and unusual punishment,' by the way, as the Americans would put it. The whole thing is preposterous."

"Are you finished?"

"No, I am not." Palmer's face was starting to redden. "What if she's killed? What then? That would be a pretty fix. You could ask the Prime Minister to ring up the President and say we're sorry about all that, but we seem to have killed one of your citizens. A young girl. Her father, by the way, happens to work for the CIA."

The Secretary started to reply, then caught himself. The two big men stood glaring at each other. Then the Secretary slowly walked away, whirled after a few steps and came back.

"I want that bomb dismantled," he said very calmly.

"I know that," said Palmer.

"I want it taken apart so Thomas can go outside with the bloody thing under his bloody arm and show the world how we can beat the IRA—put the fear of God in every Paddy with a stick of gelignite in his trousers."

"Yes," said Palmer. But you can't go that far. You can't risk the girl's life. And you don't need to."

"What?"

Palmer put a hand on his friend's shoulder. "We can still force him to cooperate. Just tell him he'd better help out or we'll lock him for good. He can help himself by helping us. Very simple. A matter of self-preservation."

For a moment, the Secretary said nothing. He was staring down at the stone floor.

Thomas had not been able to hear any part of the whispered conversation between the two men. He caught Palmer's eye, but the other man looked away.

"All right," said the Secretary.

Palmer began to smile. "That's more sensible," he said.

"On one condition," added the Secretary, rapping a knuckle against Palmer's upper arm. "I want her here. To watch. To encourage our friend when he does decide to cooperate."

Palmer looked puzzled. "That will help—just having her watching will make him help Thomas?"

"They're very vain, these Irish. Once he starts, he'll want to finish if she's watching him perform."

"Where will you put her?" Palmer asked.

"Somewhere in sight—somewhere safe," replied the Secretary. He beckoned Thomas to join them and briefly explained the situation. "Where do we put her?" he demanded.

Thomas shrugged. "I can't guarantee anything," he said. "You can never guarantee anything with explosives." A vision of the rain-swept quarry in Wales slashed through his mind, two men dangling on ropes as they lowered themselves to retrieve the body of his father. "If it explodes, there'll be a lot of debris flying around."

Thomas glanced at the girl and found she was looking directly at him. There was no trace of fear in her eyes.

"Where shall we put her?" repeated the Secretary.

The major nodded at the Strangers' Gallery at the opposite end of the chamber from the Speaker's chair. "Up there," he said.

"Right," said the Secretary. Palmer started to beckon to the policeman with the girl, but his friend caught him by the arm. "Not quite yet," the Secretary said. "Bring in Reilly."

As he entered from the foyer outside, Reilly was sniffing curiously, picking up the smell of explosives in the air. He looked for a moment at the charred pillar, his back to Thomas, and when he turned, there was a wry smile on his face. He understands, thought Thomas. He's figured it out.

Then Reilly saw the girl and the chair, and from the look of fury that flashed across his face, Thomas knew that he had guessed the whole plan instantly.

"Get her out of here!" Reilly yelled at the Secretary.

The Secretary slowly advanced on Reilly.

Jesus, he's going to hit him, thought Thomas, and wondered what he would do if Reilly were hurt and he was left on his own to dismantle the bomb.

The Secretary stopped a foot away from Reilly. He was wearing his customary double-breasted blue serge suit, but the conservative clothes did not matter. He still looks like a killer, thought Thomas, waiting for the Secretary to lose control.

"Why should we get her out of here?" the Secretary asked.

"Because that thing could go off—you know that," Reilly said. His handcuffs rattled in the quiet room as he tried to gesture. "*He* knows that," he said, nodding at Thomas.

"It goes off only if you touch it, right?" asked the Secretary. "All those clever little antihandling devices."

Reilly was looking at the girl. "There's another circuit in there," he said. He nodded at Thomas again. "He knows that. It's hitched to a timer."

"Yes," said the Secretary, talking very pleasantly now, "but is that circuit attached to the gelignite?"

"Of course it is, you twit!" Then Reilly grasped what was happening. He looked at Thomas. "You didn't know *that*?"

Thomas did not flush. He was beyond that. He waited for the next question.

"How long?" asked the Secretary. "How much time do we have?"

Reilly looked around for a clock and saw none. "It's set for six," he said.

Every other man in the room looked quietly at his watch. It was 5:13.

"Splendid," said the Secretary. "You have exactly forty-seven minutes to help us dismantle your creation—if everything goes well. So I suggest you get on with it."

The Secretary paused and glared at Thomas. "I assume you are up to it," he said, "now that I've found out for you what actually is in the bomb."

Again, Thomas made no reply. Within the space of two minutes, he had been humiliated by both Reilly and the Secretary. Get out, he thought. Quit. Let the bastards kill each other off. They're making up the rules as they go along. It's no longer your affair. Perhaps it never was.

As the Secretary started to walk out of the House, he said over his shoulder, almost casually, "Put the girl in the balcony."

Reilly saw that he had been had. They had forced him to reveal what was in the bomb. They had mistreated his girl and toyed with him, and he had no idea what would happen next. "You bastard!" he yelled at the retreating back of the Secretary. "You sadistic bloody bastard! Take your own bomb apart!"

The Secretary turned and looked back. He did not raise his voice, yet every word sounded clearly throughout the hushed room. "You will help," he said evenly, "or you will go to jail for life. I promise you that. For life."

Then the Secretary was gone and another authoritative figure Reilly did not know was approaching, talking soothingly as he came. "He's *right*," said Palmer, "and he means it. Your best chance is to help."

Reilly tried to focus his mind on the situation. He did not know if the bomb could be taken apart—he would have to count on Thomas, and he doubted the other man's courage as much as his skill. "You want me to blow my head off, is that it?" he asked Palmer. "Is that what it comes down to?"

Palmer shook his head. "We want the bomb taken apart," he said. "Safely. You have a chance, working with him." He nodded at Thomas.

Reilly waited suspiciously. "Besides," said Palmer, "you must bear in mind one fact: If you don't help, you will assuredly spend the rest of your life in jail. A British jail."

Reilly knew they had him. He had no choice at all. If he helped them, they might lighten his sentence. Might. "The bloody British," he said. "Do you wonder we love you so?"

"I can imagine how hard it must be," said Palmer.

"I bet."

"I try."

Reilly looked away. He had had enough. "Let's get on with it, then."

Palmer turned quickly and ordered the handcuffs taken off Reilly, and the girl taken up into the balcony, as the Secretary had directed. Then he beckoned Thomas in. "Your show, Major," he said.

For a moment Thomas allowed himself the luxury of thinking he would just leave, aware that he could never do it. Not now. The process had begun. Just as he had known from the beginning, there was no way he could stop it. The cameras waiting outside, the whole theatrical ambience, made him slightly giddy and drove him forward. He was performing like an actor, someone he was observing with a kind of abstract curiosity.

Phillips entered the House and walked up briskly. Thomas simply said, "All right. Let's do it." There was no sense mucking about any longer. He could not stall with the sergeant watching him. He did not have the courage. Thomas started to put into effect the plans that had been forming in his head while the Secretary was interrogating Reilly.

They had time enough, barely, if Reilly knew what he was up to. And if they did not run into any bad luck. With a few quick commands, Thomas arranged the setting to his liking, not bothering to explain to Phillips, just telling him as he went along. He sent away the guards who had been standing at Reilly's shoulders, and replaced them with three marksmen, armed with rifles, whom he stationed up in the gallery. They had a clear view of the prisoner, and yet were far enough away to have a good chance, along with the girl, to survive a blast. The three soldiers took dead aim at Reilly. As the prisoner moved around the area by the Speaker's chair, the muzzles of the rifles moved slightly, and the cross hairs on the three telescopic sights remained fixed on Reilly's head.

With his handcuffs off, Reilly sat down on the front bench of the Government, choosing the exact spot occupied by the Prime Minister when the House was in session. Watching Thomas, Reilly rubbed his wrists and waited.

The major was arranging prints made from the bomb X-rays on the great table in front of the Speaker's chair.

"So you faked the whole thing," said Reilly.

"What?"

Reilly pointed to the rear of the chamber, where a curtain was still smoldering from the explosion.

"Oh, yes, that," said Thomas, still busy. "Yes, we faked it all. It worked rather well, I must say. Got you to make a run for it, didn't it?"

"Your idea?" asked Reilly.

"What difference does it make?"

"His?" Reilly nodded toward the doorway through which the Secretary had left.

The major put down the last print and folded his arms. "What difference does it make?" he repeated.

Reilly went on. "You make up all this, too?" He gestured toward the bomb and the gallery, where the girl and her escort of two policemen were just appearing.

"Don't press your luck, boyo," said Thomas. "Not after all you've done."

That did it. Reilly felt the rage flash over him. Without a word, he rose and began advancing on Thomas. In the silence, the major heard one of the marksmen in the balcony cock his rifle—the loud, metallic click sounding clearly throughout the House—and he raised a hand to warn him not to shoot.

"What *I've* done!" cried Reilly. He reached out and jabbed the major in the chest. "What a bloody laugh! What about *you*? What about what you've done! What about all that shit in Ireland?" He fumbled for the right words. "It's *our* country. Get out of our country!"

"Your country, hell," said Thomas.

"And my father," yelled Reilly. "What about him!"

"What?"

"The bloody Prods—*you* bloody Prods," cried Reilly, "threw a bomb in his pub. Blew his legs off."

Thomas could not recall the incident—there had been so many incidents—but he did not doubt the truth of what Reilly was saying. The young man was glaring down at him with a hatred that was genuine enough.

"I'm sorry about your father," said Thomas.

Reilly did not let up: " 'Sorry,' " he mocked. "You bastards are always 'sorry.' " He pointed up at the girl. "And that," he said. "You 'sorry' about that, too? What you did to her, trussing her up like that. The law-abiding British. What a fucking laugh."

Looking up into the angry blue eyes, Thomas could feel some sympathy for the prisoner. It was partly Reilly's reference to his father—Thomas's instincts were to sympathize, without knowing the facts—and partly the scoffing remark about British law. He could sympathize with that, too. But, more important, he realized he was attracted by Reilly's honest emotion. Reilly had a cause; Thomas knew he did not. But there was no time to think about that.

"Look," said the major. "I don't like you any more than you like me, but if we don't figure out a way of disarming that bomb in—" he checked his watch "—about forty minutes, we will be very dead."

The major turned to the table that held the collection of drawings and diagrams taken from the plates. "Are you sure about that timer of yours?" he asked.

"As sure as anyone can be."

Thomas began to trace a wire through the maze that appeared in one diagram. "This is the circuit, right? Down at the bottom here?"

"Plain enough, isn't it?"

Thomas ignored the jibe. "How do we get at it?"

"You take the top off the box," said Reilly.

Thomas forced himself to look at the drawing for a moment before he replied. "All right," he said. "I thought we were cutting that shit out."

"*You're* the expert," Reilly said. "You're all over the telly saying how you can take apart anything I put together. Go ahead. Take the mother apart."

He knows I'm bluffing. He knows I won't touch it. "Remember," said the major, "your little clock is ticking away all the time."

Reilly leaned forward and picked up the print. Frowning, he studied the mare's nest of wires.

"Tricky, isn't it," said Thomas.

"I'm not sure," said Reilly. "The wires might have moved a bit after I put the lid down on the box."

Thomas pointed at the top of the paper. "Here's the capsule, right?" he said. The dark shape, rounded at the ends, was clearly discernible. The two men leaned forward, their shoulders touching slightly.

"Look here," said Reilly, "here she goes—" his finger tracked one thin line through the maze "—and then I crossed it over to the other side of the box right here. I changed directions."

"I missed that," Thomas admitted. "I'd never have picked that up."

There was no movement in the great room, no sound other than the murmured remarks between him and Reilly. Thomas felt as though he were floating in the greenish gloom, and for a moment tried to encourage the sensation—anything to put off what lay ahead.

Reilly was talking again: "It's bloody hopeless," he said matter-of-factly. "You can't take it apart. *I* can't even take it apart."

Thomas could not resist the impulse. "Just like you planned, right?" he said. "We've got to open the damn thing before we can cut the circuit that is attached to the timer. And the moment we try to open it, we jiggle the capsule and the whole thing blows up in our faces."

Reilly stared at the diagrams in silence.

"We're dead if we do and dead if we don't," said Thomas. "Right, *Paddy*?"

Reilly flushed and turned to face Thomas. "Look," he said, "Let's just get on with it. I want to open that box. That's all. You want to help—fine. If not, I'll try to do it myself, and you can watch. Then if I do it, you can go on telly and say what a fucking hero you've been."

He knows. He must know about the fear. Thomas tried to re-create the feeling that had briefly bound them together. He needed Reilly, and he knew it.

"Fair enough," said Thomas. "See here where the circuit to the capsule runs very close to the top edge of the box?" He traced the path with his forefinger. "Perhaps we can break it there. . . ."

"*Before* the microswitch in the capsule closes?"

"Yes."

"How?"

"By using some gelignite of our own."

"You're daft," said Reilly. "You'll blow the whole thing up."

For the next few minutes Thomas explained an idea that had occurred to him after learning about the details of the wiring from Reilly. The plan was to shape a small charge of gelignite so that the force of its explosion would be focused to break the wire connecting the capsule to the bomb and the battery. The problem was that the explosion would, of course, rock the capsule and close its microswitch. If the wire was already broken, it would make no difference. If the wire had not been snapped, the bomb would go off. Success or disaster would depend on what happened in a few thousandths of a second.

"You're taking a hell of a risk," Reilly said finally.

"I know," said Thomas. "What else is there to do?"

While they were talking, Phillips and an army sergeant had brought in the necessary gear and placed it on the table before the two men. Reilly watched closely while Thomas began shaping the charge of gelignite. With their heads bent together over the table, they looked like colleagues working on a common problem. Reilly made a suggestion or two that Thomas considered and accepted. For the first time in years, Thomas felt that he was working with a man who knew as much about explosives as he did.

Not only were they locked together by the bomb, Thomas realized, but they were very much the same, he and Reilly.

The major wondered if the IRA man's life was as controlled by others as was his own. Was there someone in Reilly's background, someone like the Home Secretary forcing Reilly's hand the way the Secretary forced his?

And there was more to it than that—much more. He had known instantly that Reilly too had come from a working-class background. Dozens of invisible ties bound them together. They had both taken a prompt dislike to the Secretary, for instance. In different ways, they were both driven by their fathers. More important, Thomas could even understand, vaguely, why Reilly set out his bombs. The major had been fighting the establishment all of his life. And losing. For a moment Thomas wondered if he would have planted bombs for the IRA if he had been born a Catholic in Belfast. He was not sure.

"One of us will have to hold the box and the other tape it on," said Reilly.

"It doesn't matter," said Thomas. This was the worst time, the few seconds before he began to walk toward the bomb. They both struggled into flak jackets.

"All right then," said Reilly. "I'll hold it." He picked up the charge. Thomas tore off four lengths of heavy tape and stuck them to the front of his flak jacket, so that they dangled like strange decorations for valor. Then Thomas picked up a roll of wire and handed one end to Phillips, who gave him an encouraging wink.

"All right," said Thomas. He and Reilly stood together looking at the Speaker's chair. Reilly was a half a head taller than the major, and the bulky jacket made him look huge. In the balcony, one of the marksmen moved his rifle slightly to draw a better bead on Reilly's head. Thomas could clearly see the girl sitting very erect.

It was the worst moment for Thomas—worse than he had believed it could possibly be. Suddenly a childhood prayer began to run through his mind. "Gentle Jesus, meek and mild . . ." He could not remember the next line.

Reilly could not move. He had assumed he would feel no fear when the time came. They had him: he had nothing to lose. But he could not move. "Let's do it," he finally managed to say, and a leg swung forward.

Thomas, one step behind, was pulled along as though they were chained together. The major kept his eyes fixed on the Speaker's chair. Then he remembered the other wooden box and the obliterating blue flash, the sensation of being flung against a stone wall, and the realization that Osgood was dead. The memory made him falter and Reilly, without turning his head, whispered, "Let's go."

Jesus God, said Thomas to himself, and forced himself up to the chair. He stared down at the markings and imperfections in the pine wood that had seared themselves into his mind when he was taking the X-rays. Reilly was muttering something to himself.

The miracle did not happen. This time, nothing happened. Always before, the fear had gone when Thomas actually stood over the bomb. His absorption in his task had banished every other emotion. But not this time—this time Thomas felt the terror begin to make his hands shake.

Get away! Thomas turned to run, and caught sight of Reilly's face. It was deathly white. In absolute silence, the two men stood transfixed over the bomb, each realizing that the other was also terrified. Thomas could see the beads of perspiration on Reilly's upper lip.

Balanced on the edge of panic, the two men looked at each other. Neither said a word. After a moment Reilly turned and gently placed the charge on the box. The Irishman was talking softly to himself again. "Easy," he said. "Easy." He held the charge with his fingertips, and then pressed down on the top of the box with his palms to hold it steady—to keep a tremor from passing through the wood and shaking ever so slightly, but enough—the tiny microswitch that would kill them all if it swung shut.

Thomas ripped off one length of tape and fastened the detonator at the end of his wire directly to the top of the charge. Then, swiftly, he taped the charge to the box, being careful not to catch Reilly's fingers.

"Let's go," the major said. He took two steps, and the terror came again. He would have run—he knew it—if the girl had not been watching from above. It was that absurd: endangering his life because of the risk of looking like a fool to a girl he did not even know, who might not care a whit about what he did. He glanced up at her—she was leaning forward, hands on her knees—and then walked back to Phillips at the table.

Reilly knew. He had seen Thomas tense and then hesitate and look up at Kate, and he knew that the major had nearly run. The knowledge made him feel superior to Thomas, and it broke the feeling of unity they had shared over the bomb when each had divined the other's fear. Reilly cursed himself for having been taken in—for feeling sympathy for Thomas. Thomas was one of them, one of the men trying to put him in jail. Jesus Christ, Reilly said to himself, and lashed out: "When we blow it, you going to be out in the hallway with the rest of the toffs?"

That was exactly what Thomas had been planning to do—run the wires out the door and touch off the charge in safety. But the disdain in Reilly's tone changed all that. Again, he knew it made no sense—but very little about the whole enterprise had made any sense. Reilly not only was saying he was a coward—he was expecting him to act like one. Thomas would kill himself before he did that.

"I'm staying here," he said to Reilly. "You can go if you want."

He's bluffing, thought Reilly. He won't do it. "I'm staying," he said.

Phillips interrupted. "You've got about six minutes." He was attaching an electrical detonator to the end of the wire.

With the device in his hand, Thomas turned to look at the girl. As he watched, she raised a hand to brush back a thick strand of hair, and Thomas was struck by the grace and beauty of the movement—the freshness and youth of the girl.

He could lose it all in seconds. Suddenly he felt a flash of vicious resentment against the people who had brought him to this place, fifteen feet away from a bomb that could destroy him. "You bastards," said Thomas to everyone.

Reilly did not understand. "What?" he asked, starting to look around.

"Goddamn you all," said Thomas, and turned the key.

At such close range, the explosion was so loud that Thomas's first thought was he'd done it: the main charge had blown. Then he realized that he was still alive. Phillips was there. Thomas's ears were ringing so loudly that he could not hear what Phillips was saying. The sergeant was pointing toward the chair, and Thomas, remembering suddenly what they had been trying to do, looked where Phillips was gesturing. He could see part of the box. The top was off.

Phillips shook his hand and smiled, but Thomas turned away. As his head cleared, he understood what had happened, but it was not over yet. There was still one step to go. Phillips was starting forward with a pair of wire cutters specially treated so as not to conduct electricity. Thomas grabbed him roughly by the elbow. "Mine," he said. "I have to do it."

The fear was gone, and in its place was a burning rage against everyone—the people, the system—that had brought him so close to death.

"Wait," called Reilly, but Thomas waved him back. He was going to do it by himself, goddamn it, right now, right then, and get rid of the whole fucking thing—the girl, Reilly, the Secretary, the whole bloody lot. He was going to be free, or dead, and Thomas, as he walked the last few steps to the bomb, realized that he did not care if he killed everyone else in the room in the process. He was alone: they had made him do it alone. Be a loner. Right. He had carried that burden all of his life. Well, he was bloody well alone now. The others did not count.

Reilly was yelling: "Hold the wire level!"

Yes. Thomas realized that he had overlooked that. If he cut the wire from side to side, he could force the two thin copper strands together, causing a short circuit that could fire the bomb. The fact that he had forgotten such a basic point slowed him for an instant, and then the rage to get it over forced him on again, forced him to walk the last steps and to stare down into the contents of the box. A thin spiral of smoke was curling up from one corner of the top. He could smell the almond scent. "You son of a bitch," said Thomas, looking straight down into the box.

He could see sticks of gelignite and the battery and the clock which was lying face up. The hour hand was nearly touching the nipple of metal that had been welded onto the face at 18:00.

Do it! Now! Thomas's left hand was shaking so violently that it struck the edge of the box, and for a moment he could not grasp the wire. "Jesus," he said.

Thomas knelt down by the chair and steadied his left arm on the side of the box. He watched his left hand grab the wire and turn it flat. The fumes from the explosion made him choke, and a tear started to run down his face. The wire cutters in his right hand hit the edge as he reached in. He had both of his arms in the box, up to the elbows, and his head was over the top. Locked in an embrace with the bomb, Thomas opened the cutters.

He missed the wire altogether. "Sweet Jesus," said Thomas, and leaned closer. This time he watched the gleaming jaws of the cutters pass on either side of the wire. With one convulsive movement he pressed the handles together. There was a faint snip, and the wire parted cleanly.

Thomas sat back on his heels and dropped the cutters. His head was sagging forward and his eyes were closed. His mind was quite blank. He did not feel a sense of relief; it was too soon for that. Seconds went by, and then the emotion that seized him again was the anger, only this time so strong that it made him shudder as though he had been taken with a chill. Thomas reached into the box and yanked loose the clock, snapping the wires that were attached to its face. Panting, he rose and threw the clock as hard as he could. It struck against a railing in the correspondents' gallery and shattered.

Thomas was reaching into the box for the gelignite when Phillips got to him.

"It's over," the sergeant said, taking the major by the shoulder. "You did it, Dave. It's all over."

The touch of Phillips's hand began to quiet Thomas. With an old man's care, he heaved himself to his feet. He did not know what to do with the stick of gelignite in his hand, so he simply gave it to the sergeant. His mind was not working very clearly, but he wondered about the girl. He looked up to see two officers starting to lead her away. As he watched her go, she turned her head to look down at him, and there was a gentle cascade of hair. He wanted to tell her of his gratitude that she was safe, and raised a hand to wave. The policemen were holding her by the arms. He could not tell whether or not she tried to wave back. Perhaps she did.

Reilly was there. "I didn't think you had the guts," he said.

Thomas looked right past him. "I don't much care what you think," he said.

Now a policeman had Reilly by the arm, and he looked for a way to hurt the man he had tried to kill. "Who's going to help you next time?" asked Reilly.

Next time. Thomas did not want to think about next time. "You won't be making any bombs for a while," he said to Reilly.

"There are other lads that can, boyo."

Thomas struck back. "And the 'other lads' will make mistakes," he said. "Like you. Getting the girl involved. Jesus."

A second policeman came up. "Tell them how scared you were," Reilly said. "Tell the people on the telly how you were pissing in your pants."

Thomas turned his back on the Irishman. "Get him out of here," he said.

As he was led away, Reilly passed the Home Secretary. "Some hero," said Reilly. He jerked his head over his shoulder at the major. "Something must have blown his balls off."

The Secretary brushed past Reilly without even glancing at him. He grabbed Thomas's hand and squeezed it so hard that the major winced. "Brilliant," said the Secretary. "You pulled it off brilliantly. Very well done, indeed."

Thomas was too tired to cope with the Secretary. "Thank you," he said.

"They're expecting you out front, you know," said the Secretary.

"What?"

"The BBC and all the rest. They're expecting you to go out front and show them the bomb. What you did in here."

Thomas started to walk away. "I'm not going," he said.

The Secretary picked up the box and started after him. "That's the whole point," he said. "To show you can take apart anything they put together. And now you've done it."

Thomas began to walk faster. "*You* show them the bloody box," he said.

The Secretary did not understand. "You're the hero," he said. "A legitimate hero. It all worked out perfectly. Just as we planned."

"Not quite," said Thomas.

"Why not?"

"I'm quitting."

"*Why*, for God's sake?"

Thomas reached the table in the foyer where he had left his trench coat. As he pulled it on, he studied the face of the Secretary. The man was obviously and honestly astonished. Thomas considered trying to explain how he felt, but he did not think he could reduce his emotions to words. His resentment at being maneuvered so blatantly was one thing. He might be able to talk about that—how he was an outsider who had been used by the insiders, wrung dry by the establishment. But there remained the fear. If he stayed, there would be other bombs, and he would have to go to them. He did not want to do that again. Ever. Reilly was right about that. "I'm just quitting," he said to the Secretary. "I've had enough."

The Secretary looked thoughtfully into the box he held in

his arms, then turned slowly and started to leave. He did not say good-by. One by one, the other police officers and demolition experts in the room followed him out, until Thomas was left alone with Phillips.

The sergeant had somehow found two cups of tea, and now he handed one to the major. They sat down in the metal chairs by the table in the foyer outside the House of Commons. From where Thomas was sitting, he could see through the doorway. As he sipped his tea, he could just make out the top of the chair of the Speaker of the House.

Neither Thomas nor Phillips spoke. Somewhere down the corridor there was the rich, resonant sound of two men laughing. Thomas did not even bother to turn his head to see what the commotion was about. He did not feel liberated at all. He just felt exhausted. He wondered if he could catch the late train home to Wales. Perhaps. If he hurried. . . .

Jack London

THE ASSASSINATION BUREAU, LTD.

The Assassination Bureau kills people for money. It also has a social conscience. Determined to eliminate only society's enemies, its chief, Ivan Dragomiloff, decides whether or not each murder is "justified." One day Dragomiloff accepts a contract without knowing the name of the victim—and the person marked for death turns out to be himself. . . . Unfinished when Jack London died, this thrilling novel has been so successfully completed by Robert L. Fish that the reader is challenged to find the point where one writer stops and the other begins.

Sir Arthur Conan Doyle

THE MEMOIRS OF SHERLOCK HOLMES

Sir Arthur Conan Doyle was born in Edinburgh, Scotland, in 1859 and died in 1930. He studied medicine at Edinburgh University, where the diagnostic methods of one of the professors are said to have provided the idea for the methods of detection used by Sherlock Holmes. Doyle first set up as a doctor at Southsea, and it was while waiting for patients that he first began to write. His greatest achievement, of course, was his creation of Sherlock Holmes, who constantly diverted his creator from the work he preferred. *The Memoirs* consists of eleven adventures from the crowded life of Sherlock Holmes, including "The Final Solution," with which Doyle intended to close the career of his famous detective. Holmes was a match for the author, however, and the reading public's urgent pleas for further Holmes cases could not be resisted. Doyle was later compelled to resurrect him.

Geoffrey Household

ROGUE MALE

His mission was revenge, and revenge means assassination. In return he'll be cruelly tortured, tracked by secret agents, followed by the police, relentlessly pursued by a ruthless killer. They'll hunt him like a wild beast, and to survive he'll have to think and live like a rogue male. "A tale of adventure, suspense, even mystery, for whose sheer thrilling quality one may seek long to find a parallel . . . and in its sparse, tense, desperately alive narrative it will keep, long after the last page is finished, its hold from the first page on the reader's mind"—*The New York Times Book Review*.

G. K. Chesterton

THE INCREDULITY OF FATHER BROWN

No sleuth was ever more totally amateur than G. K. Chesterton's famous little moon-faced priest with his large umbrella. He hardly knows a fingerprint from a footprint, but somehow he has unfailing intuition—perhaps a sympathy for the criminal mind. And Father Brown gets results. Here are eight quietly astonishing cases handled by the most amateur detective of all.

More Father Brown from Penguin:

THE SECRET OF FATHER BROWN
THE WISDOM OF FATHER BROWN

Graham Greene

THE POWER AND THE GLORY

In one of the southern states of Mexico, during an anti-clerical purge, the last priest, like a hunted hare, is on the run. Too human for heroism, too humble for martyrdom, the little worldly "whiskey priest" is nevertheless impelled toward his squalid Calvary as much by his own efforts as by the efforts of his pursuers.

THE QUIET AMERICAN

The Quiet American is a terrifying portrait of innocence at large; it is also a wry comment on European interference in Asia in its story of the French-Vietminh war in Vietnam. While the French Army is grappling with the Vietminh, in Saigon a high-minded young American begins to channel economic aid to a "Third Force." The narrator, a seasoned foreign correspondent, is forced to observe, "I never knew a man who had better motives for all the trouble he caused."

SHADES OF GREENE

Eighteen of Graham Greene's finest short stories, which have been dramatized for television, devastatingly demonstrate his unique talent for exploring the subtleties of human relationships. Witty, sensitive, nightmarish, comic, or merciless, every story finds its echoes in the reader's own experience.

Also:

BRIGHTON ROCK

A BURNT-OUT CASE

THE COMEDIANS

THE END OF THE AFFAIR

THE HEART OF THE MATTER

IT'S A BATTLEFIELD

JOURNEY WITHOUT MAPS

LOSER TAKES ALL

MAY WE BORROW YOUR HUSBAND?

THE MINISTRY OF FEAR

TRAVELS WITH MY AUNT

Lionel Davidson

THE NIGHT OF WENCESLAS

Young Nicholas Whistler is trapped. "Invited" to Prague on what seems to be an innocent business trip, he finds himself caught between the secret police and the amorous clutches of the statuesque Vlasta. This first book established Lionel Davidson as a brilliant new novelist of action and adventure.

MAKING GOOD AGAIN

In Germany to settle a claim for reparation, lawyer James Raison is plunged into the old conflict between Jew and Nazi. His trip becomes more dangerous as the legal aspects of the case become more complicated, and at the same time he has to cope with his affair with Elke and his involvement with her fascist aunt, Magda. *Making Good Again* is the story not only of a complicated and exciting search for the true identity of the claimant but also of a search going on in the minds of the English, German, and Jewish lawyers—a search to discover and understand Nazi philosophy.

THE ROSE OF TIBET

Charles Houston had slipped illegally into Tibet to find his missing brother—only to be imprisoned in the forbidden Yamdring monastery. Now he has to get out of Tibet quickly, for the invading Chinese army and the cruel Himalayan winter are right behind him. . . . Daphne du Maurier wrote: "Is Lionel Davidson today's Rider Haggard? His novel has all the excitement of *She* and *King Solomon's Mines*."

Michael Innes

AN AWKWARD LIE

Bobby, son of that great master of detection Sir John Appleby, finds a body on a golf course. As he wonders what to do, a very attractive girl arrives. When Bobby returns after calling the police, however, the girl has gone . . . and so has the corpse!

CANDLESHOE

What mysterious treasure lies hidden in the dark heart of Candleshoe Manor? And what breath-catching adventures will unfold before the riddle of the treasure is finally, excitingly solved?

FROM *LONDON* FAR

A random scrap of Augustan poetry muttered in a tobacconist's shop thrusts an absent-minded scholar through a trap-door into short-lived leadership of London's biggest art racket.

HAMLET, REVENGE!

The Lord Chancellor is shot in the midst of a private performance of *Hamlet*. Behind the scenes there are thirty-one suspects; in the audience, twenty-seven.

THE MYSTERIOUS COMMISSION

Tempted by the offer of a huge fee, artist Charles Honeybath accepts a strange assignment: paint the portrait of an unnamed man in an unnamed place. Is it all a trick?

Science Fiction from Penguin by John Boyd

THE LAST STARSHIP FROM EARTH

Mathematicians must not write poetry—above all, they must not marry poets, decrees the state. But Haldane IV, mathematician, and Helix, poet, are in love. They are also puzzled, for they have been studying the long-hidden poetry of Fairweather I, acknowledged as the greatest mathematician since Einstein. As they explore further, the danger for them grows; the state has eyes and ears everywhere. Will they find, before it is too late, the real meaning of the following words by Fairweather I? "That he who loses wins the race,/ That parallel lines all meet in space." "Terrific . . . it belongs on the same shelf with *1984* and *Brave New World*"—Robert A. Heinlein.

THE POLLINATORS OF EDEN

The coldly beautiful Dr. Freda Caron has waited too long for her fiancé, Paul Theaston, to return from Flora, the flower planet. Determined to learn what has happened, she begins a study of plants from Flora, and slowly she is warmed by her communion with them. Eventually she makes the trip from Earth to Flora for further research and to see Paul. What she finds is the secret of the flower planet, but in her initiation she too becomes a pollinator of Eden.

THE RAKEHELLS OF HEAVEN

In the future there will be colonial imperialism—in space! Two space scouts, John Adams and Kevin O'Hara, are sent to explore a distant world called Harlech. The Interplanetary Colonial Authority prohibits human colonization and control of those planets whose inhabitants closely resemble *Homo sapiens,* as the Harlechians do. Thus, relations with their women are strictly forbidden. But such rules were not made for Red O'Hara. From the Adams-O'Hara Probe, only John Adams returns. . . .